THE DEAD OF MIDWINTER

BOOK 1 IN THE JOSEPH STONE THRILLER SERIES

J R SINCLAIR

VOICE FROM THE CLOUDS

For Barry, Tom, and Jonathan, for encouraging me to take the plunge into crime and to write this book.

CHAPTER ONE

THE WIPERS THRUMMED BACK and forth at their highest setting, fighting a losing battle against the waterfall cascading down the car windscreen. Joseph squinted through the veil of shimmering rain at the blurred country lane covered in a veil of darkness. In the growing tempest, the headlights of their SUV could barely cut through the murk. Thank God for the Cat's Eyes down the centre of the road, like runway landing lights guiding them home.

'If it keeps up like this, the roads are going to be underwater around Warborough by morning,' Kate said as she peered out at the deluge.

'Definitely not a great night to be out driving, that's to be sure,' Joseph replied. 'Just think how we could have all been safely tucked up at home if we'd had Ellie's birthday bash there, rather than dragging ourselves all the way to Oxford.'

His wife raised her eyebrows at him. 'As we both know, that's not how the parent mafia works. Hold a birthday party at home, and Ellie would be a social pariah at school.'

'Yes, talk about bloody peer pressure to keep up with the Joneses,' he muttered.

Kate sighed. 'I know, I know. Whatever happened to jelly and ice cream birthdays, complete with the pin the tail on the donkey?'

'You realise that sounds like something straight out of an Enid Blyton book, right?'

'No, that would be lashings of ginger beer.' Kate gave him a wry smile.

Joseph laughed. 'If you say so. Anyway, I'm not sure my hearing is ever going to recover from that many screaming six-year-olds hurtling around the confined space of the play barn. As soon as we get back home, I'm having two paracetamol, followed by a stiff drink.'

'For a policeman, you do realise you have a very low mental pain threshold?'

'Oh, give me a bunch of hardened criminals any day over a herd of demonic kids having a good time.'

'But, Daddy, it was the best party ever!' Ellie said, piping up from the back seat where she'd been totally absorbed in playing on the birthday iPad that Kate's parents bought her. In Joseph's opinion, it was way too expensive a present for a six-year-old, who should be making dens in the garden rather than mucking around with that sort of thing. But when it came to Ellie and Eoin, Kate's parents wrote their own rulebook, which mostly seemed to involve a huge amount of spoiling.

'I'm glad you enjoyed your party, sweetheart,' he replied, smiling into the rear-view mirror at his daughter with her '*I Am Six!*' badge she was proudly wearing.

'It was the best birthday ever, Mummy and Daddy!' She beamed back at him, all gums, teeth and pigtails.

Even his hardened heart melted, because how could it not? All Ellie needed to do was just be her usual sunny self, and every time she effortlessly defused his grumpiest of moods.

Quite how Kate and he had produced this bundle of

gorgeousness, born on the twenty-first of December, which also happened to be the winter solstice tonight, seemed like a miracle to him. By contrast, there was their son Eoin and the last thing you could describe him as was *gorgeous*. There was one word that best summed him up, *loud*. His default mode was making noise, from yelling to crying, and all of it at volume eleven.

In his rear mirror, he could also just see Eoin's head lolling to one side. His mouth was wide open and a line of spider silk drool trailed down from his lip onto the sleeve of his rocket ships onesie. Thankfully, the car had worked its usual magic on him and within a minute of setting off, he'd screamed himself to sleep.

Despite Eoin's diminutive ten months—who, much to the delight of his mum, they'd named after Joseph's long-dead Irish Dad—he still had the lungs to put an opera singer to shame. Certainly, Eoin's performance back at the party had taken a starring role in the headache that was currently bouncing around inside his skull like an angry wasp trapped in a jam jar.

The one small blessing was that at least Joseph wouldn't have to face that hellhole again for a while, otherwise so innocently known as the Play Barn. That name really painted the wrong mental picture. The actual building was a warehouse that verged on derelict, the state of the place barely disguised by the violent primary colour scheme, bright enough to make your eyes bleed. The finishing touch to the unique ambience of the Play Barn was the distinct whiff of leaking toddler nappies that always seemed to pervade the place. And the less said about the ball pit, the better.

Joseph hadn't quite left a trail of smoking rubber in his haste to get away from the Play Barn, but not that far off. Maybe the next time one of Ellie's classmates held their birthday party there, he'd buy a discreet set of earplugs and bring enough paracetamol to tranquillise an elephant.

Ellie was humming along to some tune on her iPad as they rounded the bend. The lane opened up ahead of them. They were now on the stretch to what had slowly become one of Oxford's satellite villages and where they called home, namely Warborough. Why they'd chosen to live so far out from St Aldates Police Station in Oxford, where he worked as a constable, seemed crazy to Joseph, especially now when Kate's journalism job was also based in the city. He had a vague alcohol-steamed memory of being with friends at a barbecue where they'd tossed around the idea. Something about it being a great lifestyle choice for the kids. Then, the next thing he knew, it had become a thing. That was why he was now putting up with a daily slog of a commute to work every day—a twenty-two-mile round trip.

The things he and Katie coped with for the sake of their family.

The rain seemed to be falling even faster, and the road had been reduced to a glistening line of tarmac reflecting their headlights. Curtains of rain swirled and spun across the road, a web of shadows surrounding their vehicle on every side, as the world closed in around them.

It was little wonder that Joseph didn't spot the flooded pothole right in front of them. Too late to swerve, their SUV briefly slammed down into it, making them all bounce in their seats and sending a wave of water crashing over the car.

'Wheee,' Ellie said, kicking her feet straight out into the back of Kate's seat.

Kate scowled. 'Please don't do that, poppet,' she said, her tone restrained with a forced sense of lightness for the birthday girl, who for this one special day could apparently get away with blue murder. Kate bobbed her head several times, which Joseph knew was her tell that she was mentally counting to three, before leaning slightly towards him.

'Maybe I'll be joining you in that drink,' she whispered.

The grin that had been forming on his lips faded as their headlights reflected off a large torrent of rushing water dead ahead. The entire road had turned into a shallow river running down from the hill to their right, and crossing their path for a good hundred-metre stretch.

'Bloody hell, a flood is all we need,' Joseph muttered.

'Daddy, language!' Ellie said in her most prim and proper voice as she looked up from her screen.

'Sorry, bad daddy,' he replied, as he tightened his grip on the steering wheel.

'We could turn round, but the alternative will add an extra five miles,' Kate said, gazing out at the water rippling across the road ahead of them.

'It doesn't look too deep and if I keep my speed down, but revs high, it should be okay,' he replied.

'Thank God for that, because the idea of that drink is getting more appealing by the minute,' Kate said.

Joseph slowed to less than ten miles per hour as they entered the flood, leaning a fraction forward in his seat like a myopic senior citizen staring over the wheel. Thankfully, the rushing water barely came up to the rims of their tyres. Their SUV sent out the barest wake as they crawled through the flood.

'I'm frightened, Daddy,' Ellie said, her voice suddenly thin and weedy.

'Nothing to be frightened about, pumpkin,' he replied with his best, *I'm an adult and I've got this under control*, voice.

The silhouettes of willow trees slid past like gnarled hands in the darkness, their branches swaying in the wind as the rain hammered even harder onto the roof of the car. Joseph felt a distinct surge of relief when he saw the road ahead, rising out of the flood to reveal tarmac again.

'See, I told you we'd be okay,' he said as he settled back into his seat and pressed the accelerator a fraction to get them out of the water.

And then it happened, a split second that would change their lives forever.

It started as a blurred shape at the periphery of Joseph's vision, nothing more than a fast-moving shadow. Then something large was leaping over the low stone wall from the open field and racing across into the flooded road dead ahead of them. In the next few milliseconds, his consciousness registered that the thing was actually a stag. Its eyes were wild with fear, whites ringing them, its mouth pulled back over bared teeth.

In the handful of milliseconds that followed, Joseph just had time to yank the wheel hard over as Ellie shrieked. Their SUV responded, but its wheels scrambled for grip in the floodwater.

It all happened so fast, the stag way too close for Joseph to do anything about it. That's what he would keep telling himself in the years that followed, trying to cling to it as an excuse for the guilt that was going to eat him up forever from the inside.

They slammed into the animal with a sickening crunch of cracking bone and bending metal, audible even inside the cocooned cabin of their vehicle. The next moment, the deer was somersaulting off the bonnet and away into the night.

But even as Joseph started to lose control of the SUV, police training on skid pans was already kicking in. He turned the wheel back to steer into the sideways slide. But there was too much water on the road for the tyres to find any traction. His stomach rose into his chest as he watched helplessly, as much a passenger now as the rest of his family. They skidded straight towards the stone wall, the rocks that topped it glistening like jagged teeth in the rain.

Ellie screamed, her young voice loud and shrill as the SUV's wheels dug into the ditch on the opposite side of the road and suddenly they were tipping over. Then the world was spinning past, an alternating kaleidoscope of rain and ground as they rolled again and again. With a massive, ear-numbing bang, the airbags exploded into Joseph's face, turning the world white. Nylon smothered his mouth as shards of windscreen lacerated his hands.

Their SUV toppled one last time onto its side, shaking like a rag doll before gravity pinned him to the driver's door.

Joseph gasped in shock at the winter air flooding in through the shattered windows. As his senses rebooted, the whiff of cordite from the airbag charges that had just detonated scratched the back of his nostrils.

There was a moment of shocking silence then, just the sound of wheels spinning down and the creak of metal and the moan of the wind beyond. His eyes focused on the scene framed by their shattered windscreen. A lone figure was picked out by the headlights, at least fifty metres away, crouching by something in the field. The person slowly stood, their face hooded by a black waterproof cagoule, but Joseph got the impression from the build that the person was male. The man was carrying something in his arms as he turned towards them, black gloves covering his hands.

Joseph's chest burned as his lungs pushed against what were almost certainly several cracked ribs, as he called out. 'For God's sake, help us!'

But rather than rushing over, the figure instead paused, and then turned. With long, wide strides he headed quickly away into the swirling storm, a dark phantom vanishing into the night.

Then Joseph saw what had been at the man's feet—a deer with its head removed. Its neck was a raw bloody stump, severed arteries still pumping blood that glistened in their car's headlights. Despite the horror of what he was witnessing, his mind was already sliding away from it. Right now, his priority was getting his family out of their car in case it caught fire.

He turned his head upwards, neck muscles screaming, towards Kate, who was dangling from her belt above him.

Joseph reached out to her. 'Kate, are you okay?'

Her eyes blinked open, and she stared down at him. Then her gaze widened. 'The kids!' she screamed.

And then, the sweetest sound in the world filled their broken car as Ellie began to sob. But any relief that she was alive was short-lived because once again Joseph's police training was kicking in.

You always leave the ones making the most noise until last.

He pushed himself up on his elbows, releasing the belt that had automatically pulled him hard into his seat at the moment of the crash.

'Eoin?' Kate whispered.

No cry, no responding decibel eleven shrieks from their son.

Joseph struggled up into a sitting position and shuffled himself around, the broken glass slicing his palms with burning bursts of pain as he manoeuvred himself so he could look back at his baby boy.

'Eoin?' Kate repeated, her voice growing louder.

They say that some images stay with you forever and what Joseph was about to witness would be exactly that.

Eoin's car seat had released after its buckle had failed. The buckle that Joseph had clicked into place. The buckle that had never worked properly since they'd bought the car from a dealer. The buckle that he had kept meaning to get checked out by the garage, but hadn't got around to.

And now Eoin's car seat, suddenly released by the failed seatbelt, had been turned into a projectile. Still attached by the straps on the other side, the seat had swung his sleeping son around and slammed his head straight into the passenger window as the car had tumbled over.

Joseph stared at his beautiful baby boy, his head lying at a sickening angle to his body, and resting against the side curtain airbag like it was a pillow.

Then Kate's screaming was drowning out even Ellie's, as she struggled to break free of her seat belt.

Joseph watched, his mind numb, as she reached out toward their dead son and wailed.

SIXTEEN YEARS AND FIVE DAYS LATER

CHAPTER TWO

Ellie's eyes opened into a dim light from a single, bare bulb overhead. But when she tried to suck in a lungful of air, she became aware of a cloth gag tied tight across her mouth. The smell of damp was also clawing at her nose, as raw nausea spun through her abdomen.

There was a regular drip of water, and the hum of a machine from somewhere beyond the walls, a tickle of its vibration through her feet.

It was then that Ellie realised how dry her throat was. How long had it been since she'd drunk anything? How long had she been here?

Her thoughts were like a tumble of threads knotted together. She had a vague memory of someone in a forensic suit turning up on the doorstep of her mum's house. There had been no sign outside of the officer, John Thorpe, who was meant to be guarding her. Then the man attacked her. But she'd fought back with everything she had before a cloth had been clamped over her mouth. The next thing Ellie knew, the world was spinning as she crashed to the ground, knocking over a table. Then nothing, until now...

It felt like she was slumped in a metal chair, her hands tied behind her back to it. When she tried to stand, she lifted the heavy chair with her just a fraction, but her limbs felt as though they had been filled with lead and she could barely move.

The man had obviously drugged her. Maybe chloroform?

Then a terrifying thought took hold. The forensic suit he'd been wearing told her all she needed to know, and more specifically the demon mask that he'd also been wearing.

The Midwinter Butcher.

He had come for her tonight to finish what he'd started. This was every nightmare she'd ever had since she'd been a child. She had to get out of here, fast.

Gathering her thoughts, and shivering, she shook her head, trying to clear the wooziness.

Ellie scanned the space around her, trying to work out exactly where she was being held. In the middle of the room, there was a small table on which a strange-looking ornate dagger had been placed, two unlit candles on either side of it. There was a single door, but she also knew there was every chance it would be locked even if she had been able to move. The dripping sound was coming from a leaking section of pipes, one of many that ran through the room.

Was this some sort of basement?

She twisted around in her chair to see if there was anything else. Then her heart rose into her mouth as she took in the large occult symbol that had been daubed on the wall with a dark red substance that had to be blood. Her gaze tore back to the dagger on the table as the inevitable conclusion hit her.

That's a makeshift altar and I'm going to be the sacrifice!

With a deep breath, she fought down the rising sense of panic.

Ellie, keep it together; what would Dad tell you to do?

Her strength was slowly returning, and when she pressed

her feet to the floor, she was able to tilt the heavy chair a fraction more this time. If she could keep rocking it, maybe she could make it over to the dagger and use that...

Her train of thought rushed away and her senses became electric as she heard running footsteps getting louder beyond the door. She had a brief spike of hope. Had someone come to rescue her? But then an icy feeling of dread took over.

Had the Midwinter Butcher come back to finish what he'd started?

Heart hammering, Ellie stared at the door as the *thunk* of a lock being disengaged came from the other side.

The door squealed open, shoved by the man in the forensic suit, still wearing the strange demon mask. The figure rushed into the room. Then Ellie spotted the fine tooth saw in his hand. Was he about to cut off her head too, just like he had with his other victims, including the deer all those years ago?

Ellie screamed, but there was no one else around to hear her muffled cry for help as the masked figure advanced, getting ready to end her life, like all the others.

ONE WEEK EARLIER - 21ST, DECEMBER

CHAPTER THREE

JERICHO CAFÉ WAS PACKED, its windows fogged thanks to all the students and Oxford residents crammed into every available table. The moisture-laden atmosphere was added to by the steam currently venting from the coffee machine next to Joseph.

The detective stood patiently by the counter, waiting to collect his takeaway order. This place didn't do takeaways, but the owner made an exception in his case as Joseph had helped to solve a spate of break-ins they'd had a few years back. That had given him a golden ticket with the owners, who were eternally grateful.

Normally, the DI would grab a small table in a corner or even have one down in the crypt, nicknamed that by him thanks to its lack of daylight. But of course, right now, it was all about seeking solitude. That had meant having to cry off Ian's clumsy offer of a lads' night out to take his mind off things.

That was the last thing he needed tonight of all nights. Joseph didn't allow himself a pass on beating himself up over the stupid mistake he'd made sixteen years ago that had destroyed his family's life. No, tonight would be spent reliving that car crash and wondering exactly where the *Midwinter*

Butcher—as the papers had colloquially come to refer to the person he just thought of as the *bastard*—would strike again on this, the anniversary of what had haunted Joseph's every waking moment since.

'One aubergine parmigiana,' the smiling lad behind the counter said, handing Joseph a bag with a takeaway box inside it.

Joseph guessed the lad had to be about seventeen, roughly the age that Eoin would have been today had he still been alive. Jesus, it seemed like there were reminders everywhere right now.

Without quite making eye contact, as Joseph didn't want to suddenly lose it in the crowded cafe, he overtipped, stuffing a twenty-pound note in the jar filled with coins. Before the lad could say anything, the detective quickly stepped out into the chilly early winter's evening in Oxford.

He began unlocking his mountain bike. It was his chief means of transport these days, as he avoided driving whenever he could. That certainly made life tricky at work, where he usually persuaded someone else to take the wheel. For all these years he'd managed to avoid being pulled in for a Psych test that certainly would have raised question marks over his suitability for work. But as far as Joseph was concerned there were some traumas that you just carried with you, and no amount of poking them with a psychiatrist's sharp stick would help him.

He slid the takeaway into one of the bicycle's panniers and a short while later he was riding through Jericho, one of the trendier areas of the city. It was all boutique cafes here, restaurants and knick-knack shops that sold things like a hundred varieties of scented candles. Just how many of those damn things did people really need in their lives?

At a mini-roundabout, the detective headed over a small red brick bridge and then down onto the canal's towpath. Joseph quickly settled into the rhythm of the cycling, muscle memory synching with the soundtrack of well-oiled gears whirring within the bike's long derailleur cage.

On the opposite side of the canal, the four-storey houses of the great and the good of North Oxford slid past. Many of them had been heavily extended, but it was in the gardens where many of the occupants with their money had made full use of their water-facing properties. A number had studios and garden rooms facing out onto the canal. Every style of garden building imaginable was there, from the modern glass minimalist boxes, to one that almost looked like a Chinese temple with a dragon decorating the roof.

The finishing touches to a few of the gardens were the small jetties with boats moored to them, including the shortest narrowboat in history—it had to be only four metres long. Not that he'd ever seen anyone use any of these boats, but the dream of using them was there at least, and that was something he entirely understood.

In the darkness, the rear windows of the houses shone with golden light, drawing his eye to the jewel-like lit kitchens and designer living rooms beyond. The common feature on display was obvious affluence. Most didn't even have the pretence of curtains. As Ellie had once said as they walked along here together, '*If you've got it, flaunt it, hey, Dad?*'

Joseph was sure these million-pound-plus Oxford houses stirred a certain amount of envy in many, but not him. That was because he was completely invested in his alternative lifestyle, and that suited the DI just fine.

It was when he looked back from the palaces of glass to the towpath that he spotted the familiar stooped figure of Charlie just ahead with his beagle, Max. He was one of the city's Big Issue sellers, magazines sold by the homeless to support them-selves, whose pitch was at the main Oxford railway station where he had his fair share of regular customers among the commuters.

Joseph knew from previous chats that Charlie, a man he was very fond of, passed on Oxford's many shelters because he valued his independence. What he wasn't meant to know was that Charlie's tent was in a copse on the east side of Port Meadow. But everyone, even the force—as no one had ever complained about it—turned a blind eye because Charlie didn't bother anyone living out there. Joseph certainly would never come down hard on a man who was down on his luck, whatever the law said.

'Hey, Charlie, how are you doing?' Joseph asked as he drew closer.

Charlie glanced back, and gave him a wide smile. 'Not bad, Joseph, and how about you, my friend? Solve any major crimes today?'

Joseph pulled alongside him and his dog and slowed to match his pace, back-pedalling to keep his balance. 'Three bank robberies, broke up an international drug smuggling ring, and solved fifteen unsolved murders, all before lunchtime.'

'A slow day then?'

He winked at him. 'How did you guess?'

'Just call me psychic.' A wry smile filled the other man's face. 'Anyway, can I interest you in a copy of your regular?' Charlie took a Big Issue from his bag and thrust it towards the detective.

'Of course...' Joseph stopped and grabbed his wallet from one of his panniers, fishing out a five-pound note. In return, Charlie gave him the magazine that would join the stack of the unread ones he already had. Not that Joseph didn't enjoy them, just that there were never enough hours in the day to read them all.

Charlie dug into his pocket for some change, but Joseph

waved it away when it was offered to him. 'Have your next cup of coffee on me, my friend.'

'Not with Oxford prices I won't, but thank you for the thought anyway,' he said with a grin, exposing a missing front tooth that had been knocked out years before by some yobs.

That was how Joseph had first met him. The DI led a short but fruitful investigation into some young thugs who had targeted at least a dozen homeless victims. Thanks to Charlie doing a star turn in the witness box, they'd been put away for over a year. If it had been down to Joseph, it would have been three, if not more.

With a wave to Charlie, Joseph set off on his way again.

There was a stillness settling over the canal as he rode alongside it. The swans and ducks that normally frequented it during the day had long since quietened down for the night. But the detective liked this silence, especially when he was still so close to the heart of the city. This was Oxford all over. You didn't have to move far away from the bustle of the main streets flooded with tourists to step back into an older, quieter pulse that beat more slowly in the lanes, canals, and rivers of the city. No wonder he'd chosen to live in exactly one of those areas where he could mentally catch his breath after the pressures of the job.

Joseph's mountain bike's burn-your-retinas-out torch-beam caught a line of four narrowboats that had been moored up next to the towpath. The furthest boats were owned by two couples overwintering in the city, but the nearer craft were permanent fixtures on the canal, the people who owned them choosing to live there year-round. The first smartly painted green narrow-boat was named *Avalon*, and that belonged to Professor Dylan Shaw, a man in his late sixties who was as big a character as you could ever hope to meet. The second boat, *Tús nua*, Gaelic for *New Beginnings*, was owned by an entirely different species who was doing his best to hide away from the world when he wasn't on duty. In other words, Joseph.

The detective pulled up and hopped off his bike before lifting it across onto the prow of his boat. He then padlocked it with one of the better D-locks that would give a safecracker pause for thought. That had everything to do with his two-wheel stallion of the road being a Trek Remedy, three thousand pounds worth of serious mountain bike engineering. Buying it had been an admittedly major indulgence as there weren't exactly a lot of mountains in Oxford, although the potholes sometimes had delusions of grandeur. But as Joseph didn't run a car, he could more than justify the expense. At least so far, he hadn't been seduced by the darker side of one of those electric bicycles, although he suspected it was only a matter of time before he cracked.

Joseph unhooked his panniers and walked alongside his boat, brushing off a few of the dead leaves that had been swept from the path and onto the small array of solar panels that adorned its roof. Not that they did a lot at this time of the year when the sun was so low in the sky. But during the summer, they more than pulled their weight by making a decent contribution towards reducing the electric consumption of his very own *Fortress of Solitude*. But during the winter months, like most, he had to rely on the power hook-up post supplied by the council, for which he paid an exorbitant monthly fee.

The other thing that non-boat people invariably wanted to know about was his loo arrangements, which always made him smile. It wasn't as though he asked them about that when he went to their houses. But for those who were interested, as Joseph patiently explained on countless occasions: *no*, it wasn't a composting toilet and *yes*, it was a chemical cartridge design like you find on a caravan. Once a week, he had to hook up a trailer on his bike and slog down to the disposal point at the far end of the canal. Yep, life on a barge was a glamorous rock and roll lifestyle. But right now Joseph wouldn't trade it for any of those four-storey North Oxford houses, despite all their kerb appeal, flash gardens, and their *oh look at me* garden studios.

He was just unlocking the door to the cabin at the stern when, with a yip, a small border terrier leapt from the deck of the *Avalon* onto the towpath. The dog barrelled towards him, all white fur, black nose, and pointy ears. As usual, the beast made straight for Joseph's bag with his takeaway meal in it.

'Bloody hell, talk about cupboard love, White Fang,' the detective said. The dog's name always made him smile, apparently inspired by Jack London's book about a half-wild wolf-dog. White Fang the terrier was about as far as it was possible to get from his namesake, apart from maybe his ability to sniff out his food whenever he arrived home.

To distract the dog, because Joseph always had to, he flicked open a tin that he kept in the narrowboat's cockpit for such emergencies, and took out a doggy treat.

And just like that, mid-yap, the little dog went quiet. Now White Fang was all focused attention, sitting like he'd spent his life in obedience school as he licked his lips, a slight tremble running through his body.

'You do realise that you're going to make my dog fat,' Dylan said as he emerged from the *Avalon's* cabin.

'Hey, it's not my fault if I have to bribe White Fang to keep him distracted long enough to board my boat with my tea.'

'You try telling that to his vet, who gives me a lecture about his weight every time I take him in for a checkup.'

'You mean all those pies you share with him from the Covered Market have nothing to do with his expanding waistline?'

Dylan chuckled and ran his hand through his mad mane of hair. 'I don't know what you mean, Joseph.'

The professor was Joseph's neighbour and now firm friend. They'd first connected fourteen years ago, just as Joseph's marriage had finally fallen apart. The loss of a child, stolen away by death, had killed it like a bullet blast straight through the heart of his family.

But for all Joseph's grief, he'd been blessed by stumbling upon the parallel community of the boat people in Oxford. That was thanks to a former sergeant at the station when he'd still been in uniform working out of the St Aldates police station. The sergeant had told him over a pint that a narrowboat was a perfect choice for a freshly minted bachelor like himself, especially when one factored in the cost of property in this city, one of the most expensive places to live in the country. So it was with little surprise that Joseph had quickly been seduced by the idea.

That was how he'd found himself ploughing his share of the profit from selling the family home after the divorce into an old seventy-footer narrowboat that had needed a lot of TLC. It had also been during his search for a permanent mooring that he'd fallen into the orbit of Dylan, a retired professor from Keble who was living out the rest of his life on the water.

Dylan was also something of a local celebrity who seemed to know everyone, and they him. He certainly had his finger on the pulse of all sorts of things going on in Oxford. Joseph had more than once picked his brain over some obscure detail that only someone like him with his encyclopaedic knowledge would know about. The computerised HOLMES 2, an acronym for Home Office Large Major Enquiry system, might be good at work, but sometimes for a detail that everyone else would have missed, Dylan was your man.

With a flourish, the professor produced something from behind his back.

'What's that about then?' Joseph asked, looking at the clear glass bottle.

'A Cotswold Gin from the sunny climes of our own dear hills. It was once awarded best gin in the world, Joseph.' He made a show of peering at the label. 'And it appears to have your name on it.'

'You're telling me it's a present?'

'But of course. I've been meaning to give it to you as a thank you, after all that help you gave me repainting *Avalon* back in the summer.'

Joseph narrowed his gaze at him. 'As kind as that is, tonight's midwinter anniversary has got nothing to do with that, then?'

Charlie sighed. 'I can tell you're a detective inspector. But for your information, there is absolutely no way I'm going to leave my best friend to get through this long night all by himself.'

'I'm not sure I'll be brilliant company, Dylan.'

'You don't need to be. All I ask is that you share some of that gin with me. After all, it's number fifty-six on my bucket list of gins to drink before I die.'

'In that case, you're on, but only if you also share the aubergine parmigiana I just picked up from Jericho Café. Their portions are always enough to feed two. Although, let me grab a shower first, because the cycle from work has left me a bit rank.'

'Then, come and join me when you're ready and we'll see if we can't put a bit of a dent in that bottle tonight.'

'Sounds like a plan.' With a wave and a pat on White Fang's head, Joseph unlocked the cabin door and headed outside back to *Tús nua.*

He sat with Dylan in the cosy cabin of *Avalon*. Despite the boat's confined proportions, the professor had packed out every available wall with books. Thanks to that, the boat sat so low in the water that if narrowboats had a Plimsoll line like sea-going vessels, Joseph was pretty sure that it would be far beneath the surface.

To say that Dylan was a bookaholic would have been the understatement of the century. You weren't just talking normal dusty second-hand volumes here either. Some books in his collection looked old enough to have come straight from the vaults of the Bodleian Library. And knowing Dylan, they probably did. Somehow he was able to have them on extended loan, even though books like that weren't normally meant to be removed. But those were the rules for mere academic mortals, and Joseph's friend was of a much higher order.

The professor was also a pub quiz team's wet dream. The number of facts that he could pluck out of the depths of his mind had often left Joseph's jaw hanging. Dylan never used the internet. This guy was totally old school. He either looked it up in a book, or tracked it down to some ancient article that he'd read on one of the primitive microfiche machines that the library still had for back issues of all the major papers.

Dylan raised his glass, clinked it against Joseph's, and then sipped it. 'Ah, the fresh notes of grapefruit with the hint of juniper. That's rather good in an unostentatious way.'

Joseph took a nip. 'It certainly tastes alright.'

Dylan sighed. 'That's a serious understatement, Joseph. However, I suppose that's gushing praise coming from you.' He settled back into his well worn chair, his weather worn complexion almost taking on the same colour as the pale tan leather. He gazed at Joseph as he swirled the gin around his glass. 'So the real question is, how are you doing tonight?'

Joseph sighed. 'As well as you might expect. I've barely been able to concentrate at work. In all honesty, I should probably take this day off every year and wait it out until morning.'

'I can certainly understand where you're coming from. At least this is an improvement on previous years. Once you would have been wearing out the carpet at the police station, waiting for the report to come in about the latest case.'

'You're not wrong. As regular as damned clockwork, that psychopath cuts off the head of some poor bloody animal every year on the winter solstice. I tell you, if I ever get my hands on that bastard...' The detective gripped his glass harder.

'I know, Joseph, I know, and no one would blame you. But you're also the sort of man that will only achieve closure through playing this by the book and arresting him.'

Joseph slowly nodded. 'You're not wrong there.'

Dylan took another sip of his gin and nodded. 'Anyway, have you heard from Kate at all today?'

'Nothing so far, but there were a bunch of fresh flowers at Eoin's memorial stone in the graveyard this morning...' The detective felt sudden tears itching in the corners of his eyes.

The professor turned to look at the flames flickering in the small stove that heated his boat—a kindness to allow Joseph to compose himself. Lord, this poor man had seen enough of Joseph's snot and tears over the years on this anniversary.

'Sorry,' Joseph said, as he drew in a shaky breath.

Dylan tapped his fingernail on his glass. 'Don't be. You've already suffered enough heartache to last a lifetime. I still can't believe they haven't caught the Midwinter Butcher after all this time, and before you say it, that's no reflection on you.'

'So why does it feel like it is?' Joseph asked. 'Every year I get it thrown in my face when he does the same damned thing. Time and time again, all carried out on exactly the same night for the last sixteen years.'

'All I know is that no one could have worked harder than you have to try to catch him.'

'Maybe, but we both know that I had my part to play in what happened that night. If I had only checked that bloody seatbelt, my son would still be alive today.'

Dylan gave Joseph a look filled with such compassion that it twisted the detective's heart. 'Life is filled with *if only I'd done that* moments, Joseph. We both understand that. I could lecture you until the end of time about being easier on yourself, but if there's one person you should listen to about this, it's Kate. You know she doesn't hold you responsible for what happened, and neither should you. The problem is that you are judge, jury, and executioner in your own mind. But if you'll take one bit of advice from an old man, you need to learn to forgive yourself.'

'I'm not sure that will ever happen.'

'Well, it needs to,' Dylan said, taking another sip of his gin. 'Concentrate on what you have, namely your gorgeous daughter Ellie, who lightens up your life whenever she's here. I honestly don't think I've ever seen a father look as proud as you do when you talk about her.'

Joseph smiled at the mention of her name. 'I'm certainly Ellie's number one fan. She's flying high in her course at the Blavatnik School of Government in Oxford. Did I tell you she just won a debating prize?'

'Only half a dozen times in the last month,' Dylan said, grinning at Joseph.

He laughed. 'Fair play. I've certainly managed to bore half the team at CID to death, by going on about her all the time.'

'There's nothing wrong with that. The prerogative of a parent. Mind you, I'm also certain Ellie will have a glittering political career ahead of her, that is, if she wants it.'

'We'll see. I'd be happier if she followed her mum into journalism, or even me into the force.'

'Ellie is a woman who has always known her own mind thanks to how you and Kate have brought her up. You two might be divorced, but you both have still done a fantastic job of raising your daughter.'

'If you say so.'

'I do, and I have to say I'm a little envious of you both.'

'Why's that?' Joseph asked.

'To know the joy that a child can bring into your life. Mind you, I have been compensated by teaching thousands and thousands of students during my years at Keble College.'

'You're not going to go all *Goodbye, Mr. Chips* on me, are you?'

Dylan chuckled. 'Yes, I'm a hopeless literary romantic and the original film version of the book made me weep buckets, but I do rather like the comparison. Anyway...' Dylan raised his glass. 'Here's to you old friend, and maybe to lady luck tripping that bastard up tonight wherever he is, enough so that he gets caught at last.'

'That would be grand, and I'll certainly drink to that.'

Joseph clinked his glass against his, but as he gazed out through the portal at the night beyond, his old anxiety was already making its presence felt as a churning feeling in his stomach. Somewhere out there right now, that psychopath would be getting ready to strike again.

CHAPTER FOUR

————————

ELLIE WAS DOING her best to concentrate on her driving as her very own *Dancing Queen*, in the petite form of her best friend Zoe, bellowed out the chorus to the Abba song currently playing on the battered Ford Fiesta's sound system.

Ellie winced. Even though the song was blasting out at full volume, it was doing little to drown out the bum notes that Zoe kept hitting.

'You really should think about going on *Britain's Got Talent* with an angelic voice like that,' Ellie said.

Zoe turned in her seat and raised her eyebrows at her friend. 'Oh, bitchy!'

She gave her a crooked smile. 'Just calling it as it is.'

Her friend snorted. 'Only my bestie could get away with telling me that, especially as she's the'—she lowered her passenger window—'birthday girl!' she shouted out at a group of guys all wearing Santa hats on the pavement.

The gaggle of men who'd emerged from one of the bars on Cowley Road all turned towards the Fiesta and whooped and whistled.

Ellie hunkered down in her seat as they drove past the guys, who were blowing kisses and making heart shapes with their hands. 'God, you're so embarrassing when you're pissed, Zoe.'

'That's exactly what friends are for, keeping it real at every opportunity. Anyway, in this particular instance, I think I was doing you a favour because I reckon any one of those guys would have been up for giving you a quick birthday fumble. You could always turn the car round?'

'Even the idea of that makes me want to be sick in my mouth and I'm the stone-cold sober one.'

Zoe held up her hand to stop her. 'Hey, and exactly whose fault is that? Only you would volunteer to be the bloody designated driver on your own frigging birthday.'

'Well, somebody had to be the grown-up. Besides, as you well know, I'm never really in the mood to do anything on my actual birthday. But for some reason, against my better judgement, I let you and the girls drag me out tonight anyway.'

'We thought it might help,' her best friend said, only slightly slurring her words.

'Nothing will.' Like always, she just needed to get through this anniversary. 'But on the plus side, it was quite entertaining watching you and the others get slaughtered, especially when Sarah vomited all over that guy's expensive trainers.'

'Oh God, that was absolutely golden,' Zoe said, grinning.

'Yeah, the look on his face was brilliant,' Ellie said, laughing as she turned the Fiesta onto a side road.

'But his mate was just a bit gorgeous, wasn't he?' her friend said. 'And he was making those puppy dog eyes at you, too. You not dating is a proper crime against humanity and your dad should lock you up for it.'

'If you say so. But the truth is that I've just not met the right guy, especially on shag centre, Tinder.'

'Tinder, *shminder*. You should try dating an older guy like me. You never have to buy your own drinks, the sex is great, and they're just so damned grateful. And some of the wild parties I've been to would turn your hair pink.'

'Like the ones your mystery man has been taking you to recently?'

'Exactly, Ellie, and he adores the ground I walk on and would lick my shoes if I asked.'

'You dominatrix, you!'

Zoe shrieked with laughter as they turned onto James Street. An assistant in an Oxford medical research lab during the day, Zoe was the very definition of a wild child at night, one who certainly knew how to blow off steam.

Back-to-back cars were parked along each side, many of the houses dark, but a few shone with enough Christmas lights to turn day into night along the quiet street.

'So, when am I going to get to meet this *Mr Perfect,* then?' Ellie asked,

'Sorry, you can't because it would *A,* make you jealous, and *B,* you'd only try to steal him from me, so that's not happening.'

'Just as long as you're happy.'

'I really am, Ellie,' Zoe said with a wide smile.

'Good to hear. Anyway, here we are, your home sweet home.'

'You're the best,' her friend said as they parked up outside a maisonette with missing roof tiles and a badly patched front door.

Zoe rented an upstairs room in this building that was normally filled with students. Everything about it left a lot to be desired, from its peeling yellow walls and mouldy black patches around the windows to the strange musty smell that even a dozen scented candles hadn't been able to banish. Ellie suspected that something had died under the floorboards and was slowly decaying there. But Zoe saw this place with rose-tinted glasses because it was the first real place that she'd been able to call her own after living in care homes her whole life.

Her best friend let herself out and wobbled slightly as Ellie lowered the window.

'You want to come in and catch me up with a few drinks?' Zoe asked. 'You're welcome to stop over.'

'No, I'm all good. I've a ton of research work that I need to get through before next term.'

'What if I pointed out this is the start of the Christmas holidays?'

'I would say that my work won't research itself, now will it?'

Zoe sighed. 'Once a swot, always a swot.' She leant in through the window and gave Ellie a big hug and kiss. 'And despite that, I still love you to bits.'

'Yeah, me too.'

'Good!' Zoe clambered back, tottering away to her front door and giving Ellie a backwards wave.

Ellie smiled as she started her ancient Fiesta up again, an eighteenth birthday present from her mum after her dad had helped her find it at a car auction in Witney.

She thumbed through the music on her phone and selected an album by Einaudi, which matched her mood. It was the sort of modern classical thing that her dad loved whenever he caught a lift with her.

At first, she'd teased him about going all *Morse* on her, especially as his taste had been stuck in the era of U2. That had everything to do with a story he liked to spin about how he'd once met Bono at a party back in the mother country, and he was, to use her dad's vernacular, a *grand craic*. But then her dad met Professor Dylan Shaw and slowly but surely he'd influenced her dad's musical tastes.

At first, Ellie hadn't got it, but after listening to Einaudi and similar a few times, the more she picked up on a common thread of sadness that was woven through all of it. Of course, that was something that her family knew way too much about, especially on the anniversary that had left her unable to celebrate her own birthday.

The music soared on the Fiesta's outdated sound system as she took off into the night, but Ellie's heart didn't climb with it because tonight, the winter solstice, was the longest night for her soul in every sense.

At least she knew her mum would be fine thanks to Derek, her new husband—even if Dad still couldn't cope with the idea of her mum marrying his boss. As for Dad, he would be in good hands with Dylan tonight.

When Ellie was younger, she'd done her best to try to patch the hole that a missing sibling had left in their family. She'd spent alternating years on the anniversary of Eoin's death trying to cheer up either her dad or mum, and that had been a full-time job. But, if she was totally honest, it was always such a downer being around either of them on the anniversary. So, gradually, they'd learnt to spend the day separately for all of their sakes.

Ellie turned onto Bartholomew Road, where the Laithwaite City Farm was based and where she volunteered when she wasn't at college. It wasn't on her way home, but she'd made a deliberate diversion because there'd been several break-ins recently during which vandals had trashed the place. Now every chance she got, she gave it a visual once over to check everything was okay.

It had been a toss-up between Ellie becoming a vet, or getting into politics, her long-term plan to stand for the Green Party eventually and try to make a difference. But it had been her dad who suggested she could do both by pursuing a degree in politics, whilst working at the city farm looking after the chickens, pigs, and goats in her spare time. Her dad sometimes knew her better than she knew herself. He'd been totally right, she loved it. But Ellie was certain that her slightly obsessive love of animals was her trying to compensate after seeing a roe deer decapitated on her sixth birthday. She didn't need an inkblot psychologist test to help her work out that bit of the puzzle.

As Ellie neared the lane that led down to the entrance of the farm, she pulled up and glanced towards it. Everything certainly looked quiet, the entrance locked and not a person to be seen. It seemed that even vandals liked to take the Christmas break off. She was just thinking about turning around when she saw a flash of torchlight reflected off one of the polytunnels out the back.

'Shit!' she said to the universe at large.

She drove to the entrance and parked up. Ellie then dug her phone out of her bag and, perhaps just as importantly, the pepper spray that her dad had slipped her from work. Not that she was meant to have it, especially as it was illegal for the public to use it. But Dad said she needed to carry it for her personal protection, although she was under strict instructions to get rid of it if the police came within fifty metres of her. Most parents were paranoid to a greater or lesser degree with their kids, but her dad took it to a whole other level.

Ellie got out of the Fiesta as quietly as she could, pepper spray in one hand, phone in the other, its camera already powered up. Her dad had taught her years ago that a photo was far better evidence for identifying a suspect than trying to recall it for a Photofit. She certainly intended to nail these little buggers if she could. That would make her birthday almost *okay*.

The team who ran the farm had taken the break-ins personally. Everyone that worked there was like one big family and they all really cared about the farm. Geoff, another volunteer, had been in tears when the vandals had ransacked the place during the summer, kicking pumpkins like footballs across the field and destroying half the crop. Then, when the thugs weren't doing that, or attempting to break into their buildings or the old shipping containers where they kept their tools, they were scrawling racist slogans across the walls. You didn't need to be Einstein to realise that was something to do with the truly multinational makeup of the people who worked there.

Ellie slowly crept towards the gates. She might have been determined to catch them, but she also had a head on her shoulders, and she had no intention of tackling them single handily. Her mum and dad had brought her up to have at least some sense. But once she was certain the little buggers really were in there, she'd ring the police and let them deal with them.

Her heart sped up as she approached the gates on foot. At least she could see that this time they hadn't simply used bolt cutters to shear off the lock. Then she saw another flash of light illuminating one of the polytunnels. Okay, someone was definitely on the farm, but Ellie still wanted to eyeball them rather than wasting police time, especially when it might reflect badly on her dad.

In a single leap, she vaulted the gate and landed in a crouch on the other side. Then, seeking every shadow she could find, Ellie stole past the buildings towards the rear of the farm plot.

Although she could hear her heart beating in her ears, she was far from being afraid. She almost felt elated. Maybe it was the joy of the hunt kicking in. *No wonder Dad does this for a living*, she thought, *if he gets an endorphin fix like this whenever he's in the field, chasing down the bad guys.*

Another beam of torchlight lanced out briefly in the direction of the animal pens where they kept their livestock. On one of the more infamous break-ins, the vandals had stolen the eggs from the coops, leaving the hens half terrified to death and the farm with a hefty vet bill to deal with.

Those *eejits*, as her dad would sometimes call them if he lapsed back into full-blown Irish, had this coming.

She crept as quietly as she could on the balls of her feet, using the polytunnels as cover to close on the dancing torch-light. As far as she could tell, they appeared to be in Gandalf and Dumbledore's pen, their two kid goats named by a local primary school after they'd run a competition to come up with the best suggestions.

A sudden sharp bleat cut through the night air and she immediately recognised Dumbledore's cry. But this wasn't his usual chill tone. It had an edge to it that made the hair on her neck stand up.

Later, she'd wonder why her brain didn't put two and two together at that moment. At least some sort of red flag should have been flashed up by her subconscious. But no. Too much adrenaline had been surging through her system for the sensible part of her brain to get a look in.

Then a scream of awful animal terror came from the goat pen. It was only then that the "daughter of a policeman's" brain finally kicked in.

It can't be...

Immediately, she punched 999 into her mobile.

'Emergency, which service do you require? Fire, police, or ambulance?' the woman's voice calmly asked at the other end.

'Police,' Ellie whispered.

'Transferring you now.'

A man's voice came on. 'What's the nature of the incident?'

'Someone is attacking the animals at Laithwaite City Farm in Oxford.'

'And what's your name?' the man asked.

'Ellie Stone, I'm Detective Inspector Joseph Stone's daughter from the St Aldates Police Station. Look, you can ask me all the questions you like later, but I think it may be the Midwinter Butcher.'

There was a pause at the other end. 'And your current location is?'

She tried to keep the impatience out of her voice. 'Like I said, I'm at city farm and within thirty metres of the animal pens at the rear. Please send a patrol car here right away because he's hurting our goats.'

'One is already on the way, Ellie, but please keep on the line. Are you in any danger?'

'Not that I know of, but I can look after myself.' She gripped the pepper spray harder. *To think, after all these years, I might be the one to bring this bastard down.*

'Whatever you do, do not engage the—'

The rest of what the man said was drowned out by the scream of Dumbledore, once again filled with raw animal terror, then silence.

That was it. No way Ellie could stand there in the shadows and let this happen. She edged forward, heart racing in her chest as she reached the end of the polytunnel and peered around it.

A figure wearing a white plastic suit, just like the forensic team used. The head torch that the figure was wearing lanced down, illuminating the small goat's body lying motionless at their feet.

Just behind the man, Gandalf, the other kid goat, pressed hard against the far fence as he tried to keep his distance from the figure. He let out a high pitch bleat of pure fear that was like a knife through her heart.

Then pure rage boiled through Ellie as Dumbledore's head toppled onto the ground.

This had to be the same bastard responsible for scaring the deer that had rushed into the path of their car sixteen years ago.

And because of the Midwinter Butcher her baby brother had been killed.

Ellie focused her fury and, roaring something guttural like a Viking battle cry, she rushed to the pen.

The figure turned towards her, face invisible because of the head torch that was now shining into her eyes. But she was going to make them pay, pay for sixteen years of misery and a broken family.

Ellie's heart thundered as she closed the distance, aiming the pepper spray straight towards the figure's face, pressing the photo button on her phone at the same time. But the person reacted, bringing one arm up to shield their face, the other hand reaching down to grab something.

She hurtled towards the figure, getting ready to tackle them to the ground. But too late she registered her subject pivoting on their foot like a discus thrower and throwing Gandalf's severed head at her. Before Ellie had time to duck, the goat's skull slammed into the side of her head with a sickening impact. And then she was falling, her phone flying out of her hand as white spots swarmed her vision. As she crashed into the muddy ground of the pen, Ellie was dimly aware of blue strobing lights dancing off the surrounding trees before her world went dark.

22ND DECEMBER

CHAPTER FIVE

JOSEPH HEADED along the dimmed nighttime corridor of the hospital with a mixture of cold parental dread and exhaustion humming through his body. That hadn't been helped by his sprint across the city on his bike. He'd opted for two wheels rather than four because it was always going to be quicker than waiting for a taxi to show up. Normally, he would have considered blagging a lift in a patrol car, but the Oxford force was thinly stretched at the best of times. Especially on a Friday night, when the clubs were turning out.

Negotiating with the woman sitting behind the desk in emergency, trying to convince her he wasn't some sort of psychopath and that he really was Ellie's dad, had brought him close to punching a hole through the plexiglass screen. But thankfully, if only for the sake of his career, a deep breath or three, and a flash of his police warrant card, had been enough to eventually convince her he was legitimate. But as he'd stalked away, even he had to admit a certain grudging professional respect for that woman. She could certainly have taught some of the younger detectives at Aldates a thing or two about interrogating suspects.

A young Asian nurse, presumably the one that had buzzed him into the ward, looked up from her computer screen as he approached the nurses' desk. To cut things short this time around, he flashed his warrant card straight away.

'Detective Inspector Stone, here to see Ellie Stone.'

'You're related?' the young woman asked.

'Yes, I'm her dad. How's she doing?'

'Much better now, although she's still shaken up. But her brain scan just came back, and was all clear. The doctor just wanted to keep her in overnight for observation, which is strictly routine before you get worried.'

His shoulders sagged. 'Right...' Gradually, the snare drum of his heartbeat decelerated as he took in several longer breaths.

The nurse tipped her head to one side as she looked at him with gentle eyes. 'Honestly, we're as certain as we can be that Ellie's going to be okay. Anyway, if you'd like to see for yourself, just follow me.'

'Thank you.' The detective fell in alongside her, clenching and unclenching his fists, desperate to get hold of the toerag who'd done this to his beautiful girl.

The nurse glanced sideways at him as they walked. 'One of your colleagues has already been here to interview Ellie.'

'Who?'

'Detective Constable Anderson.'

'Don't know him. Must be one of the recruits who joined the team this week.'

'Actually, it was a woman. Megan, I think she said her name was. Anyway, your wife is already here.'

'Ex-wife,' he corrected her.

'Oh, I see,' the nurse said as she stopped just outside a set of double doors. 'Well, they're both in there. Would you like me to bring you a cup of tea?'

After the desert dryness of being dehydrated by a glass too

many of Dylan's Cotswold Gin, that sounded like his idea of nectar right then. 'That would be grand and stronger the better, but no sugar, please.'

'Coming right up,' the nurse replied with a smile. She turned and headed away along the corridor.

Joseph entered the darkened ward and began scanning the occupants of the half dozen beds, most of whom were asleep, although a few gazed with unfocused eyes at him as he passed. Around the last bed next to the window, a curtain had been partially pulled.

Joseph braced himself for whatever state Ellie was going to be in. But as he peered through the gap, an ocean's worth of relief rushed through his body when he saw his daughter sitting up. That was only tempered a fraction by the large bandage that had been wrapped around her head, reminding him of Mr. Bump from one of the picture books she had adored as a child.

Kate was sitting in a chair next to the bed, holding Ellie's hand in hers, her long blonde hair hanging like curtains on either side of her face. There wasn't a trace of makeup on her, which she wore almost like armour when working. But that was probably just as well at the moment, going by the number of tears currently rolling down her cheeks.

Mother and daughter both looked up at him as his shadow fell across the curtain.

'My darling girl, what did that psychopath do to you?' Joseph said as he entered the cubicle, unable to keep the tremble out of his voice.

Ellie just shook her head, her face pale. Then she reached out both arms to him.

Joseph crossed to her in four strides to pull her into a tight hug. She might be twenty-two, but in some corner of his mind she was still that six-year-old girl and always would be. He held onto her, then like someone had thrown a switch inside his skull, he was suddenly crying with big racking sobs. Kate, who was looking at him over their daughter's shoulder, reached out and squeezed his arm. She got it because she was wired exactly the same way when it came to Ellie, especially since they had lost Eoin.

No one said anything for a moment as Joseph wept, just holding onto his daughter, the most precious thing in his life.

Joseph never cried as a rule, but the fortified walls he'd built up around his heart after twenty years on the force instantly came tumbling down when it came to Ellie. She was his Achilles' heel, the chunk of his own soul that left him wide open to raw emotion whenever anything happened to her. From a bleeding knee from a bike tumble when she was eight, to a broken leg on a skiing trip in her teens, he was quickly reduced to snot and tears. What would the hardened criminals he'd helped put behind bars say if they could see him now?

With their roles reversed, it was Ellie who patted his back, her own face wiped dry and very much holding it together. Joseph sometimes thought that their daughter was stronger than both Kate and him.

'I'm okay, Dad, really,' she whispered into his ear as she kissed the side of his head.

He forced himself to pull away from her and then gave her face the once over. Her eyes were certainly bright, with no sign of any lingering concussion behind them.

Joseph took a shaky breath and then nodded, taking a tissue Kate offered him and blowing his nose. 'When I got that call from the station, I thought...' His throat closed up and he couldn't get the rest of the words out.

Kate nodded and squeezed his hand again. 'Yes, me too. I may have got flashed by at least one speed camera on my way over here.'

'If they had cameras on the towpaths, I think I might have

been caught for speeding too,' he replied, giving her a small smile.

They might be divorced, but Kate was still one of his best friends. When it came to Ellie, their golden-haired, blue-eyed girl, their lass was still very much the centre of a universe that they had once shared. There's no turning your back on that sort of history together, a blood bond of DNA and soul in a child that you both helped bring into the world.

Joseph gathered himself enough to ask her the question that he was burning to know the answer to. 'Ellie, when the desk sergeant contacted me, he said you disturbed the Midwinter Butcher. Is that right?'

'Dad, it has to be him because it has his MO all over it.'

He smiled at her use of the police jargon for *modus operandi*. Yes, she was definitely a police detective's daughter at heart.

'And did you see their face?' he asked.

'Like I told DC Anderson, they were wearing a head torch, so I couldn't see their features. But at least I managed to pepper spray them before they knocked me out. I think I may have got a shot of them, too, on my phone.'

He sat up straighter. 'You did? Did the DC take your phone in to check through it?'

'No, because the bastard knocked it out of my hand in the goat pen. The git probably stole it, although I gave Megan my mobile number on the off chance that it might still be turned on so they can trace it.'

Joseph sighed. 'I'm certain that whoever we're dealing with is far too careful about something like that and has no doubt already destroyed it.'

'As though I didn't already have enough reasons to already hate him,' Ellie replied.

'The important thing is that you're okay,' Kate said. 'I think I would have been terrified if I'd been in your shoes.'

'To be honest, I had little time to feel anything because it all happened so fast. But, Dad, I'm afraid there's more bad news. I doubt the forensic team will be able to turn up any DNA evidence at the scene.'

'Why's that?' Joseph asked.

'He really knew what he was doing. He was wearing a full-blown forensic suit.'

He blew his cheeks out. 'Damn, but at least that explains why we haven't turned up any DNA traces at the other animal killing sites. Anyway, the desk sergeant also told me they assaulted you with a goat's severed head. Is that right?'

Now it was Ellie's turn for tears to spring up in her eyes. 'Yes, that poor baby. According to DC Anderson, Gandalf, our other goat, is missing too. God knows what we're going to tell the local primary schools who sponsor them both.'

Kate took Ellie's hand in hers again. 'I just wish you hadn't had to witness any of that.'

'Me too, Mum. I don't think I'll ever be able to get that image out of my head, just like when—' A sob choked off the rest of her words.

But she didn't have to finish her sentence because Joseph and Kate both knew what she was going to say next. It was the same image that haunted all of them—a decapitated deer burned into their minds and forever symbolising the loss of their son, Ellie's brother, Eoin.

Joseph took Ellie's other hand. 'I'm going to ask to be put on the case and make sure that every bit of CCTV footage is checked in the surrounding area. Even if he was careful, there's still a chance that someone's private security camera might give us a clue about where he disappeared to when the patrol car turned up.'

'Dad, I'm afraid you can't get involved,' Ellie said, her tone subdued.

'What do you mean?'

'Because I'm a person of interest.'

Joseph stared at her as the ramifications hit home. 'Shite, you're not telling me because you were at the crime scene they think you might have something to do with this?'

'You know the procedure, because you've certainly told me enough times. Even if I am your daughter and I'm the one who called it in, they still have to check everything out to eliminate me as a suspect. I'm certainly not taking it personally and DC Anderson was brilliant about it. Mind you, I have to go in and make a formal statement as soon as I leave the hospital.'

'Well, I'm still bloody taking it personally and I'm going to demand to be on the case, whether or not it's a conflict of interest.' He turned to Kate. 'You need to get your *new* husband to finally put some serious resources into this case. I know Derek believes the Midwinter Butcher case doesn't warrant it, because the killer has stuck to animals so far, but the DSU's thinking needs to change, now.'

Kate nodded, not quite meeting his gaze. 'I'll see what I can do, Joseph.'

Joseph immediately felt a stab of guilt because Kate could obviously see something in the eejit that no one else could, which was why she'd married him. The problem was that Detective Superintendent Derek Walker, or *Wanker* as most detectives loved to call him behind his back, also happened to be Joseph's superintendent. To make matters worse, they had once been friends, actually doing their time together on the beat back in the days when they'd still both been in uniform.

But there'd been an ambitious streak to Derek, right from the start. When Joseph had to take time off work for compassionate leave when Eoin had died, Derek had shown his true colours and had jumped at the chance to stab him in the back. Somehow he'd convinced everyone of senior rank he was the man to be promoted to CID, rather than Joseph, who'd been in the running for the job ahead of him. The prat had even used Joseph's state of mind as evidence of his unsuitability, whispering in the right ears and poisoning the water well.

That had just been the start.

Derek had pulled whatever stunts he needed to climb the greasy pole to his current rank of DSU. Now, every chance he got, he undermined him at work and made sure Joseph could never rise above the rank of DI. There'd never been enough for him to submit a formal complaint about his treatment of Joseph at work, but just enough to make the DI's life uncomfortable. The icing on the bloody cake was Derek marrying Kate three years ago. Joseph even had to swallow his pride and go to their fecking wedding, but he only did that for Kate's sake and certainly not that gobshite's.

Ellie helped herself to some of Kate's tissues to wipe her eyes before turning back to Joseph. 'Dad, I have to ask, because you know this will already be going through the heads of anyone involved in the investigation... Do you think the Midwinter Butcher targeted the farm's goats because I work there?'

Kate's face drained of colour, but this exact thought had been rattling through Joseph's skull as he'd peddled like a madman to get to the hospital.

'I have to admit it's one hell of a coincidence, so we can't rule it out,' he said.

Kate's hands shot to her mouth. 'You're telling me that whoever this animal killer is, they've been stalking our daughter?'

'We have to look at it as a serious possibility,' he replied. 'Don't forget your photo in the Oxford Chronicle, when you covered the farm's open day, had Ellie in it.'

Their daughter's eyes widened. 'Oh God, and I was in that photo with Gandalf and Dumbledore, too, which probably gave the psychopath the idea.'

It felt like Joseph's blood was turning to ice because that little nugget of information had reduced the odds of tonight being a random event. Of course, sixteen years previously, their car crash had been all over the papers, and Ellie's name had been included by a maggot of a reporter from a tabloid. Kate had been spitting bullets about that ever since.

Joseph gazed at his daughter. 'I don't want you to worry yourself about this, Ellie, but just to play things on the safe side, I want you to stay with your mum where she can keep an eye out for you.'

Ellie gawped at him. 'What, you think they're seriously coming for me?'

'I just want you to be careful because tonight's killing marks a serious escalation with a direct assault on you. You both know that I've always been worried about where this lunatic might be headed with this one day.'

Kate nodded as she clasped Ellie's hand so tightly that her fingers dug into her skin as they both looked at him.

'Based on the profiling we've done previously, whoever this person is, there's always a chance that these animal killings were all practise ones as they build up to the main event,' he continued.

Ellie let out a small gasp. 'Bloody hell! You really think they're now actually capable of murdering someone?'

'I pray not, but that's what's given me sleepless nights for all these years,' Joseph replied, finally putting the card he had hidden from them all this time on the table.

Kate glared at him, leaving no doubt she'd be laying into Joseph about that choice fact when they were out of earshot of their daughter.

'That's it, Ellie, you're going to come and stay with me in the spare room,' she said.

But Ellie was already shaking her head. 'Sorry, Mum, but you know Derek and I don't get along. If it's all the same to you, I'll stay with Dad. And before you say anything, I know Dad's always busy at work, but there's always Dylan in the boat next door to keep an eye on me when he's not there.'

Joseph scratched his neck. 'Actually, I think you'd be better off with your mum. There's barely room to swing a cat on board *Tús nua,* as it is.'

'Please, Dad, if I have to stay anywhere apart from my student digs, I'd rather it be with you. I'll make up the spare bed on the sofa and I won't be any trouble. I'll even make you some of my famous spag bol.'

He looked across at Kate. 'Are you okay with this?'

'To be honest, as long as she's with one of us, then I am.'

'Alright then, it sounds like I have your spag bol to look forward to,' Joseph said.

'Thanks for being understanding, guys,' Ellie said.

'Let's just hope the SOCOs turns up something at the farm,' Kate said.

'Derek's assigned a full-blown forensic investigation?' Joseph asked. 'But what about keeping resources to a minimum?'

Kate gave him a small smile. 'You know Amy,' she said referring to the Scene of Crime lead. 'She's a law unto herself, as well as being a major fan of yours. You should have heard Derek arguing with her on the phone. But that woman is a force of nature, and got her way to properly investigate the crime scene with a full forensic team. She's there now.'

'Wow, Derek's costs spreadsheet will hate that,' he replied.

His ex-wife's smile widened. 'I know, and I may have had a hand in persuading him, too.'

Joseph grinned at her. 'The poor man never stood a chance,' he said as he stood up.

Kate shot him a questioning look. 'Where are you going?'

'Whether or not they want me there, I'm heading over to the city farm to check whether our SOCO team has turned up anything yet.'

Ellie pulled a face at him. 'Okay, but if anyone can, it's Amy. Please keep your head down, Dad. Remember that officially you're not meant to be anywhere near there. But unofficially, you go and nail that psychopath bastard for me.'

'Oh, don't you worry, I bloody well intend to.' He kissed first her forehead, and then Kate's, before heading out of the ward, with the stride of a man on a mission.

CHAPTER SIX

JOSEPH CYCLED straight from the hospital to Laithwaite City Farm. As he'd expected, as per standard procedure with a crime scene investigation underway, they'd already locked down the road with a patrol car parked across it. He'd learnt from the St Aldates desk sergeant that the case was being headed by DCI Chris Faulkner, who'd been assigned as the senior investigating officer. He was one of Walker's chosen few, fast-tracked for promotion just like the superintendent himself had been. Although Joseph didn't have a problem with a younger man being his senior officer, he had an issue with his snarky attitude and his barely disguised contempt. He'd once even overheard the little fecker refer to him as *the dead wood that needs trimming*. Yes, Faulkner was Walker's man.

Unfortunately, that would also mean that Joseph had zero chance of blagging his way past the uniformed officers in the car. The DI would bet on his grandma's very long life that Chris would have left very specific instructions on how he should be dealt with in case he turned up at the crime scene.

So having clocked the police vehicle, instead of trying to negotiate his way with Uniform, he'd carried on cycling straight past the lane. There, Joseph padlocked his bike to a lamppost on one of the side streets. Then he headed back to the farm on foot, his breath billowing in the freezing air like an asthmatic steam train on a hill climb.

The detective had a sketch of an idea in his head. It relied entirely on the discretion of some certain officers whom Joseph knew he could trust to keep quiet about him turning up, and to not drop him in it.

With that genius plan in place, he was now creeping through the garden of a property that backed up to the farm. The irony wasn't lost on him that if anyone spotted him—he was doing a very reasonable impression of a house burglar casing a property—it would certainly look bad.

Apart from the Christmas lights still lit in some windows, he couldn't spot the telltale ring of red LED lights that would give away the presence of a security camera mounted on the back of the house. Even if he pulled this off, any footage of the detective trying to gain entry to the crime scene through someone's private property might be tricky to explain. Irish charm could only get you so far in life.

Gentle rain began pattering down as he made his way to the end of the garden and peered through the thicket of brambles coiled like razor wire along the top of the boarded fence.

Through the gaps, he could make out several portable flood-lights that had been set up around the animal pens, illuminating a white tent that had been erected over one of them. Yep, Amy really wasn't messing around, God bless her. That tent had to be where the goat had been killed. If that wasn't a bit of a clue, the perimeter line of yellow and black tape that had been set up around it was a dead giveaway. This was all textbook stuff and, at the very least, meant that apart from him on the force, Amy was at least taking this incident seriously, too. He could almost hear Derek sobbing over his spreadsheet from here.

Joseph spotted a young constable, John Thorpe, out of the Cowley Police Station. He was patrolling the investigation site and, every so often, stamping his feet on the ground to keep warm.

A pop of light came from inside the tent, followed by a second one, both bursts throwing up stark silhouettes of at least five people. That would be the forensics team already at work and taking photos. They would do their best to secure any time-critical evidence and, of course, the tent was to protect the area of greatest interest from the elements.

The question, and the reason that Joseph was here, was would they come up with any evidence at all. Based on what Ellie had told him in the hospital, he now knew why the killer didn't leave any forensic evidence at the scene. He'd been suited up just like the team in the tent was right now. That aside, hopefully, there would be other clues that might have been left, particularly as the killer had been disturbed during his work. If they got lucky, maybe the perpetrator had overlooked something thanks to the unexpected confrontation with Joseph's daughter, and the timely arrival of the patrol car. Maybe there would even be something that would help them uncover the identity of the Midwinter Butcher. The detective just prayed that despite everything that had happened, tonight might just be their lucky night.

As far as Joseph's professional ego went, he didn't give a rat's arse about who solved the case. Even if it was the gobshite Chris Faulkner who cracked it, it didn't matter. The main thing was that his family would finally have some sort of closure when the bastard was put away for a long stretch. The only problem was Joseph was so invested that he didn't really trust anyone other than himself to lead the investigation.

At that moment, a figure clad head to foot in a white protective suit burst out of the tent, ripping off their mask as they did so. Then they immediately vomited over the fence of the pen in a spectacular yellow waterfall of chunks and stomach acid. After wiping their mouth with the back of their hand, the person pulled down their hood to reveal a face of a young woman, somewhere in her twenties, with bobbed auburn hair.

Joseph knew all the members of the forensic team, but this face was new to him. With his astonishing deductive skills, he quickly put two and two together. This had to be the same officer who had visited Ellie in hospital, namely DC Megan Anderson, who'd recently arrived on the team. Once she'd seen Ellie she must have come straight here to report back to DCI Chris Faulkner, who was also probably inside the tent, sticking his nose into Amy's team's investigations. Just like he intended to, given half a chance.

The young officer finished retching and clutched her sides as she sucked in a lungful of air. His heart went out to her. She'd obviously found the spectacle of the mutilated goat too much to handle.

Of course, most officers went through what Megan was. It was almost a rite of passage. But slowly, as case after case rolled past, nearly everyone became hardened to the grisly sights that working in murder investigations often subjected you to. Those who couldn't deal with it usually got themselves transferred to a different team or even, in a few rare cases, they dropped out of the force altogether. Hopefully, Megan wasn't one of the latter and would develop the stomach for it.

A tweak to his plan was already forming in Joseph's mind. The DC wouldn't recognise him, as she was new, unlike the rest of the people in that forensic tent. So maybe he could try talking to her and find out what had been turned up so far, before making his swift exit. PC John Thorpe, on the other hand, he was pretty sure he could sweet-talk around. That was because his dad was a sergeant at St Aldates Police Station, an old mate who had recently retired.

Okay, time to make this happen and just pray that lady luck would help him avoid finding himself in front of a disciplinary panel.

Joseph did his best to dig out a space in the brambles before pulling himself up onto the fence. He had to grit his teeth as he dropped into a thicket of briars on the other side, where the bastard needle barbs found several bits of exposed flesh and dug in. By the time he eventually forced his way through he had a number of tears in his cagoule and he could feel at least one laceration across his chin.

After a suitable amount of cursing that would have curled the toes of a priest in a confessional, the detective finally broke free of the bramble patch to find himself at the edge of freshly rotavated plots. His pa had been a keen gardener back in the day and had taught him a lot about flowers and vegetables. One day he'd have a proper garden of his own again and not just a few boxes filled with herbs on the roof of *Tús Nua*.

As the detective's gaze travelled over the freshly raked mounds, he knew enough about the prepared ground to know they'd been made ready for whatever crops they would plant the following year. More than once, Ellie had brought back some spectacular veg that put even the best efforts of the grocers in the Covered Market to shame, and tomatoes which didn't taste of the cardboard that they were packed in.

As the rain pattered the ground, Joseph made sure he kept to the paths rather than cut across the ploughed furrows. Even though the team would have already done a sweep before tightening the perimeter to the actual pen, it wouldn't be until daylight that they could be sure that the killer hadn't left a stray footprint in his haste to get away. He wouldn't exactly be popular with the SOCOs if he disturbed any prints, especially with his huge size twelves. If nothing else, a trail might show which direction the suspect had fled the farm.

As the DI closed in on the forensic tent, he lifted his head. PC John Thorpe spotted him and headed forward to intercept, already shaking his head.

'Hi, sir. I'm afraid you can't be here,' he said.

Joseph came to a stop in front of him. His slight height advantage of six-foot-three meant that he loomed over the shorter man.

'I know that, John. But I can't exactly keep away when my daughter is involved.'

'I understand, sir, but that's exactly the reason you can't be here. You know the rules way better than I do.'

It was saying something when it was a young officer giving him a lecture, but he wasn't wrong, either. Joseph knew the drill. They both did, and he would have done the same in this lad's position. Ellie, inadvertently and through no fault of her own, was now a person of interest in Faulkner's enquiries, and that was just how it was. Unfortunately, that also automatically ruled Joseph out of any involvement with the investigation. Blood is thicker than water and all that.

The added complication for the detective was that with the superintendent in his corner, Faulkner would have more than a bit of flexibility to be allowed to take over the Midwinter Butcher case permanently, especially if it was turning hot. That would be even more true if Faulkner had a real stab at solving it and being rewarded by climbing another rung on the ladder of promotion. Wheels within wheels for an ambitious yipping and yapping terrier of a DCI.

Joseph sighed as he slowly nodded towards the young constable. 'I know, John, but you've got a good head on your shoulders. You know as well as I do Ellie is innocent in this. They'll work that out for themselves quickly enough, and as soon as they do I'll be back on the case. All I need is a small favour. Just give me a moment to talk to that DC over there. DC Megan Anderson, am I right?'

John scowled. 'You are, but I could get into serious trouble for allowing you anywhere near this crime scene.'

'Just a few minutes to talk to Megan and then I'll evaporate like the proverbial morning Irish mist. Just remember you never saw me, right?'

'I'm not sure which is worse, me not stopping you, or failing to spot you entirely?'

'Such are the choices in life sometimes.' Joseph gave him a wry smile.

That elicited another shake of John's head, but a small smile, too. 'Okay, sir, but you better be quick about it. Meanwhile, I'll take myself to the other side of the forensic tent, where I can't spot you doing what you're about to do. What I can't see hopefully can't hurt me.'

'Good man, and I'll stand you a pint for this some time.'

'I'll hold you to that, sir.'

'Do.'

With another nod, John turned away and, as good as his word, disappeared around to the other side of the pen where Joseph was out of his line of sight.

Joseph slipped his police lanyard over his head. Then, head up like the detective belonged there, he made straight for the young DC who was looking slightly steadier on her feet, but was still clutching onto a post.

'DC Anderson?' he asked as he approached her.

Her gaze snapped to him. 'And you are?'

He flashed his lanyard just fast enough that she couldn't actually read it. 'I just dropped by for an update, but first...'

Joseph dug out a pack of Silvermints, a taste of Ireland back from when he was a lad. Of course, they were almost impossible to buy on any high street in England, so the detective had to resort to buying them online. He offered one to Megan, whose eyebrows crawled up her forehead like surprised caterpillars.

'A mint will help get rid of the tang of sick in your mouth,' he explained. 'A tip I learnt a long time ago is to always keep a pack of mints on you for exactly these sorts of moments.'

'Oh right, you just saw me barfing like a teenager behind the school disco then?'

He snorted. 'Yep, hard to miss.'

Megan shook her head. 'Talk about a great first impression. I can already imagine the nickname DCI Faulkner will have ready for me.'

'Don't be so sure about that. I have distinct memories of his projectile vomit after we discovered a body that had been dead for a good three weeks. His puke had almost a Jackson Pollock style in the way it splattered all over the walls.'

'Okay, that makes me feel better,' Megan replied.

'It should, as it has every other officer who's ended up barfing after their first few cases.' He offered her a Silvermint again.

This time, with a smile, Megan took one and popped it into her mouth. 'Thanks.'

'No problem.' He gestured towards the tent, feeling a brief pang of guilt at playing the young DC like this. 'So, have you found anything useful in there yet?'

'We've explored the outer perimeter, but have found nothing so far. Tomorrow the plan is to do a house-to-house search to see if anyone witnessed anything or has any security camera footage of the area. Smart doorbells, that sort of thing.'

'Hopefully, it will be possible to at least build up a picture of the killer's escape route.'

'Unless, of course, it really was Ellie who did this.'

Joseph bristled, but forced himself to keep his face calm

rather than exploding at Megan, especially as he wanted to learn as much as he could from the DC.

'Ellie is highly unlikely to be involved, especially as she was an indirect victim of the Midwinter Butcher previously.'

'Yes, I saw the case notes, and although I agree, DCI Faulkner wants to play this by the book. But it's already looking hopeful for Ellie because one of the forensic teams just found—'

'That will be enough, DC Anderson,' a woman's voice said.

A tall Amazonian with a camera slung over her shoulder had just emerged from the tent behind Megan. She pulled her hood back as she approached, revealing a sweep of blonde hair. Amy Fischer, in the flesh and looking very pissed off.

As a fellow divorcee, she and Joseph had compared battle wounds over the years and had slowly become firm friends. However, based on the sucking lemons expression currently written across her face, she wasn't exactly thrilled to see the DI here.

Amy shook her head as she reached the two detectives. 'What the hell are you doing here, Joseph? You know the damned rules,' she said, her faint German accent becoming slightly more pronounced when she was irritated with someone, which admittedly was usually Joseph.

He raked his hand through his mop of hair. 'I seem to be hearing that a lot tonight.'

Megan looked between them, and then her eyes widened. 'Please tell me you're not DI Stone?'

'Sorry. One and the same. Didn't I introduce myself?'

'No, you bloody well didn't!' Megan made a growling noise in the back of her throat.

'Let me deal with DI Stone,' Amy said.

'Yes, of course. Sorry, ma'am.'

'Don't be. You won't be the first officer that Joseph here has pulled a fast one on. He likes to play fast and loose with the rules when it suits him. Anyway, are you okay to go back in there, DC Anderson? I know that sort of thing can be hard to handle when you're first exposed to it. But it's always good to see a forensic team in action and I think you'll learn a lot from it. If you're up for it, at least?'

'Thank you, ma'am, I'll be fine.'

'Then one last word of advice. Do yourself a favour and don't mention to our SIO that DI Stone was here. It will make it easier for everyone concerned, including you.'

Megan nodded and with a final scowl Joseph's way, followed by a deep breath, she pulled her hood back up and slipped her mask back on before heading into the tent.

'Joseph, what the hell am I going to do with you?' Amy said once Megan had disappeared.

'Not dropping me in the shite would be a start.'

'And why wouldn't I do that?'

'Because you adore my winning Irish ways?' he said.

The corners of Amy's mouth trembled and just like that, that sunburst trademark smile of hers broke free. 'You bloody Irish charmer! But that doesn't change the fact that you need to make yourself scarce and fast. If Faulkner gets wind of you being here, you can guarantee there will be in a report on Walker's desk by morning.'

'I know, I know. But you know why I'm here. Just throw me a few titbits to keep me going. We both know it's just a matter of time until Ellie is dismissed as a possible suspect and then I'll be reinstated on the case.'

'I agree and I'm doing my best to come up with some piece of evidence that will do exactly that. So off the record, I can tell you that so far we have found next to nothing. We had the dog team do a sweep, but they didn't pick up anything useful. However, we did find some footprints in the pen itself and we're taking casts of those. I already have Ellie's trainers, so hopefully what's left might belong to the actual suspect.'

'Good to hear that you agree Ellie isn't in the frame for this.'

'Nobody with any sense does, Joseph. But we all still need to play our part, especially me and my team, if we're going to get her out of Chris's sights. And we will. To reassure you of that, again strictly off the record and just between us, we found Ellie's phone dropped in a deep puddle inside the pen. That's probably why the suspect couldn't find it in time before Uniform turned up.'

'Okay, that sounds more than promising. Ellie said she may have captured some photos of the killer. Have you looked at it?'

'No, but we have Ellie's passcode, so I'll begin that as soon as I get back to the station. Let's hope she actually managed to snap something useful. If she did, that could be the breakthrough we've all been waiting for.'

'I'll certainly keep my fingers crossed.'

'That's the good news.'

'Oh, shite. Then hit me with the bad stuff.'

'I'm going to give you a heads up, Joseph, but you're going to need to talk to Ellie and get your story straight.'

'Sorry, but what do you mean?'

'I mean the bottle of police issue PAVA pepper spray that was also found in the pen. As you know, every bottle has a serial number. Ellie certainly said nothing about it during the brief statement she gave DC Anderson at the hospital. But I suspect when I check it for fingerprints, it's going to have Ellie's all over it. Needless to say, it won't take much effort to check the serial number to see who signed it out and maybe even gave it to their daughter.' She gave him a pointed look.

'Double shite!'

'Double *shite,* indeed. But, Joseph, I understand, and would do the same for my child if my family had gone through what your family had. I'd certainly be jumping at every shadow and trying everything to make sure they were safe. But you know what Derek is like. If nothing else, this will give him more ammo to make your life even more miserable. You being here tonight doesn't exactly help your case there, either.'

'I know, Amy, but I can't stand by, even if it's temporarily. There must be something I can look into whilst twiddling my thumbs until I can get reinstated.'

Amy narrowed her eyes at him and slowly nodded. 'If you want to help, there is one thing you could research for me.'

'Which is?'

Amy unslung the camera from around her shoulder and pressed a few buttons. Then she turned it around so he could see its rear screen.

On it, Joseph took in the grim sight of the headless torso of one of the goats. From the neatness of the cut, it looked sawn rather than hacked with something like a machete. That fact alone bore all the hallmarks of the Midwinter Butcher's handiwork. But then his eyes locked onto the strange bloodied symbol on the poor creature's flank.

A diagonal line had been carved deep enough into the flesh to reveal the goat's white ribs and even the glistening bulge of its stomach sack. A second zigzagging line intersected the first with small circles carved into the peaks and troughs of the second line.

'Is that some sort of occult symbol?' Joseph asked.

'It certainly looks like it. We've always suspected an occult connection, especially as the animal murders happen on the winter solstice. Obviously, it's not the usual pentagram you might associate with this sort of crime, but whatever that symbol is, it marks fresh territory for our killer.'

'The escalation we've both been worried about?' he said.

'Yes, and the question is why now? That's why we need to know what this symbol is as soon as possible.'

'It could just be a sick mind's idea of a signature, or...' He gazed at the silhouetted figures moving inside the tent.

'What are you thinking, Joseph? I know that look when you think you're onto something.'

'What if he deliberately left us a clue for the first time tonight?'

'You mean he wants us to catch him?' Amy asked.

'Could be. Maybe he wants someone to stop him. Anyway, I'll head back to the station now and run it through HOLMES 2 database to see if anything is flagged up.'

'You won't find any joy on there. Information on occult rituals is fairly limited, and that symbol is as far removed from a pentagram as you could hope to get.'

As she was speaking, a new idea was already forming in the detective's mind. 'In that case, I know exactly the man who may be able to help, or at least point me in the right direction.'

'Who's that?'

'My neighbour on the canal, Professor Dylan Shaw. This symbol is obscure enough to be right up his street.'

'Then get yourself home, Joseph, and talk to him. But just as importantly, grab yourself some sleep first and be fresh-faced with a suitable cover story about that pepper spray for tomorrow, when you roll into the station.'

Joseph sighed. 'Yes, and I'll have a quick word with Ellie about it. Oh, and like you said to Megan, I was never here.' He rubbed the side of his nose.

Amy's sunburst smile flashed across her face again and she made a show of looking around her. 'Who said that?'

He grinned, turned away, and set off back across the farm to get upfront and personal with those brambles again.

CHAPTER SEVEN

THE BIRDSONG ALARM emanating from Joseph's phone slowly pulled him from the depths of his dreamless sleep. A split-second later, the events of the previous night came rushing back in and he was wide awake, staring at the ceiling of *Tús nua's* cabin.

Joseph took a mental breath as he began to focus his thoughts. His number one priority was to make sure he was reinstated on the Midwinter Butcher's case as quickly as possible. Thanks to Amy's tip-off, he had a way to make that a reality —identify that occult symbol as soon as possible and he would be as popular as a barman handing out free drinks in a pub.

He jumped out of bed and immediately swore as he bashed his head on the ceiling. Any sort of jumping antics were strictly out of bounds on his small boat.

As the chill of the cabin bit into the detective, he pulled a curtain back from over a porthole to reveal a hazed view of the morning's darkness through the ice-covered glass. A low winter sun cast long shadows from the houses across the canal, the world covered with glittering frost. A few lights were already on in some of them as his fellow early risers got ready to tackle the world—the heartbeat of a new Oxford day beginning.

The hessian flooring scratched the balls of his feet as he headed out of his tiny bedroom into his living area. That included a tiny galley kitchen where he immediately cranked his thermostat up to full and ignited the gas boiler that ran three small radiators and also supplied him with hot water. No multi-fuel stove for him on this boat as it didn't suit his lifestyle as a busy detective who didn't have the time to get a fire lit, let alone clear out the ash, even on a slow day.

Joseph heard the reassuring flutter of the pilot light catch before he turned his attention back to the large pin board filled with smiling images of Ellie. You didn't need to be a detective to see that this human being was the centre of his world, even if she was all grown up now.

He slipped his hands under the notice board and turned it around to reveal the other obsession in his life that he kept away from Ellie's eyes, his very own version of an incident board all about the Midwinter Butcher. People have their hobbies and this was his.

Joseph picked up the drawing of the strange symbol that he'd hastily scribbled on a piece of scrap paper the previous night. He pinned it near the top among the many clippings from the papers and photos of numerous animal mutilation crime scenes, taken with his police-issued smartphone. Every item on this board was a piece of a puzzle that he'd stared at for hundreds of hours, just wishing that they'd rearrange themselves so the suspect would suddenly leap out at him. But maybe this new occult symbol could be the breakthrough they had all been waiting for. Hopefully, the answer to what it was exactly, would come courtesy of his neighbour, a neighbour who'd need some serious bribing to rise him from his bunk at this godless hour of the morning.

Joseph crossed to the kitchen counter and set himself the challenge of coming up with something to help with that Herculean task. He chose a rather exceptional bean roast of Blue Dragon Vietnamese coffee from the Covered Market in Oxford. Dylan loved coffee just as much as he did. Maybe even more than gin, and that was saying something.

The detective set to work, putting the beans through the electric burr grinder while the water boiled on the stove. As it brewed the necessary eight minutes to achieve maximum coffee heaven, he pulled on some jogging trousers and a polo shirt. Then he headed outside into the shock of a freezing winter morning that immediately leached the heat from his exposed skin.

There wasn't a hint of smoke from the stainless steel chimney stack on the roof of *Avalon*. Also, there was a distinct lack of light from any of the cabin windows. Dylan didn't do mornings, so Joseph approached his boat's door with as much trepidation as a man approaching the cave of a sleeping bear that had a hangover.

He rapped his knuckles on the door, steeling himself for the tirade that would surely follow. What it actually elicited was a series of yipping barks from the other side, but no growls. White Fang had obviously recognised the pre-shower scent of the man who always had a treat for him. But apart from the enthusiastic canine response, there was a distinct lack of a human one.

Joseph tried again, this time knocking louder. 'Dylan, I need your help with something.'

'It better be bloody urgent like your boat is on fire, Joseph.'

'Yep, it's even more important than that.'

A growling sound came from somewhere inside the boat as the bear inside roused itself. That was followed by the sound of shuffling footsteps and muffled expletives, before the door opened a crack. Immediately, White Fang exploded through the gap in a bundle of doggy energy and leapt up at him.

Joseph leaned down and ruffled the dog's head. 'Good to see you too, but sorry my friend, no treats on me today.' He made a show of patting down his pockets and the border terrier made a *humph* sound and sat down, giving him a disgusted look.

When the detective glanced back up, Dylan's bleary-eyed face was there to greet him, his body wrapped tight in a red velvet dressing gown and checked carpet slippers on his feet. One day Joseph really was going to have to buy him an embroidered Fez to complete his professor's kicking-back ensemble.

'It better be really bloody important, that's all that I'm saying,' Dylan muttered.

'Trust me, it is. There's a clue from the latest crime scene and it's important that I get a move on cracking it, as I'm temporarily off the Midwinter Butcher case.'

'Why the hell is that?' the professor asked, staring at him.

'I didn't want to wake you, but after I left you last night, I got a call from the station. There was another attack, but this time it was that city farm where Ellie volunteers. It turns out she disturbed the killer whilst he was busy hacking the head off one of the farm goats.'

At that, any hint of sleep was swept away from Dylan's face. 'Oh, Jesus, and is she okay?'

'The fecker brained her with a severed goat's head, but she's fine apart from a bump on her head.'

'Oh, thank goodness, but that poor girl going through something like that.'

'I know, and there's another thing—the arsewipe carved a symbol into the side of one of the goats that so far no one recognises. I'm sure someone will eventually, but I could do with being the first one to crack it. So, as the man who knows everything, I thought you might be the chap to help me do exactly that.'

'Consider it done, but why the hell have you been taken off the case, Joseph?'

'Because of Ellie's involvement. Wrong time, wrong place and all that, but until proven otherwise, I'm afraid she's going to be in the frame as a suspect.'

'If you pardon my French, I haven't heard such bollocks in all my life.'

'My thoughts exactly, but I need your help on this, old friend. As an added incentive, there's some Vietnamese Blue Dragon coffee brewing in my cabin.'

'Oh, now you're talking my language,' Dylan said, stepping out and pulling his cabin door closed behind him.

Joseph plated up the bacon sarnies, the smell of which had slowly been driving White Fang wild, one with brown sauce for him, the other with red sauce for Dylan. Every man to his own poison.

He carried one over to the professor, who was currently studying his sketch on his incident pin board. He took a sip of his coffee as he frowned at the image.

'So what do you think?' he asked.

'This Blue Dragon is excellent. A solid eight-point-five out of ten.'

'I agree, but not that. I meant the sketch. We're thinking there's a possible occult connection.'

'I think that's a reasonable assumption, especially considering the circumstances.'

'But do you recognise it?'

'It's triggering something in the back of my memory, but I

can't quite place it yet. However, give me a while and it will come to me.' Dylan's eyes locked onto the bacon sarnie on the plate. 'Oh, is that for me?'

'It certainly is. The bacon's from McGray's, the best in Oxford.'

'Bread toasted on both sides in the fat?'

'But of course, do I look like a savage? Anyway, back to the matter at hand. Not wanting to hurry you, but how long do you think it will take you to place it?'

'It could be the time I take to eat that delicious-looking bacon sandwich, or a day at the latest. But you know me, Joseph, I'll get there, eventually. The problem is there are so many crevices in this old brain of mine. Sometimes I take a while to search through all of them to find what I need.'

'An image of an enormous library comes to mind.'

'That's the perfect metaphor, but some shelves are covered with dust and a lot of cobwebs. But I'm certain the answer is in there somewhere.' Dylan tapped the side of his skull. 'Anyway, to help me unearth that, can you give me any more context?'

'It was carved into the flank of the decapitated goat. The other goat was stolen after Ellie interrupted him.'

'Your poor daughter having to witness a despicable act like that, especially after the trauma from her childhood.'

'Exactly, Dylan. I'm worried that this may be too big a coincidence. This might make me sound like a paranoid parent, but I have to wonder if they deliberately targeted the Laithwaite City Farm this time round, because that's where my daughter works. So that's why I need to ask for another favour. She's going to come and stay with me till this all blows over, where I can keep half an eye on her. But of course, I'm not always going to be here, so I was wondering...'

Dylan waved a hand. 'Of course, I'll keep an eye on her. She's like family to me.'

'Thanks, I really appreciate it.'

'Anytime, my friend. So can I ask what you plan to do now?'

'First, Ellie and I need to get our stories straight as to why she had a bottle of police issue PAVA spray at the scene of the crime.'

'Ah, I see your problem.'

'Yeah, I know. Hopefully, we can work out something between us. I'm heading into the hospital early to see if she's ready to make an official statement about what happened. The sooner that gets done, the sooner Walker will let me back onto the case.'

'Then you better get going. Meanwhile, I'll see if I can dig up where I've seen that symbol before.'

'Good man.' Joseph took a bite of his bacon sandwich. 'If you'll excuse me, I'm going to grab a shower and then make this day happen.'

Dylan tapped his mug. 'If you don't mind, I'm going to finish this rather excellent coffee of yours, not to mention that rather delicious-looking bacon sandwich.'

'Knock yourself out.' Joseph turned to go, but paused.

'Like always, we haven't had this conversation, because apart from anything else, even I'm not meant to know the finer details yet.'

Dylan tapped the side of his nose. 'What conversation?'

'That's the spirit!'

Joseph grabbed another bite of his bacon butty and headed for a shower.

CHAPTER EIGHT

JOSEPH'S ANGER was blazing through his veins, having just visited the hospital. He crashed through the doors of the St Aldates Police Station into the reinforced glass reception area like a furious bull in a tiny china shop.

The duty sergeant, Gary Jones, looked up from his screen and frowned at him. 'What's wrong, Joseph?'

'What's bloody wrong is I just went to the hospital to discover that my daughter Ellie has been dragged in here for questioning. Where the hell is she?'

'Whoa, there!' Gary raised his hands to pacify the detective. 'To start with, she presented herself at the front desk with Kate, who dropped her off just an hour ago. She's being interviewed right now by Chris and Megan.'

Nausea pulsed through the DI. The problem with that little gem of information was that Joseph still hadn't spoken to her so they could get their cover story straight about why she'd had a bottle of PAVA on her.

'Which interview room are they in because I should be in there, too?'

'Look, Joseph, we all heard what happened and you know the drill. No can do.'

'I know, I know, but we're talking about my daughter here, Gary.'

'It's just routine, so please try to relax. Anyway, knowing you, there's plenty of paperwork you need to be catching up on, which will help take your mind off it.'

'Thanks for that, Gary, really.'

'Anytime, Joseph,' he said with a wink, as he buzzed him through.

DS Ian McDowell was already at his desk in the room they often shared, a half-eaten bagel currently being used as a paper-weight to hold down a pile of handwritten notes. On seeing Joseph enter, he made a clumsy half-attempt to quickly cover them up with a newspaper.

Joseph gestured towards them with his chin. 'Something you don't want to tell me, by any chance?'

'Sorry, Joseph, it's the statements gathered from neighbours next to Laithwaite City Farm about last night.'

The DI shot him a piercing gaze. 'So there's nothing you can tip me off about?'

'I would if I could, mate.'

'Thanks for nothing,' Joseph said way sharper than he'd meant to. But then he took a deep breath and held up both hands. 'Sorry. All this fresh nonsense with Ellie has just about finished me off.'

'I'm not surprised. But so you know, everyone is pressing DCI Fucker to get you back on the case as soon as possible and that includes me. Whatever the big opinion that guy has of himself, even he knows he hasn't got your expertise when it comes to the Midwinter Butcher. Faulkner may be the one that the Super has parachuted in to take over the investigation, but anyone with half a brain knows it should be you.'

'Those are the breaks, my friend,' Joseph replied as his anger finally fizzled out. 'Anyway, look, I didn't mean to bite your head off just now.'

'Already forgotten, but a fresh mug of tea will help mend my sensitive soul.' Ian tapped the side of his *Batman* mug.

Joseph snorted. 'Sensitive soul... I could get you banged up by the Oxford Trading Standards for spinning a whopper as big as that, but a mug of tea it is.'

'Good man,' he replied.

Ian, a detective sergeant, was as thin as a rake despite everything he managed to cram into his mouth. He was also a good man to know in a crisis, with a razor-sharp humour. No wonder they got on so well.

As Joseph gathered his mug up, Ian peered at him. 'Oh, one heads up. DSU Wanker was looking for you just now. Looked like he was on the warpath.'

Joseph's scalp prickled. It couldn't be good that Derek was after him. 'Any idea what it was about?' he asked with as innocent a voice as he could muster.

'No, but he looked bloody furious.'

'Ah, okay, thanks for the warning.'

But Ian's eyes widened, and he made a slight gesture by extending his finger the barest fraction towards something behind him. Joseph didn't need to be psychic to know who was standing there.

'What warning was that?' a gruff voice with an East End accent said.

Joseph turned to see the weasel face of DSU Derek Walker himself in the doorway. The man who was roughly the same age as him, in his mid-forties, and who'd once had a similar lean athletic build, had transformed over recent years into a Play-Doh caricature version of himself. Now the man seemed to spend most of his life behind his desk and the pounds had piled on. Why Kate is attracted to this anti-Adonis of the male species, he had absolutely no idea.

'Ian was just warning me about there being no sugar left in the kitchen,' he replied.

'Right,' Walker said, giving him a stare that said he didn't believe him for a second. 'Follow me, Joseph, because we need to have a word about that incident at the city farm last night.'

'Oh, right.' He raised his eyebrows a fraction at Ian, before following Walker back to his glass-walled office, where he kept a beady eye on the rest of the team.

The one solid wall was filled with clippings of framed articles of the cases that Walker had been involved with and had helped solve. Some might say that was a sign of insecurity and that he needed them on display for everyone to see. Joseph suspected it was an attempt by the DSU to help justify himself to other people about why he'd risen to his current rank of detective chief superintendent so quickly. Of course, if you asked Joseph off the record, he would say that Walker had more than a whiff of impostor syndrome that smelled almost as bad as his industrial strength aftershave.

That bane of his life fixed Joseph with his grey gimlet-eyed stare, before gesturing towards a seat with the disapproving look of a headmaster who'd just summoned a naughty child to discipline them for the hundredth time.

Maybe it had been John who had grassed him up, or maybe it had been their new DC, making sure she didn't break any rules during her first week in the new job. Thanks to whoever it was, this had the potential to go very badly for him. The problem was that Walker was the last man to turn a blind eye, especially when they were talking about someone like himself not following protocol.

The superintendent rested his elbows on the table, hands clasped together. 'Tsk, tsk, tsk, Joseph.' He extended his forefingers towards him like two pistols. 'Is there anything you want to tell me?'

The office suddenly seemed very stuffy, and Joseph had to work hard to keep his expression relaxed. 'About what, sir?'

A slight head shake. 'We both know, so why don't you save us a lot of time and you tell me?'

Jesus, the guy really was playing his role of headmaster to an absolute bloody T, and to think this man had once been Joseph's best friend. But familiarity also had its advantages in this specific situation, as he'd also seen Derek in enough interviews to know his interrogation techniques. Give the suspect enough rope to hang themselves with, and they usually did. Luckily, he also knew exactly the way to deal with it—play ignorant until he hit him with whatever evidence he actually had.

'Sorry, sir, you're going to need to help me out a bit here?'

The DSU glowered at him. 'Maybe this will help refresh your memory.' He pulled open his drawer and took out a sealed plastic evidence bag and pushed it across his desk.

Inside it, Joseph could see a PAVA spray canister and immediately the tension that had been building in his jaw ratcheted up a fraction.

But his best strategy was still to play ignorance and just hope Ellie had said nothing to drop him in it. 'I still don't know what you mean, sir?'

'I mean that this was found at the site of the goat killing from last night, the same location where your daughter Ellie was. I'm sure you're aware that she's being interviewed right now by Chris and he's already had her prints taken. It doesn't take a genius to work out that when that PAVA is checked for prints, we'll find hers all over it. I'm also sure when I have the serial number on it checked, it will lead me straight to the officer who supplied it to her.' Derek steepled his fingers together. 'So I'll ask once again, can you enlighten me about it, Joseph? Admit to it now and it will go easier for you. I really don't want to be forced to put you into a disciplinary procedure, which at the very best will leave you with a stain on your career. Instead, we could come to a mutually beneficial arrangement that would suit us both.'

Joseph suddenly knew exactly where this was heading. Walker was hoping to use the PAVA spray as leverage. Supplying it to his daughter certainly broke the rules, but at most, it should have meant a slap on the wrist. The problem here was that Derek would use even the smallest misdemeanour on his part to bash Joseph over the skull. Thank God the guy didn't know that he had even more heavy-duty ammo he could have used against him, specifically his highly unauthorised appearance at the crime scene last night. If anyone had said a word, he would truly be in the shite now.

The DI felt a trickle of sweat tickle down his neck as his superior fixed him with that laser-like stare of his.

'If you confess now, we can keep this conversation off the record,' Derek said. 'Then you can put in for that transfer you know would be in your best interests, maybe even head back to Dublin. Home sweet home, hey. What do you say?'

So there it was. Walker fully intended to use this to finally get rid of him. The worst thing of all is that he'd set himself up for this fall and had no one else to blame. And who knew what Ellie would say about the PAVA spray when confronted about it. Like a cornered animal, he had nowhere left to run. No wonder Walker had such a fearsome reputation for getting results in suspect interviews. He knew exactly what he was doing.

Derek held his gaze. 'Well, what do you have to say, Joseph?'

Joseph felt himself wavering. The guy had him bang to rights, but he would also never give him the satisfaction of putting in for a transfer. No, he'd resign first. Besides, there was no way on this planet he was going to move that far away from Ellie, or Oxford, which was his home.

The DI was about to respond, telling the little bollix exactly what he thought of him, when there was a knock at the door.

'Go away, I'm busy,' Walker said, keeping him pinned in his searchlight gaze.

'Please, sir, I think this is relevant to the conversation you're having with DI Stone right now,' said a voice he recognised as belonging to Megan.

Walker stared at the door and then at him. 'Do you know anything about this, Joseph?'

'I'm as much in the dark about this as everything else you've just said to me.'

'I see. Well, you can't say you weren't warned. The moment that Megan has said her piece, we're going to finish this conversation. Do you understand me?'

'If you say so, sir.'

'Oh, I do, Joseph, I do,' he whispered before raising his voice. 'Come in, Megan.'

She entered, her face the picture of mortification. 'Amy Robinson just told me they recovered a bottle of PAVA spray at the city farm last night. She said it was assumed that it belonged to Ellie Stone. As soon as I heard her say that, I knew I had to step forward.'

Oh shite, Joseph thought to himself. *She's about to well and truly drop me in it by saying I was there last night.*

Walker peered at her. 'Why, you have some extra information?'

Here it came, the perfect Christmas present for Walker.

Megan nodded. 'I do, sir. You see, it belongs to me. I still had it on me from a house search I tagged along on earlier in the day and forgot to check it back in.' She fixed her gaze on the wall behind Walker's head, hands clasped behind her back, like she was standing at attention back at the academy. 'I'm afraid it may have tumbled out of my pocket when I was exiting the cordoned-off area. I vomited and it must have fallen out when I ripped my suit off.'

Joseph stared at her, not quite able to believe the blatant lie that had just come from her lips, which were now trembling the barest amount to make her Oscar-winning performance believable.

Derek stood up, his chair scraping across the carpet-tiled floor. 'You mean to tell me you went to your first forensic investigation scene, and you managed to fucking contaminate it?'

Megan stood taller, snapping to attention like she was still on the parade ground. 'I did, sir, and I'm deeply sorry. It won't happen again.'

'You're bloody right, it won't. I can't tell you how disappointed I am, especially when you came to us with such a glowing testimonial from your last super.' He sighed. 'Okay, Megan, although this reflects badly on you, I expect you to learn the lesson and never, ever repeat it.'

'Yes, absolutely, sir.'

'Then that will be the last we say about it.' Derek pushed the evidence bag with the pepper spray towards her. 'You better get this checked back in like you were meant to yesterday.'

'I will, sir. Thank you.' She grabbed the evidence bag and her eyes briefly met Joseph's. She dipped her head by the barest millimetre, which translated to: *don't say a bloody word.*

Derek's laser-like gaze slid back to the DI. 'You can go Joseph, but just so there can be no misunderstanding, until Ellie has been cleared from DCI Chris Faulkner's investigation, you're to be nowhere near the Midwinter Butcher case. Is that clear?'

The DI bristled at the use of *Faulkner's investigation,* but before he could answer, Megan jumped in again.

'Actually, sir, that's the other reason I'm here. DCI Faulkner has finished his interview with Ellie Stone and recent evidence has come to light, exonerating her of any involvement in the actual killings by confirming her version of events. The DCI himself has asked for Joseph to be reinstated on the case.'

Walker glared at her as though she'd just dropped a steaming great turd on his office floor. 'He wants Joseph back on the case? Seriously? He actually said that?'

'Yes, sir. He asked me himself to come and fetch Joseph for the forensic briefing that's just about to begin.'

Joseph looked between them like this was a tennis match, not quite understanding what the hell was going on. Maybe he'd fallen through the cracks of their world into a parallel universe where everything was back to front and he wasn't in a shite load of trouble. Whatever this was, he knew he better play along with it.

'It will be a pleasure to work with Chris,' he said, barely able to believe just how convincing he'd made that sound.

It was pretty clear from the look that Walker gave him he knew he was taking the piss, but then he smirked.

'Yes, maybe you'll pick up a few tips, hey, Joseph?'

Joseph did Kate's trick of mentally counting to three rather than wiping the smug look off the bloated man's face with a well-aimed punch to his gut. 'Aye, maybe I will, sir.' Joseph turned to Megan. 'We better get to it then.'

She nodded. 'Follow me. Amy's just about to discuss the results of the forensic search.'

Walker shook his head as they both disappeared out of his office as fast as they could without looking like two rabbits with scalded arses.

As he closed the door behind them, Joseph immediately turned to Megan. 'Not that I'm not grateful, but why the hell did you just cover for me like that?'

'You can thank Amy. She gave me the rundown on just what your family has been through. Then I understood why you turned up like you did last night. But blimey, sir, talk about sailing close to the wind.'

'Yes, I have a tendency to do that sometimes, and you can drop the sir.'

A small smile. 'Okay, Joseph. Anyway, I've heard enough about you to know that you didn't deserve to get thrown out for a lapse of judgement, even if you were being an overprotective dad. However, as a fresh face on the team, and also because my mum knows Walker through the golf club, I was pretty certain I could get away with taking the fall for you.'

'Pretty certain, but not definite. Megan, hey?'

She shrugged. 'So you owe me. Big deal.'

'Well, I don't know quite how I'm ever going to thank you for this, let alone getting me back onto the case, as that definitely wasn't Faulkner's idea.'

'It was actually, but only because Amy seriously leant on him. She seems to be your number one fan.'

'The feeling's mutual. She's the best of the best. But what about this piece of evidence that exonerated Ellie?'

'It turns out your daughter got a photo of our suspect and it's quite a doozy.'

'In what way?'

'It's better if you see it with your own eyes.'

Before he could ask Megan another question, she turned on her heel and strode away, with Joseph hurrying to keep up with her and not quite believing his luck.

CHAPTER NINE

THE MEETING ROOM was already filled with six officers, one of who was Ian. That was more than Joseph would have expected Derek to allocate to this considering it wasn't actually a murder investigation. However, the good news for him was that it suggested that the DSU was at least taking the escalation of the assault on his daughter seriously. No doubt Kate had an awful lot to do with that softening of attitude. At the head of the table, DCI Chris Faulkner sat next to Amy, who immediately gave him a not-very-discreet thumbs-up. In contrast, Chris's withering look made it obvious that he was less than delighted to see Joseph here.

Chris had the lean, muscular build of a featherweight boxer. His other notable feature was what could be best described as a Roman nose. His hair was very well groomed, suggesting he spent a bit too much time in front of the mirror, his broad jaw always seemed to be set to serious, and he had what could only be described as calculating eyes. Constantly guarded, he was very much Derek's man, but that didn't make him a bad officer. However, more often than not, he was a right royal pain in the arse, as he always did everything by the book. No wonder Derek loved him so much.

The DCI pointed a remote at the screen behind him and powered it up. 'Okay everyone, I'm going to start with an overview of the case, together with preliminary results of the investigation into what appears to be another killing perpetrated by the Midwinter Butcher. As I'm sure you're all aware by now, the latest incident bears all the hallmarks of the previous cases. A goat's head was severed and removed by the suspect. However, a second goat was also abducted from the scene, which marks something of a departure from the killer's usual MO. The suspect was interrupted by Ellie Stone, our very own DI's daughter.'

All eyes briefly flicked towards Joseph, but there wasn't a hint of surprise in any of their gazes. Obviously, that little snippet of information had spread like wildfire through the station.

'But most significantly, as I'm sure you will have all heard, Ellie was assaulted. Thankfully, apart from some bruising and a minor concussion, she has made a complete recovery.'

People nodded, and several *goods* were muttered. This time, no one looked his way apart from Megan, who gave him a genuinely sympathetic look. But she was too new to realise that the rest of the team did their best to bury real emotion when on duty, anything else could get in the way of getting the job done. However, the truth was when they were down at the pub, Joseph knew he wouldn't be buying any drinks for himself for some time. That was how they looked out for each other, less with words, and more with understated gestures like that.

'Anyway, Ellie has been extremely helpful,' Chris continued. 'She may have turned up something significant that Amy will brief you on in a moment, along with several other clues that have been found at the scene. However, before we get to that, initial investigations have turned up little so far.' Chris clicked on his remote and a satellite map of Laithwaite City Farm appeared on the screen.

'The red box highlights the goat pen where the animal slaughter took place. The blue marks the outer perimeter of the search area, where unfortunately, nothing was found. However, as the only road access was cut off by a patrol car, that suggests our suspect was on foot and likely climbed one of the fences that border the farm. We are going to extend the search area to see if any domestic CCTV systems picked up anything during the time in question, within a radius of two miles of the crime scene.'

Joseph's shoulders, which had been tensing, relaxed a fraction. Hopefully, if they were just checking the footage around the time of the incident, no one would notice the eejit detective who'd taken it upon himself to turn up uninvited to the crime scene a couple of hours later.

'I'll now hand it over to Amy, who has some better news on the evidence front, and she'll also be presenting the pathology report,' Chris said as he handed the remote over to her.

When Amy looked out at everyone, the room fell instantly silent. That was an entirely normal reaction to her. In fact, whenever she took the floor, everyone listened, whatever their rank, and with good reason. Amy had an astonishing track record, which was why she'd risen to the top in her specialist field. She'd personally had a hand in identifying key forensic clues across dozens of investigations, which had often led to major breakthroughs. It was little wonder she was a SOCO legend throughout the Thames Valley Police Force.

Her blue eyes swept the room. 'As Chris said, this latest incident resembles the previous cases of the Midwinter Butcher. Goat A'—she clicked a button on the remote and the gruesome headless torso of the animal appeared on-screen—'had its head removed with a fine-tooth saw. The marks through the vertebra indicate it was exactly the same bone saw used in the previous Midwinter Butcher killings, according to the pathologist report.'

Next to Joseph, Megan shuddered and dropped her gaze to the floor. Not another person in the room even blinked. That's how hardened everyone present all became to this sort of thing and Megan would too, given time.

'As for goat B...' Amy clicked again and a brown goat appeared. By the look of it, the image was from the farm's website. 'We believe it was abducted by the suspect, maybe because Ellie surprised them, so they didn't have time to complete what they'd started. However, goat A's head was, as in previous cases, removed, possibly as some sort of trophy.'

For years, Joseph had tried to get into the headspace of the person behind all of this. He'd often discussed with the others that the heads might be trophies. It certainly wasn't hard to imagine that the psycho had them all mounted on plaques on the wall in his shed—or even better, a basement—probably lit with a dim sixty-watt bulb and...

The DI's attention snapped back to the room as Amy clicked the remote again to reveal a bar chart, with a blue bar that was far higher than any of its neighbours.

'Toxicology analysis after the postmortem has once again confirmed that there was a significant amount of ketamine in the dead goat's system. Analysis of its stomach contents confirm partly digested apples, which suggests that they were the delivery system used for the drug.'

Megan, whose eyes were back on the screen, leaned towards Joseph. 'Ketamine, as in the date rape drug?'

Joseph nodded. 'That's right, but in this case, the sick bastard appears to use it to paralyse the animals whilst they hack the poor creatures' heads off.'

Megan shuddered. 'God, talk about being a serious psychopath.'

'Aye.'

Amy clicked the remote again and this time it was Joseph's turn to shudder as a photo of Ellie appeared, the bruise to the side of her forehead revealed in all its blue and brown glory.

'As you can see, the impact mark and swelling are in line with Miss Stone being knocked out with the head of goat A, when it was used as a weapon and thrown at her,' Amy said.

'Of course, as per procedure, before Joseph could be allowed to work on this case, his daughter needed to be ruled out of the enquiry as a suspect,' Chris said, jumping in. 'And I'm sure the more astute of you will have already deduced by Joseph's presence at this briefing, she has now been cleared of any involvement.'

Gazes pivoted towards him, and Joseph cleared his throat. 'Which, as we all know, was always going to happen. Not that I'm not grateful, but how were you able to rule her out so quickly?'

'That was because of the photo your daughter took of the suspect before she was knocked out,' Amy replied. 'My team pulled it from her phone, which was recovered from the crime scene.'

Just like that, the entire atmosphere shifted and became focused. People sat up straighter, leaned forward, some took out notebooks. Amy had well and truly got everyone's attention now as she clicked her remote.

But any expectation that they were on the verge of a breakthrough was swept away by the photograph that appeared on the screen. The image almost appeared to be a selfie, with Ellie's face partly filling the screen, a severed head of a white goat caught as it flew at her, and a blurred hooded figure behind both with an arm raised as if it had just thrown the goat's head. The problem was that although this photo clearly supported Ellie's version of events, her assailant's face was obscured because of the head torch they were wearing.

'Oh God, you had us going there, Amy,' Ian said. 'I thought you were about to pull a rabbit out of a hat.'

'Patience, Ian,' Amy replied with a small smile. 'This is the unprocessed file, but thankfully, Ellie had the RAW option on her phone turned on, capturing far more useful data than a JPEG file. With that, the technical forensic team worked their usual magic, adjusted the brightness curves and ran an AI sharpen filter. You'll see the result of their efforts in the next image.'

Joseph could tell by Amy's tone that she was onto something and his mouth grew dry. Could this be it, the vital clue they had been looking for all these years?

If the atmosphere had been tense before, you could almost taste the static of it now, it was so electric. Was Amy about to pull off yet another extraordinary breakthrough?

Then, without so much as a drumroll, she pressed the button, and they had their answer. Although still distorted, a face was now visible, but beneath the hood of the forensic-style suit, the person's complexion was bone white...

Then Joseph's brain caught up with what he was actually seeing. The person was wearing a mask, but not just any old mask. It was a stylised face made from white shiny plastic, not unlike the one that the activist group Anonymous based on Guy Fawkes. But instead of a pencil-thin beard, this mask had two demonic-style horns protruding from the top.

Several people shook their heads, but it was Ian who once again said what everyone was thinking, even if it was stating the bleeding obvious.

'Are you telling us that we're no closer to identifying this psycho?'

But before Amy could reply, Joseph jumped in. 'Actually, I don't know about the rest of you, but that mask looks like it might be a clue to me. I mean, has anyone here seen anything like it ever before?'

Everybody was shaking their heads.

'Exactly,' Amy replied. 'My team has already checked listings on Amazon, eBay, and every fancy dress shop we've been able to track down. So far, we've drawn a complete blank.'

'Do you think it could be homemade?' Megan asked and was immediately rewarded with several nods.

'Without seeing the original, it's hard to make a call on that, but if it is handmade, it's professionally done.'

'So that suggests it may be someone who is very handy, maybe even has some art training,' Chris said.

'Possibly, but we may be getting ahead of ourselves,' Amy replied. 'There's still a chance it was mass-produced, but either way, you have a line of inquiry that's worth pursuing.'

'Sounds like one for you to cut your teeth on, Megan, as you raised it,' Chris said.

Joseph actually felt a bit of grudging respect for the DCI, suggesting that since it wasn't an insignificant lead. If Megan was successful in tracking it down, it would certainly raise her stock with the rest of the team.

'Thank you, sir. I'd love to,' Megan replied with maybe a bit too much enthusiasm. Although this was important police work, she probably had no idea how boring it would actually be. Trawling through a lot of online content and contacting manufacturers, not exactly the stuff of investigative wet dreams.

'I'll have another team member work with you and assist with that,' Chris said.

Megan gave him a grateful look.

Once again, Amy's gaze swept the room. 'Also, we have another piece of significant evidence that needs looking into.'

She clicked the button on the remote and this time a new image of the decapitated goat appeared, laid out on a slab in the morgue. On its side, the symbol that Amy had shown Joseph the night before on her camera was visible.

'What the hell is that?' Ian asked.

'That's a good question and so far we're coming up blank, although I think it's fair to say that in conjunction with the demon mask we saw, it would suggest that there is some sort of occult, even satanic connection here,' Amy replied.

'That's something that I've long suspected because of the nature of the previous killings, but this is the first time we've had any actual proof of it,' Joseph said.

'So what's changed, and why show his hand now?' Chris asked.

'It might be a very bad sign indeed, sir,' the DI replied. 'I'm on record about being worried that these were practice killings and, at some point, the suspect might escalate to murdering someone.'

'Look, Joseph, I know we can't take chances, but the profiling still suggests that the killer is in a steady pattern here and is unlikely to progress to people if he hasn't done so in the last sixteen years.'

Joseph glowered across the room at the DCI. 'I'm afraid I don't quite see it like that, sir.'

Chris gave him a thin smile. 'Then we're going to have to agree to disagree. Granted, the man's obviously a psycho, but beyond needing to stop him from hurting animals, his MO has never extended to people.'

Not for the first time, Joseph had to keep his irritation in check. The man was making an educated guess and every instinct in his body, as it had been ever since his son's death, told Joseph he was completely wrong.

'Who can look into this symbol?' Chris continued like the

DI's statement was a silent fart in a lift that no one was going to pay any attention to.

But then, like a kid in class, Joseph found his hand rising by itself. 'Leave it with me, sir.' At least Amy gave him an approving look.

'Then it's yours, Joseph,' the DCI said in a tone that suggested he didn't in a million years think he'd get to the bottom of it if Amy couldn't figure it out.

Joseph couldn't wait to wipe that smug look off the man's face when his neighbour Dylan came up with the answer for him.

'Okay, Amy, if you've got nothing else to—' Chris started, but Amy raised her hand to stop him.

'Actually, I have,' she said. 'We have one other piece of key evidence that came to light during my examination of goat A.' She clicked her remote again and this time a closeup of the stump of a headless goat's torso filled the screen.

Megan grimaced and dropped her gaze to inspect her shoes again. But the thing was, Joseph knew from experience the best way for her to get over squeamishness was to confront it.

Joseph leaned over to her, dropping his voice to a whisper. 'I know you don't want to, Megan, but my advice is to make yourself look.'

Her eyes met his, and she slowly nodded. 'Yes, sir.'

'Like I said before, it's Joseph.'

'Yes. Sorry, sir—. I mean, Joseph.' She gave him a small smile. But as she made herself look at the monitor, a slight shudder passed through her body.

'As you can see from Ellie's photo,' Amy was saying, 'the suspect was wearing a forensic-type suit, so we weren't very hopeful of finding any DNA evidence, which also explains the distinct lack of any evidence recovered from the previous killings. However, on this occasion, it appears the Midwinter

Butcher may have made a mistake.' Another click and we were treated to an extreme closeup of the ragged line of the goat's neck.

A slight tremor went through Megan, but stoically she kept her gaze fixed on the screen.

The image was straight out of a horror movie. The cut line was incredibly neat, testifying to the very fine saw blade used. The bloody mess of flesh, sliced vertebra, and severed arteries didn't offer any clues. But then Joseph spotted a fine long silver hair protruding from one side of the ragged hole of the oesophagus.

'Is that some sort of human hair in the wound?' he asked.

'Ten out of ten for keen observation skills, Joseph,' Amy said. 'Yes, it seems like our perpetrator, despite all their caution, left a hair behind. This has only just come to light and it's being run through DNA testing in the lab right now. Also, because of the location of this hair, it's unlikely to belong to anyone other than our suspect. The likelihood is that it became entangled in the wound when the killer was sawing the goat's head off.' And just like that, Amy's sunburst smile once again broke out on her face and the entire atmosphere in the room changed as everyone began talking at once.

Chris stood and held up his hands to quieten everyone down. 'Yes, this might just be the breakthrough that we need to track down and arrest the Midwinter Butcher. We are obviously going to cross-check it against previous suspects who have been brought in for questioning, as well as check it against the national database.'

Almost unconsciously, Joseph found his hand in the air again.

'What is it this time?' Chris asked, as though the DI was stealing his moment of glory.

'I'm concerned that Laithwaite City Farm may have been targeted for a very specific reason.'

'Which is what, exactly?'

'Because my daughter works there.'

Chris's expression went from one of incredulity to one of amusement. 'You're telling me that the Midwinter Butcher has been stalking your daughter all these years?'

'I hope with every fibre of my being that I'm wrong, but we can't afford to overlook it, sir,' Joseph said as his phone buzzed in his pocket.

'Oh, come on, Joseph. You do know that sounds like outright paranoia?'

Joseph could see from everyone's expressions around the table that they were thinking the same, but he didn't expect to see that look on Amy's face as she shook her head.

'Joseph, the most likely explanation is that it is simply coincidence, nothing more,' she said.

'But what if you're wrong?' The phone buzzed in his pocket again, and he continued to ignore it. 'I really feel we should explore every single avenue, however unlikely.'

But Chris was shaking his head. 'If we had the resources, I'd say yes, of course, but as you well know we're stretched thin as it is on this case. Anyway, we've got some promising lines of investigation to pursue and besides, based on his previous behaviour, we have an entire year to track him down before the Midwinter Butcher strikes again.'

Joseph could understand where the DCI was coming from, but he had a grinding feeling in his gut that told him the SIO was being too blasé about this. However, he also knew he wasn't going to win this argument, especially when every other person in that room, even Amy, seemed to agree. He needed to choose his moment before tackling this again with Chris.

'Of course, sir,' he said, trying to keep his exasperation out of his voice.

'Good, I'm glad we understand each other.' He turned to the rest of the team. 'Okay, let's make this happen, and you'll update us as soon as you have the DNA results from the hair, Amy?'

'Of course I will,' she replied.

'Okay, let's get to it, everyone,' Chris said.

Megan turned to him as his phone buzzed for a third time.

'Joseph, I just wanted to say—'

Joseph held up his hand. 'Just give me a sec, I need to check my phone.'

The DI pulled his police mobile out to see he'd two missed calls and a text from Dylan. However, his frustration of a moment before was swept away as he read his text.

'Joseph, you have to come see me at the Bodleian library. I've identified that symbol, and you're going to want to see it for yourself.'

He pocketed the phone. 'Right, I've got somewhere I need to be in a hurry. Megan, do you drive?'

'Of course.'

'In that case, I need a lift to the Bodleian. I think we may have just had a breakthrough regarding that symbol.'

CHAPTER TEN

MEGAN PARKED the unmarked police Peugeot within sight of the iconic Georgian Radcliffe Camera, the strikingly beautiful, honey-coloured, stone circular domed building in the heart of Oxford. Within moments of exiting the car, the two detectives were having to squeeze between the tourists taking selfies with the Hertford Bridge in the background. Unofficially, and far more popularly, the ornate arched bridge was also known as the Bridge of Sighs, famous for its similarity to its namesake in Venice. However, rather than being built over a canal with gondoliers travelling it, this one spanned a cobbled street populated with cyclists. With these two famous Oxford landmarks within close proximity of each other there was little wonder they were such a draw for visitors.

Joseph and Megan picked their way through the throngs of tourists, and unintentionally photo-bombed at least one shot with a young couple doing bunny ears over each other's heads. Then, at last, they were clear of the rabble and entering the old Bodleian quad, surrounded on every side by five-storey stone buildings and arched leaded windows. This was the older part of the Bodleian Library, as opposed to the fancy and also very impressive Weston Library wing built in 2015 on the opposite side of Broad Street, all glass and pale stone.

As the two of them made their way towards the doors in the corner, they passed the bronze statue in the middle. Dylan had once told Joseph that it was the Earl of Pembroke, who back in the day had been the Chancellor of the University.

The two officers stepped through the door into the library to see a woman on the other side of a glass window glance up from her computer screen.

'Can I help you?' she said.

Joseph presented his warrant card, and Megan followed his lead.

'We're here to see Professor Dylan Shaw,' the DI replied. 'He's expecting us.'

The woman scanned her screen and nodded. 'Yes, the professor left a note for you. He's over in the study room in the Radcliffe Camera. I can call someone to take you to him, if you like?'

'Thank you, that would be grand.'

As they waited, Joseph noticed Megan was almost bouncing up and down on her feet.

'What's up with you?' he asked. 'Need a loo stop?'

'No, I'm just really looking forward to seeing inside the Radcliffe Camera.'

'Yes, it's normally not open to the public, just the Oxford students and professors. But this is one perk of our job, Megan. Sometimes we get to see the hidden side of this city that many mere mortals never get to witness.'

At that moment, a young man appeared with an academic pass lanyard around his neck. 'You're after Professor Shaw, I believe?'

They both nodded.

'Then please follow me, and I'll take you straight to him.'

The man unlocked the door, and they followed him. But rather than head straight out through a doorway into Radcliffe square, as Joseph expected, he led them to some stairs. A few moments later, the detectives were heading through an underground corridor lined with shelves.

'What is this?' Joseph asked.

Before their guide could respond, Megan jumped in. 'This is the Gladstone Link, and there's an even lower level to this, with more reading rooms. This passageway links the Radcliffe Camera to the Bodleian Library. At the moment we're passing under the square.'

'That's one way to avoid all those bloody tourists,' the DI replied with a smile.

Megan nodded, but her attention was focused on the spines of the books that they were passing. Joseph had a strong suspicion she was going to get on mighty well with Dylan when they were introduced.

They reached the end of the passageway and entered into a space that was in stark contrast to the minimalist modern styling of the corridor.

Megan stopped dead for a moment, her gaze sweeping around and soaking up every detail of the architecture. It certainly wasn't hard for Joseph to see why. The vaulted circular room they were standing in was spectacular. Pale carved stone arches ringed the circular structure, with bookshelves and highly polished wooden desks filling the alcoves. At the centre of the space was a round desk, light pouring down onto it from the ring of windows beneath an intricately decorated ceiling.

'Nice isn't it?' Joseph said.

'*Nice* is a bit of an understatement. In my mind's eye, this is the very picture of what a library should look like. Breathtaking.'

'Aye, that it is,' he replied with a wider smile. Joseph was quickly warming to the DC, and it was great to be with someone who was seeing this city with fresh eyes. Megan was also definitely going to get on with Dylan, who'd often waxed lyrical about the Radcliffe Camera in similarly glowing terms. All Joseph knew was that it was so much better for not being crowded with tourists.

They followed their guide across the room to an alcove where Dylan had set up camp. Piles of books were stacked around him on the desk. He was so engrossed in the ancient-looking book he was currently reading that he didn't look up as they hovered over him.

'Professor Dylan, your guests are here,' their guide said.

Dylan's half-moon specs flashed up at them, blinking as he surfaced from whatever he'd been reading.

'So, you tracked me down at last,' he said with a smile. 'Thanks for making sure they didn't get lost in the vaults, Gavin.'

'No problem, Professor,' the young man replied. He nodded to them and then headed back the way they had just come.

Dylan's eyes immediately zeroed in on Megan as he stood, hand outstretched. 'And you are?'

'DC Megan Anderson, and apparently Joseph's private chauffeur.'

Dylan chuckled. 'Yes, you need to watch him like that. He loves to take advantage of anyone with a vehicle.'

Joseph raised his eyebrows at his friend as they sat down in the two vacant seats on either side of him. 'Only if they're willing. Anyway, what do you have for us?'

The professor gazed at Joseph over his specs. 'You know how I said I'd seen that symbol before? Well...' From the pile of books next to him, he withdrew the second one from the top. Its black leather cover was embossed with *The Occult Compendium* in gold lettering and a stylised eye was intricately engraved above the title. The author's name, *Aaron Fearnley,* was also picked out in gold.

'That looks rather ancient,' Megan said.

'Actually, it isn't,' Dylan replied. 'This was only printed a couple of years ago, but with a limited run of three hundred copies, most of which went straight into the hands of collectors. Mind you, it was a solid investment, thanks to their rarity. I believe the last one exchanged hands for thirty thousand pounds in an open auction at Sotheby's.'

Joseph whistled. 'That's one hell of a markup.'

'You could say that. The rest were snapped up by several libraries, including Bodleian, although in its case the author is a local man who donated a copy for the library's archives. Obviously, they were more than happy to accept it, as it's something of a textbook for scholars for researching the vaguer aspects of the occult. Certainly, you'll find information in this book that you won't with an internet search. No doubt the remaining copies are locked away in private libraries of the sort of people who actually believe in this type of rubbish.'

Joseph drummed his foot. 'As fascinating as that is, Dylan, let's cut to the chase. Did you find the symbol in there?'

'Patience, Joseph, I'm building up to the big reveal.'

Megan looked between them. 'Hang on, an occult symbol. Does this have anything to do with the Laithwaite City Farm incident?'

Joseph sucked air through his teeth, realising that she was putting two and two together. 'It may,' he replied.

'So tell me if I'm wrong, but you shared a confidential piece of evidence with a member of the public and, based on the fact that you've only just been reinstated on the case, you must have done so when you weren't meant to have anything to do with it?'

Dylan pulled a face, but remained mute, leaving it to Joseph to claw his way out of the bog that he'd landed them both in.

It looked like this woman already had a detective's instinct.

Joseph shrugged. 'What can I say, Megan, but you have me bang to rights. The thing is, Dylan is one hell of a valuable resource with a wide range of expertise in a variety of areas. I've certainly confided in him more times than I care to remember on the trickier points of a case. Hell, if Sherlock Holmes was a real person and he were alive, he'd head to Dylan for advice.'

Megan frowned. 'And DSU Walker has authorised this?'

'What do you think?' he replied.

Megan sighed. 'Why do I feel like working with you will be exceptionally bad for my career?'

But Dylan, who'd been looking between them like an umpire at a tennis match, cleared his throat. 'Actually, Joseph here is one of the best detectives on the force, even if he hasn't received the rank he should have been given. You could learn a lot from him, Megan, even if some of what Joseph loves to do is off the record, so to speak.'

'Thanks for the vote of confidence,' the DI replied.

Dylan shrugged. 'Anytime, because it's true.'

Joseph smiled at him before focusing his attention back on Megan. 'Look, we can debate the finer points of this later when we get back to the station, but right now, the sooner we find out about that symbol, the sooner we can pursue it as a line of inquiry. What do you say?'

'Since when was this a *we* situation?' she replied.

'A word of advice: I wouldn't put up too much of a fight, Megan,' Dylan said. 'When Joseph rates someone highly, as I can tell he does you, based on the fact he's even giving you the time of day, they rarely get a lot of say in the matter. Anyway, before you two start arguing again, let's get down to the real reason you're here.'

Dylan turned to a page he'd marked with a white feather. This was the professor's trademark alternative to a bookmark.

He always had a selection he'd picked up from around the city. Once, when Joseph had been thumbing through a book on his boat, so many feathers dropped out it was like an angel had been shedding its wings.

The professor pointed to the open page. 'See what you think of that.'

Megan and Joseph leant to either side of him to get a better look.

The pages themselves appeared to be made from cream-coloured vellum rather than everyday paper. Obviously, no expense had been spared in creating this volume. Even the writing was some sort of flowing script that almost looked like it had been handwritten, rather than the usual font selection you'd find in printed material.

Joseph found himself gazing at an etching of an angel-like figure. Its black wings were stretched forward and curved around to envelop a man crouching before it. It was obvious the crouched man was having a bad day because his head was thrown back and looking upwards, his mouth wide and twisted.

The DI's eyes immediately flicked to the left-hand side where there were stylised symbols, all of which seemed to be variants of the same design. And then he saw it, towards the bottom of the page, the same zigzagging design with small circles that he'd last seen carved into the goat's flank during Amy's briefing.

Joseph stared at Dylan. 'You beauty, you found it!'

'It would appear I have,' Dylan replied, settling back into his seat with a satisfied smile.

'So you're telling us this symbol has something to do with an angel?' Megan asked, frowning.

'Not just any old angel...' The professor turned to the previous page to reveal the title of the section that they had been looking at.

'The Archangel Azrael – The Angel of Death.'

There were other names beneath it, written in different languages, one of which looked like Arabic.

'Okay, you've more than piqued my interest now,' he said. 'What else can you tell us?'

'That Azrael's name varies slightly across different cultures and his precise role does too. However, his underlying responsibility was for transporting souls to heaven.'

'You think that this is related to the animal sacrifices?' Joseph asked.

Dylan shrugged. 'All I can do is supply you with the relevance of this symbol. The rest is for you to piece together. However, there is also another significant factor that came to me once I realised it symbolised Azrael. That's the fact that two goats were involved, and not just one. I could kick myself for not seeing it before.'

'I'm not sure I follow,' Megan said.

'Are you aware of the origin of the word scapegoat?' Dylan asked.

Megan shook her head.

Joseph narrowed his eyes at him. 'No, but I'm sure you're going to enlighten us.'

'Absolutely, because I love discovering the origin of an expression. In this instance, we are talking about the well-known phrase scapegoat. In Hebrew, it's *Saʿir La-ʿazaʾzel* which translates to *goat for Azazel*, which is another variant of Azrael's name. Within the Old Testament, you'll find the ritual of Yom Kippur, where a kid goat is symbolically burdened with the sins of the people and released into the wilderness, taking with it all their impurities. A second goat was sacrificed to God.'

'Shite,' Joseph said, as he slowly nodded.

'Hang on,' Megan said, pursing her lips. 'If you're saying the

Midwinter Butcher is re-enacting an ancient sacrificial ritual, there is one glaring problem with that theory.'

'Go on?' Joseph replied.

'The murdered goat had Azrael's symbol on it. Shouldn't it have been the other way round? The dead goat would be a sacrifice to God, so wouldn't that symbol be more likely found carved into the missing goat's side?'

'Yes, you're not wrong, and that bit puzzled me too,' Dylan said.

'Maybe the killer was covering the odds and intended to sacrifice a goat to both Azrael and God just to make sure?' Joseph said.

Dylan scratched his chin. 'Possibly, but there's also a darker explanation, and it's everything to do with what you've been worried about all these years, Joseph.'

'You mean that this might finally be the start of an escalation?' he replied.

'I do. However, we also need to keep in mind that originally it was a purification ritual. It was looked at positively. Maybe that means the Midwinter Butcher is about to sign off, and this ritual was the cleansing of all previous sins. Or the alternative explanation is...'

'That the killer is preparing the groundwork for upping his game.'

'What do you mean?' Megan asked.

'Azrael is the bringer of souls,' Joseph replied. 'This sacrifice is our suspect setting out their stall as they get ready for the main act.'

Dylan nodded. 'I think that's a valid conclusion.'

'Bloody hell, you're being serious?' Megan asked, looking between them.

'I wish I wasn't, but yes,' the DI replied. 'Our killer has been content to restrict his killings to animals until now. But this could be the red flag that they're ready, after all his practise killings, to take things to the next level.'

'Okay, if you're talking about him murdering someone, are we talking a random event here or something planned?'

'Planned, absolutely,' he replied. 'Nothing our suspect has ever done has ever been random. Just look at the care he's previously taken to not leave any DNA behind. So I would bet that he's already studying his next victim, laying the groundwork to...' His words trailed away as an awful thought struck him.

'Joseph, you've gone very pale, what is it?' Dylan asked.

'You being here, that's what's wrong. I thought I asked you to keep an eye on Ellie, because if she's alone on my boat...'

'Stop right there and please relax,' Dylan replied. 'Her friend Zoe turned up and is with her.'

'Okay, okay...' Joseph took several breaths, trying to slow the spin of adrenaline that had surged through him.

'You really think the killer might go after your daughter?' Megan asked.

'I think we have to consider it as a possibility.'

'Okay, and I can see where you're coming from, but based on the killer's previous pattern, it's going to be another year before they kill again. So surely we have plenty of time to arrest this person, long before they ever take the chance to escalate things?'

'Jesus, you're sounding just like Faulkner now,' he said.

'Why? Don't you agree?' Megan asked.

'There are a lot of things about this incident that make me uneasy,' he replied. 'Any change of behaviour is a worrying sign.'

'True, and what with Azrael's symbol and the demon mask, that's not exactly reassuring,' Megan said.

Dylan sat up straighter. 'Demon mask?'

Megan tipped her head backwards. 'Me and my big mouth. Sorry, Joseph.'

'Don't sweat it,' he said. 'As the cat's out of the bag, we might as well tell you that Ellie's assailant was wearing a mask with horns, Dylan.'

Megan sighed. 'In for a penny, in for a pound.' She dropped her gaze back to Dylan. 'Yes, a demon mask, and I've been tasked with trying to track down the source of it. The problem is it's an unusual design and so far the forensics team hasn't been able to trace where it came from.'

The professor scratched his chin. 'I see... In that case, can I make a suggestion that may help?'

'Knock yourself out,' Joseph replied.

Dylan closed the book and tapped on the name of the author. 'Why don't you talk to the author of this book, namely Aaron Fearnley?'

'Not a bad idea, as he is the closest thing to an expert that we know. I don't suppose you have the contact details for him so I can give him a ring?'

'Actually, you can do better than that and have a word with the man himself as he works at the Pitt Rivers Museum. Aaron is an expert in all things occult and even recently put together the witchcraft exhibition at the Ashmolean. Of course, the museum has an extensive collection of ancient masks, so if anyone can help with where your suspect's mask came from, I think Aaron's expert knowledge may be as good a starting point as any.'

'Thank you for the tip,' Megan said. 'We will certainly follow that up.'

'I told you, Dylan is a useful man to know. There is one other thing that's still bothering me.'

'What's that?' Megan asked.

'What's happened to the other goat? If the killer is following this scapegoat ritual, even if they've adapted it a bit, shouldn't they be sending the other into the wilderness carrying their sins? If so, the question is where?'

Megan raised her shoulders. 'Maybe a random field out in Oxfordshire, or even take it out to somewhere further away and really wild like a moor?'

'I think Derek would have a cost-induced heart attack if I asked for a police helicopter to search half the country for a wayward goat,' Joseph replied.

'You never know,' Dylan said. 'A member of the public might just spot someone acting suspiciously when they try to bundle a goat out of a truck and into a field.'

Megan smiled. 'Particularly if they're wearing a demon mask.'

Joseph rolled his eyes at her.

23RD DECEMBER

CHAPTER ELEVEN

Max bounded ahead of Charlie, his nose seeking out every fresh scent in the copse at the edge of Port Meadow, where the man's tent was discreetly hidden deep in a thicket.

The world around them had been transformed by the intense hoarfrost that had wrapped all the branches in fine prickly icicles the night before. Charlie followed the wagging tail of his dog, the grass crackling under his feet as he made his way among the trees.

Mondays were always good for business thanks to the commuters being particularly generous. He always made a point of stocking up with plenty of copies of The Big Issue on Sunday, as the following day was often his best day of the week. Friday, on the other hand, Charlie often wondered if he'd become invisible. People tended to be blinkered, seeing nothing but their phones or an invisible point in the distance, focused on getting through the day as fast as possible so they could get home again and start the weekend. Yes, Fridays weren't great.

His breath clouded around him as he carefully positioned his hand on the barbed wire running along the top of the fence. He lowered it just enough for him to hop over, his lower back complaining like it always did, more so in this cold weather. He knew he was getting too old for this game, but what choice did he have?

Charlie wrapped the orange puffer coat tighter around himself against the chill of the day. That item of clothing came from a kind hearted soul who'd spontaneously emerged from an office to give it to him when it had been snowing one day. There were still some kind people around.

Max cocked his leg on a fence post, and the next along just for good measure, as Charlie made his way down the slope onto the edge of Port Meadow. A thick river fog hung low to the ground, tinged with the gold of a rising sun hidden somewhere beyond it. He knew it wouldn't be long before it burned off. But in the meantime, when the weather was like this, it was hard not to imagine that he'd stumbled through a backdoor into Narnia, a story he remembered fondly from when his mother had first read it to him as a child.

He set out across the meadow, and even with no visible landmarks, he could still use his well-honed instinct to guide him to the far side. Once there, he would pick up the path and cut across to the canal, before heading into town and his final destination, the railway station. Max trotted alongside, his faithful friend and companion.

As Charlie walked, the fog increased its otherworldly spell, even sounds deadening.

Perhaps I've fallen off the edge of the world, he thought to himself.

But then a shape began to take form in the fog as he moved forward, whatever it was standing motionless. However, far from being worried, Charlie smiled to himself as the ghostly shape revealed itself to be one of the wild ponies who roamed free across the meadow. The mare, with her dusty white coat, almost perfectly camouflaged in the fog, turned an expectant head towards him.

'Ah, Mable, I was wondering if I might run into you,' he said.

Charlie knew all the ponies by sight and had names for all of them. And they knew him, the man who always had an apple in his pocket.

As he trudged towards the animal, Max hung back and sat down, waiting patiently for the transaction to be completed. The ponies didn't take kindly to dogs, however well-behaved they were, so Max had learned long ago to keep his distance.

As Charlie got nearer to the pony, he could see that Mable was covered in hoarfrost, her mane hanging with a chandelier's worth of jewelled icicles.

'Hey girl, you look like you've had a hard night of it,' he said, reaching out and gently rubbing Mable's neck.

The pony began nuzzling his jacket.

'Yes, yes, cupboard love, but yes, I've got something for you.' He dug into his pocket and withdrew an apple. That elicited a snort of approval from the pony. Charlie held it out to her in his flat palm.

Mable dipped her head and with a brush of teeth and gums on his skin, plucked the apple cleanly from his hand and began munching on it.

As she ate, Charlie ran his fingers over her mane, trying to free her from some of her icicle burden.

'You poor old thing, but it won't be long till the sun burns through this fog to warm you up.'

Swallowing the apple, the pony gave a soft whinny as though she agreed. But then her ears angled forward as her head came up, her muscles stiffening beneath her ice-laden coat.

'What is it, Mable?' he asked, turning and half expecting to see a dog bounding towards them.

Nothing was there, although Charlie could hear a faint bleating. That immediately piqued his interest, as he'd never seen a sheep on Port Meadow. Then the animal's cries became more desperate.

Max turned, his ears pricking forward. Then, with a lolloping run, he set off to where the sound was coming from, and disappeared into the bank of fog.

'Great, looks like I'm going to get involved whether I want to or not, Mable,' Charlie said, giving the pony one last pat.

He headed off in the direction that his dog had disappeared, his own concern mounting when he heard another distressed bleat dead ahead. It was then that the fog thinned just for a moment and he saw two figures in white suits of some kind.

Of all the things that he might have expected to see on Port Meadow, he never would have imagined this. One of the figures was holding a kid goat, which was struggling to get free.

Charlie almost laughed. So much for it being a dog attacking an animal. But then the oddness of the situation struck him. Why was anyone out here with a goat anyway, and dressed like that?

The taller figure put the goat down on the ground, and it immediately bounded away bleating into the fog.

Charlie's curiosity was well and truly up now. Why release a goat out in the middle of Port Meadow? Was it some unwanted pet that they were abandoning? And what was the deal with the white suits?

Desperate to find out what was going on, Charlie called out to the mysterious figures. 'Interesting choice of pet you've got there.'

Both people froze, and then slowly turned.

Shock surged through Charlie as he took in the white demon masks they were both wearing, and he immediately backed away.

'I don't want any trouble,' he said, raising his palms.

Without saying a word, the shorter of the two figures withdrew something from a bag—a strange-looking dagger with a thin blade. The other person reached out a hand to grab the shorter one's arm, but they shook it off. Slowly, that person advanced towards Charlie.

Charlie's blood pounded in his ears as he spun around and began to walk back the way he had come. Bitterness tanged his throat as he tried to lengthen his stride, but his tired old muscles didn't obey. He dug into another pocket for the mobile phone that he kept for absolute emergencies.

Adrenaline powered him into a half run, half hobble, as he tried to get away. 'Leave me alone!' Charlie called out as he heard his pursuer gain rapidly on him.

He started to dial 999 as the dark ribbon of the River Thames appeared just ahead, cutting across Port Meadow and also his only way to escape.

Charlie heard the click of a connection on his mobile as he frantically glanced back to see the other figure less than three metres away.

'Help me—' The rest of his sentence was drowned out by his own scream as the figure lunged forward, knocking him to the ground.

'Hello, hello,' a tinny voice said from his phone as it was yanked from him by the person and thrown with a splash into the river.

Then Max streaked out of the fog, barking frantically behind them. Charlie's eyes locked onto his pursuer's as they knocked him down, rolling him over to kneel on his chest, squeezing the air out of his lungs. A sense of absolute terror coiled in the old man's gut, as his killer raised the dagger, getting ready to strike.

No one around to help. No witnesses.

CHAPTER TWELVE

As THE HEAVY fog lapped around Joseph, he felt considerable relief when he turned his mountain bike off the main road. The only reason he'd not been taken out by a driver in the freezing fog was thanks to his LED lamp, which would give a searchlight a good run for its money. On days like today, being a cyclist rather than driving came with distinct disadvantages.

The detective pedaled slowly through the car park out at the end of Port Meadow, trying not to skid on the frozen puddles. The fog was so thick he was almost on top of a van with RSPCA written on its side before he realised it. As he padlocked his bike to the railings next to it, he waved to the driver who was sitting inside talking to someone on his phone as he peered out at the featureless grey expanse of mist.

The reason that the DI was here at all was that he'd been roused from his bed first thing by a call. It had been St Aldates station saying that the local division of the RSPCA, one of the groups that had been asked to report any unusual sightings of a goat turning up somewhere random, had been in contact with a hopeful lead. Apparently, a member of the public had been out walking their dog across Port Meadow just thirty minutes earlier, and had reported finding a goat half frozen to death and abandoned in the middle of the common.

It was a long shot, but the detective was hoping it might turn out to be the second goat and that would help support Dylan's theory that this was a variant of the scapegoat ritual.

Wishing he was wearing an arctic-level insulated jacket, the DI walked up to the driver's window and tapped on it. The man's gaze took in the cycling kit that he was wearing as he lowered the window. He then held up a finger for Joseph to wait a moment as he listened to someone at the other end of the line.

'Okay, just send through your location,' the man replied. A moment later, his phone pinged. 'That's great, Luke. I just got the GPS marker; I'll be with you in ten minutes.'

'Hi, are you Jesse Walsh?' Joseph asked as soon as he finished his call.

'Yes, and you are?'

'DI Stone from the St Aldates Police Station. We had a report from your office about a goat being found out on Port Meadow.'

'You're a DI?' The guy gave Joseph another once over with a slightly incredulous look.

'Obviously plain clothes and currently disguised as a cyclist.' Joseph took out his warrant card and waved it at him.

He nodded. 'Sorry, yes, I was told to expect you. In my head, you guys always turn up in a classic car rather than...' He gestured with his chin towards the mountain bike.

'Cut backs, I'm afraid.' Joseph gave him a wry smile that made the other man snort. 'Anyway, do you know where this goat is located?'

The RSPCA officer clicked on his phone and pulled up a map with a marker on it. 'I do now. That was Luke, the guy I was speaking to just now, who found it. He's stayed with the kid goat and just sent his location through to me. I'm certainly going to need it to find him in this thick fog. Anyway, you're more than welcome to join me, but we need to get a move on before the goat freezes to death. The guy who found it tried to pick it up, but every time he gets within a few feet of the goat, it just runs away.'

'Of course, let's get going,' Joseph said, taking his helmet off, before they headed through the gate in the fence.

A short while later, using his phone with the map marker that Jesse had shared, Joseph was leading the way walking into the meadow. Jesse followed a short distance behind, his hands full with a large plastic transport carrier and a pole with a noose on it to catch the goat.

The entire meadow was still engulfed by the pea soup bank of fog, with no sign of the city skyline and spires to the south.

The saturated air was coating Joseph's cycling jacket with water droplets that were freezing instantly into beads of ice. The grass was frozen solid too, crumping beneath their feet like the sound of fresh snow. The detective was starting to seriously fantasise about a warming coffee when Jesse broke the silence.

'I've got to ask, Inspector, why are the police interested in a goat being dumped in the middle of Port Meadow?'

'I'm afraid I can't talk about an ongoing investigation,' the DI replied.

'So nothing to do with the Laithwaite City Farm goat murder, by any chance?'

Joseph glance back at him. 'How the hell do you know about that?'

'It was in the Oxford Chronicle all over the front page. I grabbed a copy early this morning.'

'Oh shite. They were meant to keep that quiet for the time being whilst we carried out our investigations.'

'Well, I'm afraid someone must have blabbed.'

Joseph sighed inwardly. He was going to have a word with

Kate, who had obviously taken matters into her own hands. That was if Derek hadn't roasted her already over this. Certainly, the control freak that was DCI Chris Faulkner would be apoplectic when he found out that the news embargo he'd insisted on had been broken. If Joseph had been running the case, he would have been working with the press and using them as an asset to get the word out there. That was what Kate had presumably decided to do, rather than keeping them at arm's length like the DCI had done. Each man to their own, even if Faulkner was totally wrong about how they were handling this.

Joseph drew the zip of his jacket all the way to the top to shield himself against the biting cold as they steadily closed in on the map marker. They were down to ten metres when a man with a black Labrador sitting on its haunches suddenly appeared out of the murk.

'Luke?' Jesse asked.

'Yep, and thank God you're here at last; I've been freezing my nads off waiting for you,' the man replied with a Brummie accent.

'So where's this goat, then?'

'Just over there.' The guy turned and pointed to a small brown goat ten metres behind him on the ground.

The detective pulled up the photo of Gandalf that Faulkner had shared at the briefing to help identify the goat should he ever turn up. The animal trembling before them was an exact match.

Jesse put the carrier on the ground, opened its cage door, and took out a blanket that had been tucked inside. 'The sooner I get that goat back to the van, the sooner I can get him warmed up.'

'Good luck with that,' Luke said. 'I must have tried a dozen times to get hold of the little guy, but every time I get close, he dances away, out of reach.'

'That's why I brought this,' Jesse said, showing the other man the pole with the hoop on the end.

'Nice one.'

As the two spoke, Joseph's brain was cranking into gear. So Port Meadow passed for a suitable wilderness in the Midwinter Butcher's mind. If so, that would confirm Dylan's theory about this being a variation of the scapegoat ritual.

Joseph turned to Luke. 'I don't suppose you saw anyone acting suspicious around here?'

'Are you with him, or just some random guy trying to help?' he replied.

Joseph flashed his warrant card. 'DI Stone.'

The guy's eyes widened. 'Oh right. No, sorry. If you mean catching sight of the idiot who abandoned a young goat out here in this weather, sadly not. But whoever did it should be locked up, because the little guy could have died in this.'

'Don't worry, I'm working on tracking them down.'

'Good to hear,' Luke replied.

As the other two got to work rounding up the goat who was now on his feet, bleating at them, Luke kept the black labrador on a short leash, Joseph examined the ground in the immediate area, hoping to find some sort of clue. But despite several minutes of searching, all he could find were their own footprints in the frozen grass, along with the goat's hoofmarks.

Jesse was extending the hoop towards the goat's head. 'That's it, that's it, don't move, little fella,' he whispered.

The detective gazed at the trail of hoofprints leading away from the goat and into the fog, just as Jesse slipped the hoop around Gandalf's neck and tightened it.

'Got you!' he said, quickly shuffling the pole through his hands, before grabbing hold of the goat, who was now frantically bleating. With the no-nonsense approach of a man who'd done this hundreds of times, within moments Jesse had Gandalf wrapped in a fleece blanket, and was carrying him towards the carrier. 'See, that wasn't so bad, little fella.'

As the RSPCA officer passed Joseph, he saw something glinting from around the goat's neck.

'Hang on a moment,' the detective said.

Jesse stopped as Joseph leaned in for a closer look. Around the animal's neck was a small gold crucifix hanging from a fine chain.

'A scapegoat sent out into the wilderness for God, so everything is reversed,' Joseph muttered to himself.

'Pardon?' Jesse replied.

'Don't mind me. Just thinking out loud.' He glanced at Luke. 'You don't have a poop bag, do you?'

'Of course, I'm a responsible dog owner, unlike some round here.'

'Could I have one?'

The man nodded, dug in his pocket and handed Joseph a bag, giving him a puzzled look.

A moment later, with his gloved hands, Joseph carefully unfastened the gold crucifix and placed it in the poop bag.

'Potential evidence,' he said, meeting their questioning looks.

'Oh, right,' Luke replied, bewildered.

'Speaking of which, if you can try to keep the goat isolated for a while, our forensic team will want to check to see if they can find any evidence on it.'

'Wow, you guys are really taking this seriously,' Luke said.

'You could say that,' the DI replied, exchanging a look with Jesse.

'I better get this goat back to the van and get him nice and toasty,' Jesse said as he nodded towards Luke. 'Thank you for taking the time to stay with him. You almost certainly saved his life.'

'Anytime, the least I could for the little guy,' Luke replied with a broad smile.

'Before you go, can I just take your details in case we need to be in contact?' Joseph asked.

'Of course. Happy to give evidence if it will help put the bastard who's responsible for this away.'

'Thank you,' the detective replied as his gaze returned to the trail of goat hoofprints again.

Joseph's hunch of following the goat's tracks had paid dividends. He stood, his breath billowing around him, the tips of his fingers already numb with cold despite the cycling gloves he was wearing. Before him was what appeared to be a crossroads, with at least two sets of tracks converging on the same spot. The grass was heavily trampled in one area and included boot imprints in the compressed, frozen grass alongside the goat's hoofprints. This had to be the spot where the Midwinter Butcher had first abandoned the goat, and recently, too. The trails through the grass were fresh and the detective strongly doubted that the young goat could have survived the night on the meadow during such icy conditions.

He realised he needed to work quickly. As soon as the grass thawed, any signs of the trails would quickly disappear.

The DI dropped a pin on the map on his phone's screen so he could come back later and check over the location thoroughly. But right now, he needed to follow one of the trails whilst it was still visible. One set of footprints appeared to head roughly in the direction of the car park where he'd left his bike next to Jesse's van. But there was a second trail of footprints that came from the eastern side of Port Meadow and almost converged on the same spot. Could it belong to an accomplice, or maybe someone that just crossed the same location later on? Another dog walker, maybe?

But then the detective noticed another trail leading away, two lots of footprints almost now on top of each other, and heading west towards the river. The fact that they so closely overlapped suggested that one person had been following the other...

Joseph's blood grew colder than even the arctic conditions around him. The DI set off at a stride, walking parallel to the combined tracks, praying that his suspicions weren't true and this was just a coincidence. But the fog pressed in, the frozen grass crunching with every step as that dark sense of foreboding grew inside him.

This bloody weather was the perfect cover. No witnesses to see what had happened.

Joseph kept glancing at his map as he headed steadily towards the Thames. Ahead, the mist was thinning at last and the river was becoming clearer with every passing moment, the trail of both sets of human footprints still heading straight towards it. The slow-flowing water had taken on the colour of copper in the muted sunrise, the stillness in the air extending to its surface where there was barely a ripple. Beyond the river, the trees stood like shadowy figures on the far bank, sentinels to whatever had occurred here.

Then the detective heard a quiet whine, and he looked ahead to see a dog he recognised at once, limping towards him.

Joseph raced over to the wounded dog. 'My God, what happened to you, Max?' Then he cupped his hands around his mouth. 'Charlie, are you round here somewhere?'

No answer came back, not even the faintest murmur of sound. The DI's sense of foreboding was through the roof now, instinct telling him that something awful had happened here. His mind raced as he put the pieces together. The second set of tracks hadn't belonged to an accomplice, but an eyewitness, someone that had stumbled across what was happening and then had been pursued by the Midwinter Butcher towards the Thames. And that man had to be Charlie.

Max whined again, as Joseph dialled the RSPCA officer.

Jesse picked up in two rings. 'Hello.'

'It's DI Stone, please tell me you're still in the car park?'

'Yes, but I'm about to head back with the goat to the vet, why?'

'Then hang on, because I've just stumbled across an injured beagle that's limping badly. He needs to see a vet, too.'

'Okay, bring the dog to me and I'll deal with it.'

'I would if I could, but I'm going to need you to come to my location.'

'Why's that? If you're worried about moving the dog—'

'No, not that,' Joseph said, cutting him off. 'I've found something else and I'm afraid I can't leave it.'

'Okay. Send me a pin then.'

The detective did as he asked, and a ping down the phone indicated that Jesse had just received it.

'I'm on my way, Inspector.'

'Thank you.' Joseph clicked the end call button, and gently ruffled Max's head. 'You stay here, the cavalry is on its way.'

Max sat, his paw raised to keep the weight off it, as Joseph headed the short distance towards the river embankment. As he got closer, he spotted a tangle of footprints and something glistening like rubies across the ground.

'Oh, shite,' the detective said as he squatted to examine dark red splatters of blood. Beyond it were scrape marks of something heavy being dragged straight towards the embankment where the trail abruptly ended. Then leading away at a right angle was a single set of boot prints, well spaced, of someone running back in the direction of the car park.

Joseph's mouth grew dry as he selected a contact on his phone and pressed the call button.

'Hello, St Aldates Police Station,' Gary's voice said at the other end.

'Hi, it's DI Stone. You need to rouse the troops because I think I may have just stumbled across the scene of the Midwinter Butcher's first human murder.' Joseph looked down at the copper river and shook his head as he became lost in the memory of a kind soul who had never harmed anyone in his entire life.

CHAPTER THIRTEEN

Joseph watched the trail of bubbles snaking through the deeper section of the Thames as they had for the past thirty minutes. The last of the fog had burned away to leave a bright, sunny day, which was in stark contrast to how he was feeling. An incident scene had been taped off around the embankment area where three yellow numbered tags had been placed. One for where he'd found Max injured, another for the drag marks through the embankment to the river, and a final one for the blood splatters that had already been sampled.

The detective already knew in his bones that Charlie was dead. Too much experience combined with the evidence he'd already seen left him without much in the way of hope for a positive outcome.

Joseph was watching the SOCO team at work when Ian headed towards him with a cup of coffee in his hand.

'Here you go, Joseph,' Ian said. 'I heard you'd been out here for hours and thought you might appreciate this.'

'Thanks, I'm freezing my arse off here. A hot drink is exactly what I need to thaw out.' The DI took the cup from him and wrapped his hands around it in an attempt to warm them up.

'No problem. Anyway, we just heard from a couple of officers who checked Charlie's usual spot at the railway station. He wasn't there and there's no sign of him on any of the CCTV footage covering the area, either.'

Joseph took a sip of what turned out to be lukewarm instant coffee and did his best not to pull a face. 'I think that just confirms what we already know, Ian.'

'Yeah...' The DS gestured towards the trail of bubbles. 'Has the diver found anything yet?'

'If you mean a body, nothing so far. But the river could easily carry the corpse downstream into Oxford. We already have sniffer dogs on the embankments there in case a body has washed up.'

'Right, and I hear Charlie's dog was injured too?' Ian asked.

Joseph grimaced at the memory of Max limping towards him. 'Yes, and according to the vet, although the poor chap had some broken bones that seemed to have been caused by someone kicking him, he's going to make a full recovery.'

'At least that's something, but we need to catch the scumbag responsible for it and put them away sooner rather than later. Maybe we'll get lucky today and find some fresh DNA evidence. Such a shame that the silver hair from the goat killing was a bust.'

The DI stared at him. 'That's the first I've heard of it.'

'The lab report came back this morning,' Ian replied. 'Not a single match on the national database.'

Joseph shook his head. 'That doesn't actually surprise me. I've always suspected that the killer is someone who's flown under the radar for a long time. I bet they probably haven't ever had so much as a parking fine.'

'That's certainly a possibility.'

The DI nodded. 'Until recently, the Midwinter Butcher hasn't taken any chances, but seems to be getting careless. First

Ellie and now taking the next step that I've been worried about all these years, to murder a human victim. My hunch is that Charlie stumbled across our suspect releasing the second goat.'

'So why kill him and not Ellie...' Ian's words trailed away as he grimaced. 'Sorry, me and my big mouth,'

Joseph had to suppress the shudder that went through him. 'It's nothing I haven't thought about already, Ian. If this pans out like I think it's going to, then that tells me exactly how lucky my daughter is to be alive. Maybe, if the patrol car hadn't got to the farm so quickly, we would be searching for her body right now.'

Ian stared down into his coffee. 'Thank God it isn't, Joseph.'

'Amen to that, but I'm not going to be able to shake what could have been,' he replied.

Both detectives looked back at the river when a flurry of bubbles broke the surface. Then, like a black seal surfacing, the diver's head appeared, a phone held aloft in his hand. He waded towards the embankment and handed it over to a forensic officer, who took it from him with gloved hands.

'That looks promising,' Ian said.

'It is. There was a report of an aborted 999 call, from a male caller asking for help before being cut off,' Joseph replied. 'Although he wasn't on the line long enough to triangulate his position from cellphone masts, we have a rough location of him being somewhere around the Port Meadow area. But I have more than a strong hunch that once they check it, they'll discover it belonged to Charlie.'

'I certainly wouldn't bet against it.'

Joseph's phone vibrated in his pocket and when he pulled it out, he saw St Aldates Police Station displayed on its screen. The DI immediately pressed the call accept icon.

'Hi, Joseph. I thought you should know that we've just had a report of a body found by Magdalen Bridge,' Gary's voice said. I'm afraid it matches the description of the missing homeless man you called in. Chris is already at the scene with Megan. Amy and her team are on their way there now. Anyway, I thought you might want to get yourself over there as well.'

'Oh shite, part of me was holding out hope that he might turn up okay, but thanks for the heads up, Gary.'

'No problem,' the desk sergeant replied.

'Bad news?' Ian asked as Joseph pressed the end-call button.

'Yes, it seems like Charlie's body may have turned up further down the river like we guessed. Any chance you could give me a lift?'

'Sure.' Ian drained the last of his thermos coffee as Joseph discreetly threw away the rest of his.

They set off together back across the meadow just as the diver's head disappeared again beneath the surface, searching for more grim clues that might hopefully include the murder weapon.

Joseph and Ian sped through the streets of Oxford in an unmarked police BMW Series 3, blue lights flashing and siren blaring. Somehow with the rear seat folded down, they had squeezed the DI's bike into the back. Now commuters' cars and buses parted before them. Even the cyclists pulled over to let the unmarked car pass, which was a minor miracle in itself. But that was little wonder as they could probably hear Ian approaching like a bat out of hell. The DI was certainly regretting his choice of Ian to be his taxi driver. His knuckles were turning white while he hung onto the handle above the door as they tore around a bend onto the high street, wheels squealing.

'Alright, Ian, you're not auditioning for the Top Gear show,' Joseph said through a clenched jaw.

The DS glanced over at him. 'You want to get there as fast

as possible, don't you, before Chris has everything neatly tied up with a ribbon?'

'Yes, but preferably in one piece.'

'Alright, alright.' Ian dropped their pace to somewhere just below light speed as they hurtled along the high street, the shops blurring past.

Just ahead, at the start of Magdalen Bridge, were at least six marked police cars all parked up. Beyond them, a line of pedestrians had stopped and were peering over the edge of the bridge's balustrade. A couple of PCs in high-visibility vests appeared to be standing guard at the top of the steps where a yellow cordon tape had been hung.

With a totally unnecessary emergency stop, Ian stood on the brakes, and they came to a shuddering halt behind the last parked-up police car.

'That will be ten pounds, *guvnor*,' Ian said with a genuinely awful cockney accent.

'Yeah right, eejit,' Joseph replied, arching his eyebrows at the DS as they got out of the BMW.

PC John Thorpe, one of the two uniformed officers standing guard, turned towards the detectives as they approached. 'They're down at the quay,' he said, answering their unanswered question.

'Thanks.' Joseph gestured to the crowd. 'And could you do me a favour and have someone clear away the sightseers? We could do without photos of the crime scene being splashed all over social media.'

'I'll deal with them, sir,' the other officer said, heading off to tackle them.

'So what's the situation down there, John?' Joseph asked.

'DCI Faulkner and the SOCOs are already on site. I think they're about to pull the body from the water.'

'We better go and see if it's your friend, Joseph,' Ian said.

'You knew him?' John asked.

'I'm pretty sure it's Charlie, that Big Issue seller who has a regular spot at the railway station.'

'Seriously? But he doesn't seem the sort to take his own life.'

The DI peered at him. 'What do you mean?'

'When DCI Faulkner first turned up, he was working on the assumption that it was a drunk homeless guy who fell off the bridge,' John said. 'But as far as I know, Charlie never touched a drop.'

'He didn't. Thirty years dry, and that was something Charlie was really proud of.'

'So you're saying this wasn't an accident, then?' John asked.

'Correct, and I'm afraid it's linked to another Midwinter Butcher incident further upriver.'

'Oh, bloody hell,' John said as lifted the tape for the two detectives.

At the bottom of the stairs, Joseph and Ian headed towards the boathouse next to the quayside. A few punts had been lined up there for the really hardy who fancied taking a boat trip in the middle of winter.

Joseph spotted Amy easily enough among the other forensic officers, standing in a boat and towering over everyone else. She was taking photos of a body floating facedown in the water, who was wearing a orange puffer jacket that he recognised as the one Charlie had always worn in the winter. Four more of Amy's team were on the quay, suited and booted in forensics suits, doing a fingertip search of the area. The lack of any numbered markers showed they had found nothing so far.

An ambulance crew waited with a gurney next to their vehicle, a body bag already unzipped and ready for the body. Not for the first time, it struck Joseph that the end of a life should never look like this.

Chris was off to one side taking photos of the bridge with his smartphone, which suggested that he was still convinced that this was just a drunk falling off the bridge into the river below.

Ian headed off to report in, and the DI was about to follow when he spotted Megan vomiting into the river on the far side of the punts. At least the Isis' current, the name that the locals used for the section of the Thames that ran through Oxford, would carry her puke away so it wouldn't interfere with the crime scene.

Joseph headed over to her, Silvermints already in his hand. 'Hi, Megan. Not doing so well, I see.'

She raised her face from the water. 'What gave it away, Joseph?'

'That trail of sick snaking along the Isis like a yellow oil slick gave me a bit of a clue.'

To her credit, she managed a half smile. 'You could be a detective with deductive skills like that.'

'Always good to have one's abilities recognised.' Joseph smiled as he offered her a mint.

She took one this time without any hesitation and sucked it. 'You're a lifesaver.'

'Aye, I like to think so. Anyway, based on your reaction, I'm guessing you had a good look at the corpse?'

Megan grimaced. 'Yes, I was first on the scene with Chris after it was reported. We even beat Uniform to it.'

'Yeah, our DCI loves to grab all the glory when a body is found.'

She frowned at Chris, who was deep in conversation but kept casting glances their way. 'If that's his idea of glory, he can stuff it up his...' She did a small headshake. 'Sorry, sir. There's something about the guy that just rubs me up the wrong way.'

'Don't worry, you're not the only one. And once again please drop the *sir* routine.'

Megan nodded, and this time gave the DI a wider smile.

'Okay, we're ready to move the body,' Amy called out.

Joseph turned to see she was back on the quay and her team was making their way out along the two adjacent punts that the body had been wedged between.

'Maybe, look the other way for this bit, Megan,' Joseph said, handing her the rest of his mints.

She nodded and gazed out down the Isis, a small tremble passing through her shoulders.

The DI headed towards Amy as she stepped over the cordon and pulled her mask down.

'How's it going?' he said as he approached her.

'Another grim day at the office, I'm afraid, Joseph.'

'I don't suppose you know what the cause of death is yet?'

'I can tell you he didn't drown, otherwise, he'd be at the bottom of the river, at least until the bacteria in the gut and his chest cavity produced enough gas to float him back to the surface. My best guess is the victim entered the water facedown, trapping the air in his lungs and that's what kept him buoyant. Skin colouration suggests he hasn't been in the water that long either. Of course, that could support Chris's theory that the guy fell from the bridge.'

Joseph shook his head, in no way surprised that their illustrious DCI would settle for the easy option as a way to wrap up the case.

'I'm absolutely certain that's not what happened,' the DI said.

'Yes, I think even he's starting to realise this is something more sinister,' Amy replied. 'I'm guessing something to do with the crime scene you reported in at Port Meadow?'

'The very same.'

The SOCO team, who'd knelt in one of the punts, got their hands on either side of the body.

Amy and Joseph turned to watch as one of the men called out, 'Get ready to lift. Three, two, one, now...'

The body was hauled out of the water, droplets splashing down from the orange puffer jacket. Charlie's bedraggled grey hair hung down on either side of his head.

The forensic team, carefully manoeuvring the body with the punts rocking beneath them, carried the dead man back to the quay and then turned him onto his back.

The DI looked down to see Charlie's mouth was open wide like a gaping fish, his grey skin was slick with river water. Moisture beaded his beard and eyebrows, his skin a sickly mottled grey, lifeless eyes staring up towards the sky.

Joseph had to fight the impulse to cross the tape barrier, push the forensic team aside, and close the man's eyes. Charlie was as gentle a man as they came and didn't deserve any of this.

Megan must have turned and seen Charlie's face too, because once again she was retching as quietly as she could into the Isis.

Amy crouched over Charlie and began taking photos, the camera's LED light panel illuminating Joseph's friend's face with stark clinical light.

Chris wandered over. 'A terrible business, Joseph,' he said with an almost respectful tone when he reached him. 'Ian just updated me about what happened in Port Meadow, so this looks like it's linked to the goat incident that you were investigating.'

'I'm certain it is, sir,' Joseph replied, doing his best to be just as respectful. 'I believe Charlie disturbed the Midwinter Butcher and was killed for his trouble. Then it appears his body was thrown into the river.'

Chris sighed. 'Then it looks like I owe you an apology. Like DSU Walker, I was certain that our man wouldn't escalate things, especially after all these years have passed, since...' His gaze met Joseph's. 'Well, you know.'

Joseph gave a small shrug. 'We all get it wrong sometimes, sir.'

'Yes, it would seem that we do.'

The DCI's attention was pulled away by Megan, making another retching sound.

He shook his head. 'I had such high hopes for her, too.'

'I'm not sure I follow?'

'Well, look at her. She obviously hasn't got the stomach for working on a murder investigation.'

'Most officers don't when they start.' Joseph gave him a knowing look.

Chris frowned at him. Neither of them needed to mention the Jackson Pollock incident by name. 'Be that as it may, I have an instinct about people, Joseph. I honestly don't think she's going to stay the course.'

As good as your ability to judge whether a suspect might escalate from animal ritual killings to murder? Joseph kept the thought to himself and instead, said, 'If you're thinking about throwing Megan overboard, in my opinion, you need to give her a proper chance first.'

'Look, I haven't got time to wet nurse someone who isn't up to it.'

A spike of irritation ran through Joseph. Faulkner's type got to where they were by trampling over people on their way up the greasy pole. Well, he wasn't going to let that happen on his watch.

'Tell you what, sir. I'll take her under my wing and mentor her. I think Megan has real potential.'

'If you're prepared to waste your time, be my guest. But please don't teach her any of your bad habits.'

'No, but maybe I'll encourage her to develop a few of her own.'

And just like that, what had amounted to a brief truce between the two detectives was swept away.

Chris glared at Joseph, but before he could slap him down, Amy appeared, camera clutched in her hand. Behind her, Charlie was being zipped into a body bag by one of the other forensic officers.

'You're both going to want to see this,' Amy said as she reached the detectives. She turned the camera around so they could see its rear viewing screen. On it there was a closeup of Charlie's face, a black hole in the middle of his forehead.

'Is that some sort of bullet wound?' Chris asked, peering at it.

But Joseph was already shaking his head. 'It can't be because the edges are square rather than round.'

'Well spotted, Joseph,' Amy said with obvious approval.

He raked his hand through his hair. 'It could be a screwdriver, something like that?'

'We'll hopefully know for sure once the pathologist has finished the autopsy.'

'All I know is that DSU Walker is going to be demanding we crack this and quickly,' Chris said. He gestured towards a few people who, despite the officer's best efforts, were still on the bridge taking photos. 'Once word gets out, the press will be all over this like nappy rash and we're going to need to supply them answers, and quickly.'

'I agree, sir,' Joseph said. 'But it's looking increasingly obvious that the occult connection is real. So if it's alright with you, there's a lead I'd like to follow up on with Megan.'

'Is that contacting the man who wrote that Azrael occult book you mentioned in your report?' Chris asked.

Joseph stared at him, surprised. 'You actually read it?'

'Yes, of course I did. I know we don't always see eye to eye, but I value your opinion and experience, especially with a case that you've been working so closely on for years.'

Joseph gave him a look, trying to work out if the DCI was taking the piss. But no, once again he seemed to be extending an olive branch. Chris had obviously got out of the right side of the bed this morning.

'Aaron Fearnley, the man who wrote that occult book, actually works at the Pitt Rivers Museum,' Joseph replied. 'I'm hoping that maybe he can clarify why someone would go around carving symbols for an archangel into the side of a goat. We're also hoping that he may have some thoughts about where that demon mask came from. But on that subject, I have another idea that may help.'

'Which is?' Chris replied, looking at him suspiciously.

'I think it may be time to hold a press conference.'

'You mean in case a member of the public recognises the demon mask?' Amy asked.

'Why not? It's got to be worth a shot.' Joseph gestured towards the people on the bridge. 'Besides, this story will be out there before long. We might as well try to get ahead of it so we can have some control over it.'

'Okay, that does actually makes sense,' Chris said. 'I'll run it past DSU Walker and see if I can get his blessing. I'll also be asking for extra resources now that this has turned into a murder investigation.' Nodding to Joseph and Amy, he headed off towards the stairs.

'You do know he's going straight back to the station to take credit for your idea,' Amy said as they watched the DCI go.

'And do I look like I care?'

'No, you don't.' Her sunbeam smile suddenly made the day feel a little brighter even as Joseph turned back to the ambulance to watch Charlie's body being lifted into its glowing interior.

'Good, because the only thing I care about is bringing the bastard who did this to justice. Charlie was in the wrong place at the wrong time. But if the killer has done it once, they can do it again. We're in uncharted waters here, Amy, and we all need to up our game before the Butcher kills his next victim.'

As the ambulance doors were closed and Charlie's body bag disappeared from view, Amy reached out, gently patted his arm, and nodded. 'We do, Joseph. We all do.'

24TH DECEMBER

CHAPTER FOURTEEN

THE PRESS BRIEFING room was crowded with journalists, a few of the broadsheets' heavy hitters, and staff from several online news sites. There were also a few of the less savoury reporters, jackals from the tabloids that Joseph had locked horns with occasionally over the years.

Because of his expertise on the previous animal mutilation cases, Derek had insisted that Joseph attend along with himself and Chris. Of course, Joseph also suspected the superintendent was going to use him as a lightning rod if the briefing went south, especially if the questions focused on why they hadn't previously been able to track down the Midwinter Butcher. If their DSU got the opportunity to throw him under the bus, Joseph doubted he'd hesitate to do exactly that.

From the audience, Kate gave the DI an encouraging look. Even though she knew it had been his idea to hold this press conference, she also understood the professional risk it was for him.

Joseph took a sip of water whilst they waited for their DSU to swan in and start proceedings. If he could draw any comfort from being put in the spotlight, it was that Chris looked just as apprehensive about it as he felt. He had run his finger around the inside of his collar as though he was being strangled by it several times since they'd taken their seats. Of course, taking the step to allow the case to become high profile with the press meant the scrutiny was now well and truly on. None of them would have much in the way of wiggle room with even minor slip-ups after this briefing. This was a calculated gamble for the entire team.

He scanned the back row of the audience to see Jane Robins, the press officer who'd advised them all to stick to the key message: find out if anyone could identify the demon mask, or had any other information that might lead to the arrest of the killer.

Jane had specifically warned them not to get drawn into the quagmire about the killings escalating. '*Stick to the facts and don't fall into the trap of speculating that this could be the start of a serial killing spree,*' she'd said.

Megan caught his eye in the back row. Despite it being Christmas Eve, she'd finally got hold of Aaron Fearnley, the author of the book on the occult that Dylan had pointed them to. As soon as this press briefing finished, Joseph intended to head over to the Pitt Rivers Museum to pick his brain.

The door opened to his right, and all eyes were immediately on Derek as he stepped into the room, a black leather A4 binder under his arm. The journalists who'd been chatting to each other powered up laptops and got recorders out, including Kate, who gave him a nod.

Derek opened the binder to reveal a prepared statement. He also took out a slim remote for the screen behind them that was currently displaying the TVP logo.

He turned first to Chris and then to Joseph. 'Are we ready to begin, gentleman?'

Chris nodded, again pulling at his collar.

'As we'll ever be,' the DI said.

Derek pressed a switch in front of him that turned on the three mics positioned before them, and all conversation fell away.

The superintendent glanced down at his notes and then cradled his hands together.

'Okay, everyone, I'd like to begin this briefing,' Derek said.

Many of the journalists, including Kate, pressed the buttons on their recorders and held them forward as several photographers took photos.

Lights, camera, action! Joseph couldn't help but think to himself.

'As I'm sure all of you in this room know, a body washed up under Magdalen Bridge early yesterday,' Derek continued. 'The forensic team has confirmed that this wasn't an accident and that the victim, Charlie Blackburn, of no fixed address, was murdered with a sharp instrument that penetrated his skull, causing instant death.'

The clicking of multiple photos being taken filled the room like a background soundtrack, as many of the journalists rapidly typed notes on their keyboards.

Derek glanced briefly at his notes again. 'We believe this murder was perpetrated by the individual that has come to be known as the Midwinter Butcher.'

Dozens of hands shot up in the air, but Derek was already shaking his head. 'We will take questions at the end. Anyway, now I'm going to hand it over to the SIO on the case, DCI Chris Faulkner.'

Chris took a sip of his water and leant forward, the slightest tremble in his hand. 'For those of you that have been following the Midwinter Butcher case, you'll know that the most recent animal killing happened three days ago at Laithwaite City Farm, where one of their goats was killed. This followed the pattern of previous animal killings that have all taken place on the midwinter solstice. However, this latest incident was different in one key detail, and that was that a second goat from the same pen was abducted. My colleague, DI Stone, who was the officer who recovered the second goat from Port Meadow, will brief you about that now and the relevance of this to Charlie Blackburn's murder.' He nodded at Joseph.

This was it, the DI's moment in the spotlight and hopefully, it would be as short as possible. Joseph relished dealing with the press with about the same level of enthusiasm that he approached dental treatment.

Joseph dropped his gaze to his own notes. 'We received a report that a goat had been found around six-thirty AM on the 24th December, called in by a dog walker. I attended the scene, and after the goat was rescued, discovered an injured beagle that had been attacked, which I recognised as belonging to Charlie Blackburn. Upon further investigation, it became clear that the owner could have been injured as well and might have fallen into the Thames. We now believe that Mr Blackburn was actually murdered by the Midwinter Butcher, and his body dumped into the river. It then drifted downriver until it washed up near Magdalen Bridge.' He brought his gaze up to meet the looks of rapt attention across the faces of the journalists, no doubt already imagining their front-page headlines. Joseph cleared his throat. 'I will now hand it back to DSU Walker to conclude.'

Derek tapped his thumbs together as he looked out over the audience. 'We obviously need to identify the individual responsible for Mr Blackburn's murder and the animal killings, and as quickly as possible. As this is an active investigation, certain aspects have been kept out of the media until now. For the first time I can reveal that during the Laithwaite City Farm incident, the suspect was disturbed by a member of the public, who, although assaulted, was able to take a photograph of the person. However, as you're about to see, the suspect was wearing a mask.' He picked up the remote and pressed the button.

The TVP logo was replaced by Ellie's photo of the masked figure.

'As you can see, although the image is blurred, it's still clear enough to see that the suspect is wearing some sort of stylised demon mask. However, so far, we have been unable to locate the source of what is obviously a unique design. We hope that it may lead us to the identity of Charlie Blackburn's murderer. And this is where the public can help. If anyone recognises this mask and where it came from, or indeed has any other information relevant to the investigation, we need you to contact the hotline number that has been set up especially for this and that we will put up on-screen at the end of the briefing. I'll take questions now.'

Nearly every hand shot up into the air, apart from Kate's. If anyone had the inside track, it was her, and she already knew the answers, even if she had agreed to sit on them until this news conference was out of the way.

Derek selected one of the reporters from the local TV news team.

'Have you been able to secure any DNA evidence from either the Laithwaite City Farm incident or from Charlie Blackburn's murder?' the woman asked.

This was one of the many areas that Jane had told them would almost certainly come up.

'I'm afraid we can't talk about sensitive information such as that, as this investigation is ongoing,' Derek replied.

This was one of the agreed upon answers because they didn't want to tip off the suspect about what they had. The less the murderer thought they knew about their identity and their ability to prove it was them, the more likely they were to catch them.

Derek selected another reporter, this time from one of the broadsheets.

'Do you think the killer may have switched their targets from animals to concentrating on the homeless?'

Derek nodded at Chris.

'Yes, I'll take that,' he replied. 'We've no reason to believe that, although nothing is being ruled out at this moment. Although we don't want to speculate on motives right now, our belief is that Charlie Blackburn's murder wasn't premeditated. He may have simply stumbled upon the suspect as he was releasing the goat in Port Meadow, the reasons for which we're still looking into.'

A man's hand shot up in the same row as Kate.

'If that's true, Inspector, why wasn't DI Stone's daughter, Ellie, also killed when she disturbed him at Laithwaite City Farm?' asked Ricky Holt, a tabloid journalist who was as sleazy as they came.

Joseph clenched his fists as cold fury burned inside him at the man for dragging his daughter's name out into the open.

Derek, to his credit, immediately killed the mics and leant across to Joseph. 'You don't need to answer that, Joseph.'

'I'm not sure I've much choice now that the cat is out of the bag,' he whispered back.

'Okay, but try not to bite his head off,' Derek replied as he looked down at Kate, who was glowering at the reporter.

'I'll do my best.'

Derek nodded and turned their mics back on.

Joseph took a deep centring breath before he met the gobshite's eye. 'I don't know where you got that information, but to answer your question would be sheer speculation on our part at this stage.'

He could see by the tiny curl at the corner of Holt's mouth the reporter wasn't going to let it go because he thought he'd rattled him.

'So as a father, you're not worried about the Midwinter Butcher targeting your daughter again, especially as this isn't the first time her path has crossed his? Isn't she the same Ellie Stone who was in the car that you were driving and crashed because of the deer the Midwinter Butcher scared out into the road sixteen years ago?'

Kate was on her feet. 'How dare you drag that up!' she shouted at the man.

'What's it to you?' Holt asked, giving her a surprised look.

'Because she's my daughter, you arsehole, and not material to pad your crappy paper with.'

Joseph stared at her, half in shock and half in admiration. But before he could get his response in, the eejit, with an obvious death wish, came back with another response.

'But you must be worried...'—Holt's eyes sought out her press badge—'Kate, that he may come after her. Especially as there may even be a satanic connection to all of this.'

That was it—the blue touch paper of his anger had been lit and Joseph was on his feet. 'Stop fishing, you little gobshite...' Suddenly his voice dropped in volume as Derek killed the mics. But he was in full flood now and he simply raised his voice to compensate. 'If I see one mention of our daughter in your fecking paper, I'll—'

Derek grabbed hold of his arm and shook his head. 'Don't.'

Joseph locked eyes with him, but it was seeing Kate give him a slight head shake that finally defused him, and he slumped back onto his seat.

The superintendent fixed the reporter with his laser-gaze. 'I apologise on behalf of my officer, but yours wasn't an appropriate question. Anyway, I think that's enough for now. You will all be supplied with the information pack on the way out, including the hotline contact number. Thank you for your time, ladies and gentlemen.'

The DSU stood and made a sharp gesture for Joseph to follow him.

Joseph made sure he didn't look at the journalist, who he knew would be smirking, as he headed out through the door. The DI closed it behind him to cut out the explosion of unanswered questions that were being called out.

Exactly as he expected, Derek hung back to talk to Joseph, but as Chris passed him, he raised his eyebrows before he disappeared down the corridor.

Just like that, Joseph knew he had given their superintendent all the ammunition he needed to put him on a disciplinary.

But instead of hardness in the superintendent's expression, Joseph was caught off guard by the actual look of understanding.

'Joseph, I'm so sorry that scumbag pulled a fast one in there. I would have thought that he would have some integrity about Ellie being off limits, but we're talking the gutter press after a sensational headline here.'

'One that I seem to have handed him on a silver plate.'

'Maybe you did, but on this one occasion, I'm going to turn a blind eye to it. Although, I have to admit I loved it when you called him a gobshite and Kate was pretty magnificent, too.'

Joseph found himself smiling as he dragged his hand through his hair. 'She was, wasn't she?'

Derek nodded. 'A lioness protecting her young.' A smile crept across his face. 'Just don't do it again. Do we understand each other?' His smile broadened.

'Absolutely understood, sir.' Joseph resisted the urge to snap him a salute.

'Good...' Derek met his gaze with his. 'Look, Joseph, I know we haven't always been on the same page about a lot of things, but I want you to know I'll do everything in my power to make sure Ellie is kept safe. If we really think there is a credible threat to her life, then I'm fully prepared to post an officer on security detail to protect her.'

'I don't think we're there yet, especially as there's still a chance that Charlie's murder may be a one-off event.'

'Do you really believe that?'

Joseph slowly shook his head. 'No, I think our suspect has crossed the line and if he's done it once, he can do it again.'

'I'm afraid I think you may be right. Anyway, if you'll excuse me, I better go and calm that lioness before she tracks down that tabloid reporter and punches him on the nose.'

A grin filled Joseph's face. 'Aye, you better had.'

As the superintendent headed away down the corridor, Joseph watched him wondering at what point he'd fallen through into a parallel world where Derek was a half-decent guy.

CHAPTER FIFTEEN

WITH A LEATHER BINDER under her arm, Megan and Joseph headed through the exhibition floor of the Oxford Natural History Museum. Columns rose around them like tree trunks to support the vaulted cathedral-like glass roof. It had often reminded the DI of the grandeur of a Victorian era railway station, but considerably cleaner without the diesel fumes to pollute the pale stone work. A soft diffused light made even the greyest of days seem brighter within the museum.

They made their way between the display cabinets filled with stuffed animals and information panels, passing what Ellie had insisted when she was a young girl was a woolly mammoth, refusing to believe it was actually an Indian elephant.

'This is quite something,' Megan said, taking in the magnificent architecture.

'You've not visited before?' Joseph asked.

'First visit, but I'll definitely be back based on what I've seen already.'

'You should, but wait until we get to the next gallery.' Joseph gestured towards the big double doors ahead of them. In contrast to the bright space they were currently walking through, the area they could glimpse beyond looked like a dark cavern. 'That's the Pitt Rivers Museum through there, filled with mysteries and wonders of bygone eras.'

'If you say so.'

'Oh, I most certainly do,' he replied.

As they entered through the doors, a woman with tightly curled ringlets and a broad smile at least six feet wide, approached them with a clipboard. He couldn't help noticing that she, along with her female colleague, had angled herself so that they would be funnelled past the voluntary contribution box for the museum on their way down the steps. Not that Joseph ever put anything in the box, although without fail he felt a pang of guilt every time he walked past pretending he hadn't noticed it.

'Hi, would you like an information sheet?' the woman with Helen written on her name tag asked.

'No, we're actually looking for Aaron Fearnley,' he replied. 'We have a meeting with him.'

'And you are?' the woman asked, her eyes narrowed.

'DI Joseph Stone and DC Megan Anderson from the St Aldates Police Station,' he said.

A smirk flashed across Helen's face for a moment before she suppressed it. Then her eyes lingered on Megan, looking her up and down.

What was that all about? Joseph thought to himself.

Helen's attention returned to him. 'You'll find Aaron working on the witchcraft display towards the rear of the lower gallery.'

'Can you tell us what he looks like?'

'Like George Clooney, but slightly hotter,' Helen said.

'Really?' Megan asked.

Helen raised her eyebrows. 'Very easy on the eye, as you'll

see for yourself in a moment. Anyway, you can't miss him. He's wearing one of his trademark silk waistcoats today.'

'Okay, thank you for your help,' the DI said, ushering Megan away.

The detectives headed down the steps into a labyrinth of dark wood display cabinets filled with an astonishing selection of objects, from model temples to pots of every design and shape. But as this was Megan's first visit, Joseph deliberately took her straight towards a particular cabinet and paused before it.

The DI turned to Megan. 'Believe it or not, there used to be shrunken heads in there.'

'Seriously?'

'Seriously. But they finally removed them because they felt it wasn't *culturally sensitive*. Anyway, when Ellie was eight, she asked if we could have one.'

Megan snorted. 'Kids, hey?'

'Yep, you better believe it. So let's see if we can find this George Clooney lookalike.'

'Don't forget the *hotter* part.'

Joseph rolled his eyes as they headed towards the rear of the gallery, where a tall totem pole with carved figures stacked one on top of the other rose to the high ceiling.

They spotted Aaron easily enough, wearing a blue silk waistcoat, his head buried in one of the open display cabinets. As they approached, Joseph took in the curious collection of objects the man was looking at. There appeared to be all manner of things in there, from amulets to long horns with stoppers, and even a wooden box with some unidentifiable shrivelled animal inside.

'You've got quite the collection here, Mr Fearnley,' the DI said.

Aaron almost dropped the small bottle he'd been about to place back in the cabinet as he looked up.

Even the DI could tell that the guy was quite handsome, with his chiselled features and penetrating blue eyes. The sweep of grey hair certainly didn't age him, but made him look distinguished instead. With his designer stubble beard, he was one of those men who was almost effortlessly good-looking. It was alright for some.

'And you are?' Aaron said, but then his gaze alighted on Megan and a smile filled his face.

'I'm Megan, I mean DC Megan Anderson, and this is DI Joseph Stone. I spoke to you on the phone.'

The DI couldn't help but notice the blush that spread up her neck as she shook Aaron's hand. Yes, it seemed like she found him rather easy on the eye.

'Ah yes, I was expecting you,' Aaron said, his eyes lingering on hers. 'Just let me place this love potion that one of our Oxford college labs was desperate to analyse back in this case. Turns out it was nothing more than tea mixed with thyme and a dash of rose water.'

'I expect someone sold it for a lot of money to whoever needed it,' Joseph said.

'Almost certainly,' Aaron replied with a smile.

Megan wrinkled her nose as she peered at the contents of the display cabinet. 'Are all those items to do with witchcraft?'

'Absolutely,' Aaron replied as he carefully placed the glass bottle next to a labelled number and then closed the cabinet again. 'Everything from curses, to spells involving dead animals found sealed in chimney breasts, to talismans to ward off evil spirits.'

Joseph shook his head. 'It's amazing that people believed in that sort of thing.'

'Some people still do,' Aaron said, pulling a pendant out from beneath his designer shirt.

He held it up for the detectives to see a round silver pendant with a stylised eye design in the middle, surrounded by runic symbols.

'And that is...,' Megan said, leaning in for a closer look.

'An Eye of Horus amulet. It's an ancient Egyptian symbol of protection, power, and good health.'

'We'll have to take your word for it that it works,' Joseph replied.

'I certainly have nothing to complain about,' Aaron said, as his gaze was once again drawn back to Megan.

'I'm sure,' the DI replied. 'Anyway, is there somewhere we could have a word? As I'm sure DC Anderson told you, we need your expert advice on a certain matter.'

Aaron frowned briefly, but it was gone as quickly as it had come. 'She did, and I'm very intrigued. It's not often we have the police here on official business.' He locked the cabinet with a small key. 'Please follow me.'

He set off, and the detectives followed him along the line of display cabinets. As Aaron reached the end and headed through a glass doorway, Megan stopped and pointed at the large cabinets to their left.

Joseph turned to see a large collection of masks from every continent and every style and design, but nothing that was even a close match.

Megan shook her head. 'So much for hoping to get a lead about the mask here.'

'Don't be so quick to judge. A huge amount of the collection isn't on the display, but is held in storage in the vaults.'

'Oh, right.' Megan's expression brightened considerably.

Aaron's head reappeared around the corner of the door. 'I thought I'd lost you.'

'Sorry, we were just admiring the masks.'

'Yes, they are rather striking, aren't they?'

'It's an impressive collection, along with everything else in here,' Megan said as they followed Aaron down a set of steps.

'It's certainly unique,' Aaron replied as they went through a door marked staff only. 'The collection is arranged according to how the objects were used, rather than their age or origin. That has everything to do with the theories of the founder of this collection, George Pitt-Rivers himself. He intended his collection to show how human culture evolved from the simple to the complex, hence the sometimes almost random association of objects in the cabinets.'

'It certainly sounds fascinating, and I'll have to come back another time to have a proper look round,' Megan replied.

'You should, and let me know when you do,' Aaron said, smiling at her a fraction too long.

'I'll happily be your guide.'

I bet you would, Joseph thought as the man showed them into a small meeting room.

'Can I interest you in some tea?' Aaron said. 'I have a rather excellent stash of lapsang souchong hidden away from the other members of staff, if you fancy a cup?'

'No, we're both grand,' Joseph said before Megan could leap in with a response. 'The reason we're here is that a good friend of mine pointed us in your direction. He said you were the closest thing to an expert that we have in Oxford about the occult, having written a book about it.'

'Ah yes, *The Occult Compendium,* that was a passion project. But if I'd realised it would become so successful mone-tarily, I would have printed a lot more.'

'That's hindsight for you,' the DI replied.

'It is indeed, Inspector. Anyway, I'm guessing that something of an occult nature has turned up in a case, hence you coming to me?'

'You're right. So first of all, have you heard of the Midwinter Butcher?'

Aaron gave him a surprised look, his face clouding for a moment. 'If you mean that maniac that has been mutilating animals every year, then, of course. It's hard to live in this city and to not have heard about him. I've always wondered whether there was some sort of occult connection with the animal sacrifices, especially as they happen on the winter solstice.'

'The police do now as well. In the latest incident, a goat from the Laithwaite City Farm was beheaded and another one was abducted.'

'Yes, I read that in the Chronicle and thought how odd that was because it almost sounded like it might be something to do with the scapegoat ritual.'

Megan narrowed her eyes at him. 'If you suspected that, why didn't you come forward and tell the police?'

Arron shrugged. 'I thought I was jumping to conclusions. You see, when you start writing about the occult, you tend to see signs of it everywhere. An overactive imagination on my part is something of an occupational hazard, I'm afraid.'

'I see,' Joseph replied. 'But in this particular incident, it's hard not to come to the same conclusion.' The DI took out his phone and flicked through the images that he'd downloaded from the case files. Joseph finally found the one of the decapitated goat, the engraved symbol clearly cut into its side, turned his mobile around and pushed it across the desk.

Aaron leant forward to look at the screen and jerked back so hard that his chair rocked on its legs. 'Good grief, you could have warned me.'

'Sorry. But I need your opinion about that symbol carved into the goat's flank.'

Aaron's, lips thinned, leant forward for a closer look, and then his eyes widened. 'That's one of the symbols for Azrael.'

'Yes, we realised that after coming across the symbol in your book,' Megan said.

'If that's not enough by itself to confirm some sort of occult ritual, the other goat turned up today, abandoned and freezing to death in Port Meadow,' the DI added. 'Based on the assumption that we are dealing with someone recreating the scapegoat ritual, we believe the other goat being sent out into the wilderness was part of that. However, there's one important proviso. The goat we found alive on Port Meadow yesterday had a golden crucifix around its neck. Unfortunately, forensics has already reported back to say there wasn't any human DNA evidence on it.'

'I see...' Grimacing, Aaron pushed the phone back across the table towards Joseph. Then he slowly shook his head. 'However, that doesn't make sense. Based on the original Hebrew scapegoat ritual, the beheaded goat should have been sacrificed to God and the other goat set free for Azrael. But based on what you've told me, it's the other way around.'

'Exactly,' Megan said. 'Do you have any idea why somebody would reverse the ritual in that way?' Megan asked.

Aaron tapped a finger on his lips. 'Interesting, very interesting. Well, animal sacrifices and offerings are usually part of a religious ceremony, or even to appease or seek the favour of a deity. So with the scapegoat ritual in this instance being dedicated to God and the other goat sacrificed to Azrael, that could suggest the purpose of the ritual is reversed too. So, rather than a cleansing of their sins, maybe the killer is announcing their intent to embrace their darker nature. However, it's the goat sacrifice to Azrael that I find particularly troubling.'

So Aaron was confirming what they already suspected.

'Why exactly?' Joseph asked.

'Because Azrael's role is to transport souls to heaven. This may mean that this individual is signalling their intention not to step away from murder, but to fully embrace it.'

Megan grimaced. 'That's what we were worried about.'

Joseph doubted Aaron would have heard yet about Charlie's murder as they had come straight from the press briefing, so the man wouldn't realise yet that things had already escalated. The question was, where did it go next?

The DI narrowed his gaze on Aaron. 'So you're saying this could be the start of a killing spree?'

'Obviously I hope not, but as you said, the reversal of this ritual gives cause for concern.'

The DI sat back in his chair, his worst worries confirmed. 'Jesus, I fecking knew it. All those animal slaughters really were practice for someone building up to the main act.'

Aaron gave them both an earnest look, his hands clasped together. 'I'm sorry I couldn't be the bearer of better news and be of greater help to you.'

'Actually, there is one other area you still might be able to help us with,' Megan said. She thumbed through some more photos and, having selected Ellie's photo of the guy with the demon mask, showed it to Aaron.

Aaron frowned, lines appearing around his eyes. 'My goodness, where was that photographed?'

'It was taken by a woman who interrupted the killer when they were killing the goat at Laithwaite City Farm. As you can see, they are wearing some sort of mask. So far, we've had no luck tracing it, and we were wondering if you had ever seen anything like this before. We already had a quick look at your mask collection, but couldn't see anything that matched.'

Aaron shook his head. 'I'm afraid it doesn't even match any of the masks that we have in storage. The closest thing that I've seen to that, stylistically, would be the Japanese *noh* masks, some of which we do have here in the collection. But by the shape of the face and the far more minimal design of this mask, I would say it originated in the west and is a far more modern design. Could it be handmade? A one-off maybe?'

'We're exploring all possibilities,' Joseph replied.

'I see. Well, have you considered the psychological aspect of wearing a mask?'

'In what sense?' Megan asked.

'From an anthropological aspect, there are many origins of the word mask. However, one that may be relevant here is a theory that the word mask was originally derived from the Spanish *más que la cara*, which literally means, more than the face, or added face.'

Joseph rubbed the back of his neck as he tried to order his thoughts. 'So you're suggesting that we may be dealing with someone with a split personality?'

'Not necessarily, but maybe they find it liberating and are able to do things they wouldn't normally dare to do, literally taking on the role of the demon.'

'In other words, a licence to murder?'

'I'm afraid I believe it may be.'

'Oh feck, a real bona fide psychopath.'

Aaron nodded. 'It would certainly seem so. That aside, is there anything else that I can assist you with?'

'No, but you've been a great help. We may contact you in the future to pick your brain, if that would be alright.'

'Of course.' An almost calculating look filled Aaron's eyes. 'However, there is one last thing, and I don't mean to tell you how to do your job, but on the occult connection side, I assume you've looked into people who work with animals for a living?'

'Yes,' the DI replied. 'We ran that through the profiling model after the first few cases, everyone from abattoirs to vets, but nothing came up.'

'What about people who work in a lab who are involved in experiments with animals? After all, Oxford is a leading centre of new drug trials that frequently involve using animals and often dissecting them. It may be an area worth looking into, if you haven't already. Maybe someone there has taken their enjoyment of killing lab mice and the rest to the next level.'

The DI gawped at him. 'Bloody hell, that one slipped under our radar. But thank you for the suggestion. I'll personally make sure we look into it.'

'As I said, I'm just glad to be of service. Here, let me give you my card with my mobile number. Contact me anytime, night or day.'

Joseph couldn't help but notice that Aaron handed the card to Megan rather than to him, the man's gaze once again lingering a moment too long on the DC's eyes. Yes, definitely a lady's man, if not something of a player.

'He was rather *interesting*,' Megan said a short time later as they headed away back down the corridor.

'Not getting pulled in by his seductive good looks, are you?' Joseph replied.

'Of course not,' she said, grinning at him.

He shook his head at her. 'You Tinder generation you. Anyway, that was a very productive meeting. We should start drawing up a list of everyone who works in the labs and cross-reference them. If anything is thrown up by that, we can go and interview anyone of interest.'

'Absolutely, but that's going to be tricky to do at the moment.'

'Why's that?' the DI asked, turning to her.

'Because it's Christmas Day tomorrow, Joseph, and pretty much everything will grind to a halt for the next few days.'

'Oh feck, I've lost track of time. Talk about bad timing.'

'I know. But please tell me you've made plans? I've heard

you're something of a confirmed bachelor who will probably fall asleep in front of the TV watching White Christmas.'

'You've been talking to Ian, haven't you?'

'Maybe I have.' She grinned at the DI.

'Don't trust a word that man says,' he said, winking at her. 'But to answer your question, I actually do have plans. It's my turn for Ellie to be with me this year, so I'll make a dash around to the shops and see if I can grab a few things.'

'Wow, talk about cutting it close.'

'I know, but I've had other things on my mind,' Joseph replied as they headed back out into the main museum.

They had almost reached the exit when his mobile buzzed and Ian's name came up on the display.

'What is it, Ian?' Joseph said as he took the call.

'Christmas has just come one day early, that's what. You won't believe this, but we just received an anonymous tip about that mask, thanks to the news briefing. The guy just saw the article posted online and recognised the mask straight away, and to use your language, it's a *cracker* of a tipoff.'

'Okay, don't keep me in suspense here. Where does the mask come from?'

Megan's eyes widened as she listened in.

'Apparently, it's used by members of a very select club who wear it to very special private parties to hide their identities.'

'When you say *special*, do you mean what I think you do?'

'Basically, yes. Not to put too fine a point on it, our informant, who is a member himself, told us they are basically orgies where anything goes.'

'Right. And do we know who organises these private parties?'

'Actually, we do. Lord Alistair Saxton hosts them at his private manor.'

'You're kidding me. Not that local eccentric guy, half-hippie with all the unofficial wives?'

'The very same. I thought you would also like to know that Faulkner is already heading over to steal all the glory with a warrant to search the guy's property.'

'So much for the softly, softly approach.'

'Tell me about it. Typical Chris, charging in with all guns blazing.'

'I don't suppose you've got Saxton's address, do you?'

The DI's phone pinged.

'Just texted it through to you.'

'Thanks, mate, I owe you.'

'I'll just add it to your tab.'

Joseph snorted and hung up before turning to Megan. 'Did you hear most of that?'

She nodded. 'Sounds like a very promising lead.'

'I think it could be huge. So I was wondering if there was any chance of you running me up there?'

'But what about your last-minute Christmas shopping?'

'That will just have to wait, and if it's Maccy D's for lunch tomorrow, so be it.'

'Are you deliberately trying to sound tragic now?'

'Maybe...' Joseph smiled at her and she chuckled.

'Then we better get a move on before Chris steals all the thunder.'

As they headed outside, Joseph pulled up Ellie's number on his phone. He'd get his apology in now and suggest she spent Christmas Day with her mum instead. Unfortunately, he had a strong suspicion this might turn out to be a long night.

CHAPTER SIXTEEN

JOSEPH AND MEGAN were driving up a long driveway on private grounds, winding up the side of a hill that overlooked the stretched-out expanse of Salisbury Plain. Darkness was descending, and silhouetted against the skyline was a large mansion above them, its windows glowing in the winter gloom.

Megan peered out at the trees on either side of the driveway, festooned with white lights. 'This is a regular winter wonderland up here.'

'Lord Saxton is obviously a big fan of Christmas,' Joseph replied as they reached the large gravelled area in front of the house.

Apart from the three marked police cars—two of which he could see belonged to the Wiltshire force and had no doubt been liaised with for what amounted to a raid—were some very expensive-looking vehicles. They were visible in a large garage to one side where the doors had been left open. Among the half-dozen vehicles were a silver Lamborghini, two Range Rovers, and a white Bentley.

Overhanging the slope to the right of the manor was the largest infinity pool that Joseph had ever seen. Then, just to make sure that you weren't left in any doubt that the owner had serious money, a silver helicopter was parked on a landing pad on the other side of the house.

'Wow, being a hippie obviously pays well,' Megan said, taking in the view as they both got out of the car.

'I believe it's everything to do with old family money, so he doesn't exactly have to worry about it.'

'It's alright for some,' Megan replied as they headed across the driveway, the gravel crunching under their feet.

Ahead of them, the large double doors had been thrown wide open, and a SOCO carrying a large box emerged, heading towards a white van.

'What have you got there?' Joseph asked as he passed them.

'No idea, but the SIO ordered us to take anything that looks like files, as well as seize any computer.'

'Do I take that to mean Lord Saxton isn't cooperating?'

'That would be the understatement of the century, sir. He had a blazing row with the SIO about his rights, and has already called his solicitor to lodge an official complaint about police mistreatment.'

'Then let's see if we can't pour some oil on those troubled waters,' Joseph replied.

'Good luck with that, sir,' the officer said as he continued towards the van.

The two detectives headed through an oval hallway with a vast Christmas tree in the middle, decorated with hundreds of silver and blue baubles, and a galaxy's worth of twinkling lights, maybe even two. It was framed by a sweeping grand staircase, the bannisters of which had been covered with ivy, dried flowers and even more lights, along with a huge painting that more than demanded attention. It was of a naked woman at least twenty feet high, her body made up of swirling words and sentences that flowed throughout the image.

'Not bad if you like that sort of thing,' Chris's voice said from behind them.

They turned to see the SIO standing there wearing blue latex gloves.

'Apparently, Lord Saxton did that piece himself and it's based on one of his poems,' Chris continued.

'I actually rather like it,' Megan said.

'Me too, but I think I'd have trouble squeezing it into my narrowboat,' Joseph replied.

Her eyes widened. 'You live on a boat?'

'Don't get Joseph started on that subject, or he'll bore you all night about it,' Chris said. 'Anyway, exactly why are you both here?'

'A little bird tipped us off that you've come across a major lead on the demon mask, so we're here to help,' Joseph said.

'I certainly appreciate all the bodies we can throw at this. Even if it is Christmas Eve, this is too big a lead to leave until after the holidays.'

Joseph nodded. 'So, have you found anything useful yet?'

'Nothing concrete so far. Lord Saxton hasn't been particularly helpful either. Keeps muttering about the data protection act and member confidentiality. Anyway, the SOCO team has already removed his computers and external drives to see if they can unearth anything, but that may take some time as they seem to be heavily encrypted.'

'Ah, okay. Do you mind if I have a go talking to him?'

'Good luck using your Irish charm on that one. He didn't seem receptive to anything I tried. I'm tempted to throw him in a cell overnight for obstructing an investigation.'

'I'm not sure that would work out too well, especially as it's Christmas Eve,' Megan said.

'Is this the part where I say humbug?' A rare smile flitted across Chris's face.

'Probably.' Joseph raised his eyebrows at him.

'Okay, go and knock yourself out. He's just through that door there in his study. Last time I saw him, he was pacing, and wearing a groove in an expensive Persian rug.'

'Then we'll see if we can sweet-talk him round.'

'Then good hunting,' Chris said as he turned and headed up the stairs.

When Joseph and Megan entered the study, they found a man in his mid-sixties, wearing a white cotton shirt and trousers. He was also still doing exactly what Chris had said he'd been doing, walking up and down the room with his hands clasped behind his back. The study was filled with large black-and-white photos of nude men and women, who appeared to be having real rather than simulated sex. The highly decorated Christmas tree standing in the corner had presents piled beneath it, which seemed slightly incongruous by comparison.

The man spun around. 'And who the hell are you?'

Based on the hostility carved into Lord Saxton's expression, his hackles were obviously well and truly up thanks, no doubt, to Chris's confrontational style. Five seconds in the room and Joseph could already tell that he was going to have to take a much more nuanced approach if they were going to get anywhere with him.

'Hello, Lord Saxton. I'm DI Stone and this is my colleague DC Anderson.' The DI held up both hands. 'First, I'm sorry we've had to descend on you like this. It must be particularly upsetting as it's Christmas Eve.'

'Bloody right, it is. Your DCI and his goons just marched into my home, upsetting my family, who were forced to take shelter in the pool house whilst your fellow officers ransack my home.'

'I can assure you that every care will be taken going through your family's things, but we are only doing this because of the urgency of the situation,' Megan said, picking up on Joseph's softly, softly strategy.

'That's as may be, but there are ways to handle a situation, and I can assure you I'll be putting in a formal complaint about your DCI. That's not an idle threat as I'm very well connected.'

'You must do as you see fit, but I can't help thinking that we got off on the wrong foot, especially when we need your help so urgently,' Megan said.

Lord Saxton's face visibly softened. 'Yes, this business of one of our Asmodeus masks being worn by the killer who murdered that homeless man is awful. However, I can assure you that I knew nothing about it until your DCI turned up here mob-handed and demanding to see my records.' Lord Saxton crossed to a sideboard where a decanter on a silver tray sat and poured himself a very large glass. 'Can I interest either of you in a drink? This is a very fine twenty-year-old Armagnac.'

Megan shook her head. 'Sorry, I'm on duty.'

But Joseph raised his eyebrows at him. 'Well, technically I should have gone off shift by now and as it's Christmas Eve, maybe a small one.'

Megan gave him a sideways stare that he pointedly ignored. This was all about getting the man onside and if that took sharing a drink with him, so be it.

Joseph watched Lord Saxton pour him a drink that was at least half the size of his, but still easily a double. Then the man gestured to a bright blue velvet sofa for the detectives to sit on, in front of a giant fur rug and beneath another pornographic image that appeared to show a couple in full bondage gear getting it on.

Saxton handed the DI the drink as he sat down in a chair that was covered in zebra-print fabric. Joseph took a sip, and the Armagnac was very smooth. Notes of sherry combined with the best brandy. Dylan would approve.

'Oh, now that's very good,' he said, pulling an appreciative face.

'I should hope so at over £600 a bottle,' Lord Saxton replied.

Joseph almost sprayed the Armagnac out of his mouth, but just managed to stop himself as Megan's eyebrows crept further up her head at the DI before she turned back towards Lord Saxton.

'You said it was an Asmodeus mask... May I ask what that is?' she asked.

'Ah, that will be everything to do with my exclusive club of the same name. Here, have one of our cards.' He leant across and took a business card and handed it over to Megan. It appeared to have a strange triangular-shaped symbol on it and the only writing on it was an email address.

'For a business card, that doesn't exactly tell us a lot,' she replied as she gave it to Joseph for a look.

'That's the general idea. We run very discreet and exclusive parties from my home.'

'Organised orgies, in other words,' Megan said without batting an eyelash.

'Goodness, you're rather direct, unlike DCI Faulkner, but I do find that a refreshing approach. Anyway, to answer your question, yes, sexual soirees of the highest taste for the open-minded, and only between consenting adults. However, we do have a strictly no filming rule. What happens in the Asmodeus club stays in the Asmodeus club.' He tapped the side of his nose and smiled.

'Is the name itself of any significance?' Joseph asked.

Lord Saxton took a sip of his drink and nodded. 'Most certainly. You see, Asmodeus is one of the seven princes of hell, second only to Lucifer and Beelzebub. His job description, so to speak, is to tempt us with carnal desire.' He gave the detectives a wolfish grin.

'And these demon masks, do they have any particular purpose?' Joseph asked.

'They do. People who join our club are guaranteed absolute anonymity. Of course, that wouldn't work very well if someone well known, such as a famous actor or politician, could be recognised at one of our soirees. Hence the need for masks that all our guests wear from the moment they arrive until the moment they leave.'

'A sort of sex masked ball?' Megan said.

'I do like you. You're absolutely right again, Detective.'

'So where exactly do you source these masks from?' Joseph asked.

'We actually 3D print them on-site for each member when they join.'

Megan tightened her gaze on him. 'So what about the reason that your home is currently being turned upside down? Namely, because you won't release the membership list of the Asmodeus club?'

Lord Saxton sighed and finished the rest of his brandy in one gulp. 'As I tried to explain to DCI Faulkner, I would help you if I could, but my hands are tied. You see, there is a legal contract in place that guarantees our members anonymity. Even though I told the detective chief inspector that I keep no records here, he has insisted on seizing all of the computers and mobiles for your forensic team to go through. They won't, of course, find any records because any computer, however secure, can be hacked by someone with enough determination. That's the reason why the only memory stick with a list of members is held in my solicitor's firm's safe. They have been instructed not to give that up without a considerable legal battle and that's going to take a lot of time as it will drag on through the courts.'

'Look, I completely appreciate your position, but you also need to appreciate ours,' Megan said.

'I do, but I'm duty-bound to fight this to the best of my ability.'

'Even if that means the murderer, who could well be a member, kills again?'

Lord Saxton grimaced. 'What can I say? It's an awful situation, but there really is nothing I can do to help your investigation. My hands are legally tied in this matter.'

'I see,' Joseph replied, putting the rest of the drink down on the table. 'Then let's just hope for your sake that nobody else is harmed, because you'll have that on your conscience for the rest of your life.'

'I'm afraid that my soul is already fairly burdened thanks to my lifestyle,' Lord Saxton said. 'But that doesn't mean I won't wish you the very best of luck catching this murderer.'

'Right...' Joseph stood up.

Lord Saxton gestured towards Jospeh's drink. 'Aren't you going to finish that?'

'For some strange reason, I'm no longer thirsty.'

'In that case, I wish you both good luck with your investigation.'

Joseph gave him a curt nod and had to fight the urge to slam the door behind him as they left the study.

'What an absolute jerk,' he hissed as they crossed the hallway, and almost ran straight into Faulkner emerging from another room.

'Any joy?' the DCI asked.

Joseph shook his head. 'No, stonewalled us all the way, sir. It was all I could do not to pick him up by the ankles and try to shake it out of him.'

Faulkner arched his eyebrows at Joseph.

Megan quickly jumped in. 'DI Stone was the model of restraint in there.'

'Glad to hear it,' the DCI replied, giving Joseph an unreadable look before heading on his way.

As they walked outside, Megan leant in towards the DI. 'If you had wanted to punch the smug git in the face, I wouldn't have seen a thing,' she said.

'I'll bear that in mind next time.' He gave her a faint smile. 'I can't believe we've come so close to a major breakthrough, and it's been snatched away from us.'

'About that, Joseph, I have an idea.'

'Fire away because I'm prepared to do anything right now, even if it means severely bending the rules.'

'Fortunately, my idea is strictly legal and one that even DSU Walker would approve of,' she said as they headed across the gravel drive towards the Peugeot.

Joseph glanced at her. 'Go on?'

'Did you notice that red light camera on the junction of the main road that we passed before entering the gates at the bottom of the drive?'

'Not particularly. Why?'

'Well, you know how most of the public don't realise those cameras register their number plate, even if they don't jump the red light? So I was thinking...' A slow smile filled her face.

He gawped at her. 'Oh, you little genius. You're saying we run the plates of all the vehicles that pass through it on the first Saturday evening of every month, the time of Lord Saxton's soirees?'

Megan beamed at him and she nodded. 'By comparing the plates on different dates, we should be able to whittle it down by cross-referencing them.'

'You realise that's going to take a considerable amount of time because thousands of vehicles will probably have been captured by that camera?'

'Yes, but once local people have been ruled out, we'll probably be left with a very close match to Lord Saxton's precious membership list that he's so determined not to give us. The only problem is, I'm sure it'll take several days of serious number crunching by our tech team to come up with a shortlist. But once that's complete, then if we have to, we can interview every single person that the vehicles are registered to, checking their alibis for the key dates.'

'DC Anderson, I do believe you just made my Christmas,' Joseph said.

'No, that will be me rushing back to the city so you can get in that last-minute shopping so you don't end up having Maccy D's for Christmas dinner.'

'Thank God for your mercy then,' he replied with a wide smile. For the first time during this investigation, he felt a sense of lightness as they got into the car. They were closing in on the killer, Joseph could feel it in every fibre of his being.

CHAPTER SEVENTEEN

Joseph headed down the cycle path on his mountain bike, with the few meagre bits of food that he'd managed to pick up from the twenty-four hour supermarket mini-store in the city. It was one of the last places that had been open late on Christmas Eve, and it had already been stripped almost bare by the last-minute shoppers who were obviously as disorganised as the DI.

The houses backing onto the canal had their windows lit up by Christmas decorations of every sort, and all very tasteful. No inflatable snowmen or Santas in this part of Oxford. Oh no.

He was on the home stretch when he noticed *Tús Nua* had gone through something of a transformation since the last time he'd seen her. She was now illuminated with hundreds of white fairy lights from stem to stern, surrounding the canal boat in a golden halo.

The curtains on Dylan's boat twitched as he approached, and before he'd even pulled up, both Ellie and the professor were on deck and grinning at him like two eejits.

Joseph flapped a hand towards *Tús Nua*. 'I'm guessing you two had something to do with this handiwork?'

Dylan nodded towards Ellie. 'This was mostly your daughter's doing, but I helped out a bit.'

'I should have known,' the detective said, smiling at his daughter as he parked up and unhooked his pannier.

'Your boat looked so sad for the holidays, with not so much as a single festive light on her,' Ellie said. 'We can't have you getting a reputation as the local Scrooge on the canal.'

'As Chris would say, *humbug!*' Joseph winked at her.

'You seem in a much better mood than when you left this morning,' Dylan said.

'That's because I am,' he replied. 'We may be on the brink of a breakthrough on the Midwinter Butcher case.'

'Seriously?' Ellie asked.

'Seriously. Although there's going to be a lot of data crunching and tracing to get us there. But we may be able to draw up a list of potential suspects before the holidays are out. I'm certainly in the mood for Christmas now.'

'That's good to hear,' Dylan said.

'And you've got all the food in for tomorrow?' Ellie asked, looking sceptically at his panniers.

Joseph grimaced and held them up. 'I'm so sorry, love. The case well and truly pulled me in over the last few days, so I haven't had time to prepare. I hope you're okay with a ready-meal chicken curry because that was the closest thing I could get to a turkey.'

Ellie traded a raised eyebrow with Dylan.

'I told you,' he said.

'Told her what, exactly?' Joseph asked, narrowing his eyes at the professor.

'That you wouldn't change a habit of a lifetime, and actually be prepared for Christmas for once. I mean, it's not like they shift the date every year to deliberately catch you out.'

'I know, I know, and what can I say? It's one of my many failings.'

'Shall you tell him or shall I?' Ellie asked Dylan.

'Why do I feel like I'm in the middle of a conspiracy?' Joseph said, glancing between them.

'Because you are,' Ellie replied. 'I went with Dylan to the covered market to pick up the turkey that he ordered for you from the butchers back in October. We also got all the trimmings from everywhere else, so chicken curry absolutely isn't on the menu for Christmas Day.'

'Thank God for that, but you do remember that I don't have a massive oven on my boat, right?'

'That's why we're going to be cooking together,' Dylan said. 'I'm soaking the turkey in brine overnight and then will cook it on my gas barbecue.'

Joseph stared at him. 'On a barbecue?'

'Before you throw your hands up in horror, it's one of the best ways to do it. Really lovely moist meat, made especially succulent thanks to the brine.'

Ellie beamed at him. 'Then we'll do all the trimmings in the ovens of both boats. I've already prepped the homemade bread sauce that Mum gave me the recipe for.'

'You two have really thought this through,' he replied.

'Oh, we most certainly have,' Dylan said. 'Anyway, I must leave you as I have some salmon baking that I love to have on Christmas Eve, but I will see you both tomorrow.'

'Looking forward to it, my old friend, and thank you.'

'No problem. But credit where credit's due, Ellie was the driving force in this, and you haven't seen everything yet.'

Joseph turned to her as Dylan disappeared into his boat. 'Why, what else have you been up to then, wondrous daughter?'

She hooked her arm through his. 'You better come and see for yourself.' She towed him towards the cabin of *Tús Nua*.

As they entered the narrowboat, the air actually caught in his throat at the level of transformation. There were lights and decorations everywhere, including a small Christmas tree in one corner of the cabin.

The detective scraped his hand through his hair as he took everything in. 'Wow, talk about a regular Santa's grotto.'

Ellie gave him a searching look. 'But you like it?'

'Love it, you mean. But this all looks like a lot of work?'

'It was, but Zoe helped me with this bit when she popped over to keep me company. That was after she realised she couldn't drag me out to a bar, especially without having a police escort in tow.'

'How is she? I haven't seen her this side of forever.'

'That would be because of her very active love life, and apart from that, she's still very much the wild child.'

'She could be Irish with all that red hair and spark to her. No wonder I've always liked her best out of all your friends.'

'Don't let Zoe hear you say that. She has a thing for older men.'

Joseph pulled a face at her. 'I don't think so.'

'God, no. Apart from anything, she'd eat you for lunch. Anyway, I hope you don't mind, but I invited her to join us for Christmas dinner tomorrow. Otherwise, she'll be spending the day by herself.'

'Well, we can't have that and the more the merrier will make it a grand old craic.'

'Brilliant. Thanks, Dad!' She leant in and kissed him on the cheek.

It was then that Joseph noticed the three presents under the tree. 'Please tell me you haven't got me anything?'

'They're not all for you, one's from me to Zoe. But the other two are yours. The small package is from Dylan and the larger one is from me.'

'Oh, Christ, that's lovely and everything, but you know how he said I've been sucked into the case at work...'

Ellie held up her hands. 'I sort of already guessed you wouldn't have time to get me anything. But before you sweat it, don't worry. You can make it up to me by taking me around the sales and buying me something then.'

Joseph peered at her. 'Does that mean waiting for you to try on lots of shoes and clothing?'

'Yes, it most certainly does. View it as your penance.'

'I'm going to make sure I get you a present next year.'

She laughed. 'Honestly, the best present is spending the day with you.'

'Don't let your mum hear you say that.'

'Oh, don't worry, I tell her exactly the same when I am with her at Christmas.'

This time, it was Joseph's turn to laugh. 'You are so my lass.'

'You better believe it.'

As Joseph slipped his jacket off, he realised for the first time that the tension that he'd been carrying across his shoulders had begun to let go. For the first time in maybe a long time, despite the grim way that the day had started with Charlie's death, he had a sense of fresh hope inside him.

Joseph headed over to the galley kitchen. 'Do you know what? I think you may have actually succeeded in putting old Scrooge here in the mood for Christmas. Do you fancy a cinnamon hot chocolate?'

'If you're going to put a shot of Irish whiskey in it, absolutely,' Ellie replied.

'When did you grow up?' Joseph asked.

'Maybe when you were looking the other way.'

'Aye, isn't that the truth,' he said, as he began to take the mugs out of the cupboard.

25TH DECEMBER

CHAPTER EIGHTEEN

As Joseph pushed away his empty plate, Zoe raised a glass to Ellie, Dylan, and him, who were all gathered around the small table in the detective's boat. White Fang had taken up a prime position beneath the table, and had been given more than his fair share of tasty morsels throughout the meal.

'I'd like to propose a toast to our two astonishing chefs,' she said. 'Honestly, that is some of the best turkey I've ever had, and I can't believe it was cooked on a barbecue.'

Joseph clinked his glass against hers. 'Yes, bravo, Dylan. I raise my glass to your culinary skills.'

The professor beamed at them, his Christmas cracker hat at a suitably jaunty angle. 'The secret is soaking it in brine overnight. It really brings out the flavour.'

'I agree, but those roast potatoes were mighty fine too,' Joseph said, smiling at Ellie.

'That will be the goose fat,' she replied. 'It makes all the difference.'

'Yes, that was a veritable feast,' Dylan said. 'I don't know about anyone else, but I'm going to have to let my dinner go down before I tackle any Christmas pudding, otherwise, I think I may be in danger of bursting a few buttons.'

'I absolutely agree,' Joseph replied.

'In that case, it's time for presents,' Ellie said, looking as lit up as she had when she'd been a child on Christmas morning.

'That sounds like a grand plan,' Joseph replied.

Zoe clapped her hands together. 'Fantastic, because I've something for you, Ellie.' She dug into her bag slung over the back of her chair, took out a gold foil-covered parcel and held it out for Joseph's daughter. 'This is for you, bestie.'

'In that case...' Ellie grabbed the soft parcel from under the tree and handed it to her friend. 'But you should open that when you're alone.'

'Don't be daft, I'm among friends.'

Before Ellie could stop her, Zoe ripped into the snowman patterned wrapping paper, and then withdrew an embroidered scarlet basque. 'Oh, I likey,' she said, holding it up for them all to inspect.

Ellie blushed. 'Bloody hell, that was meant to be my secret present to you.'

'Sorry about that, but I just love it. You know me so well.'

Dylan and Joseph traded raised eyebrow looks as the two women hugged each other.

'Anyway, you need to open my present, because I have to dash in a moment. I'm meeting my man tonight for a romantic liaison.'

Ellie grinned as she opened her present to reveal a bright blue rectangular box. She opened it, and her eyes widened as she took out the pendant. The design was two cats—one black and one silver—curled around each other, like the yin-yang symbol.

'Oh wow, this is beautiful,' Ellie said.

'It's a friendship pendant. If you do this, the two halves come apart and we can each wear one.'

'That's just perfect. Thank you, Zoe.'

They hugged again and then Ellie put the black pendant on, as Zoe did the same with the silver version of the cat.

'Right, I better get going and make myself all gorgeous for my man,' Zoe said as she stood. 'He said he's taking me somewhere magical and bringing plenty of champagne.'

'Sounds very romantic,' Ellie replied.

'You better believe it.'

Zoe kissed Ellie on the cheek as she stood, pulling her bag strap over her shoulder.

'Thank you so much for one of the best Christmases I can remember, guys,' she said to the two men.

'It's been a genuine pleasure, Zoe, and we should all do this again,' Joseph replied.

'That would be amazing.' She blew first him and then Dylan a kiss, and then, grabbing her jacket, headed out of the door like a woman on a mission.

'That woman is a force of nature,' Dylan said.

'You better believe it,' Ellie said as she cradled her half of the cat necklace in her hand, before looking up again.

'Okay, phase two of present giving.' She took the last two gifts and then handed both to Joseph.

'The smaller one is from me,' Dylan said.

The detective grimaced. 'Like I said to Ellie, I didn't have time to get you anything.'

He waved a dismissive hand at his friend. 'Nothing a good bottle of craft gin can't sort out in the New Year.'

'You're on.' Joseph began unwrapping the brown paper to reveal a blue rectangular box with *Waterman* written on the lid. He opened it to discover a beautiful blue lacquer pen trimmed with gold.

'You're always borrowing my pen, so I decided I'd better get you one of your own. I would have bought you a fountain pen. However, I thought a rollerball would be more practical in your line of work, rather than ending up with ink all over your fingers.'

'This is perfect, thank you.'

'Anytime, just no more stealing my pens, understood?'

Joseph chuckled. 'Understood.'

'Okay, mine next,' Ellie said.

He held it up and gave it a gentle shake. 'Something for the boat?'

'Nope, and that was your first of three guesses.'

'A bedazzled police truncheon.'

Dylan chuckled. 'I can definitely see you with one of those.'

'Sadly not, but I'm making a mental note of that for next year's gift,' Ellie said.

Joseph felt the weight of the present. It was relatively light, whatever it was. 'Something for my bike?'

'You're getting toasty warm now.'

'An air horn to scare those pesky pedestrians out of my way?'

'Nope and that's it—no more guesses.'

'Fair enough.' Joseph pulled the holly print paper off to reveal a plastic box, the top half of which was clear with a small rectangular-shaped camera. 'Oh, it's a cycle helmet camera.'

'I thought you could use one, especially when those taxi drivers cut you off. Now you can capture their number plate, have them arrested, and throw them in jail for life.'

'If only it worked that way,' Joseph said with a wry smile. 'But seriously, this is great. Whatever did I do to deserve such a gorgeous daughter as you?'

'You got very lucky,' Ellie said with a grin.

'Aye, that I did.'

Dylan sat up in his chair. 'I don't know about anyone else, but how about a Christmas movie? Something like, *It's a Wonderful Life.*'

Joseph smiled at him. 'You absolute traditionalist, Dylan, but sounds great to me. Maybe accompanied with a wee dram of something. I have some excellent Dead Rabbit Irish Whiskey that will hit the spot.'

'I'm certainly not going to say no to that, either,' Ellie said as she headed into the kitchen to fetch the tumblers.

———

Dylan was stretched out on his bench seat sofa, fast asleep, a tumbler balanced on his rising and falling chest, with White Fang snoring at his feet. Ellie had made something approaching a nest out of cushions on the floor, whilst Joseph was stretched out in his one and only armchair. He'd lowered the white blind from the roof on which they'd projected *It's a Wonderful Life*. Then they had moved on to some Christmas-themed episode of a sitcom that Joseph never normally watched.

'Do you fancy any more pudding, Ellie?' he asked, seeing his daughter open her eyes.

'Oh God no, I'm absolutely stuffed.'

She looked up at him from her nest and gave him a sleepy smile. 'This has been the best day, Dad.'

'It has, hasn't it? And most of that is down to you and Dylan pulling out all the stops.'

'That's what family is for and he's definitely family,' she said, gesturing towards the professor.

'Aye, that he is.'

Joseph gazed down at his daughter, so beautiful and always full of life. He felt a huge surge of love for her like he so often did.

Ellie had obviously noticed something in his expression because she tilted her head to one side. 'What?'

'Just thinking what a lucky dad I am to have a daughter like you.'

'The feeling is more than mutual,' Ellie replied.

'You do know how proud I am of you, don't you?'

'You only tell me every other day, so yes, I have a pretty good idea.' She gazed at him, and then her eyes widened. 'We haven't taken our traditional Christmas Day photo to send to Mum.'

'Oh right, better sort that out pronto then.'

'Hang on, my phone is under these cushions somewhere.'

'Don't worry, you can use my police smartphone and email it to her from it.'

'Okay, but hand it over, because you might be a skilled detective, but your photographic skills aren't exactly known for being great.'

'I can't help it if I keep cutting people's heads off.'

'Exactly, so give it to the professional Instagrammer in the family.'

Shaking his head, Joseph gave Ellie his phone. As she opened it, something fluttered to the ground. He glanced down to see Lord Saxton's Asmodeus club business card lying there.

'Hey, where did you get that?' Ellie asked, staring at it.

'It's part of our investigation. I don't suppose it would hurt telling you, but it's to do with that lead I was telling you about. You see, we had an anonymous tip about that devil mask that your assailant was wearing. It turns out it is used by members of this very exclusive and pretty dodgy club.'

His daughter's gaze tightened on him. 'When say dodgy, what do you mean exactly?'

'Without putting too fine a point on it, it's basically a very racy sex club where apparently anything goes.'

'Bloody hell!' Any semblance of sleepiness had vanished from his daughter's face as she sat up. 'Zoe said her guy had taken her to some parties that would turn my hair pink, but I never imagined it might be something like that.'

Joseph stared at her. 'Are you trying to tell me Zoe is dating someone who is a member of that club?'

'I'm just guessing here, but I saw the same business card in her bag.'

Immediately, any alcoholic Christmas Day haze was swept away as Joseph's mind burst into action. The killer targeting Laithwaite City Farm where Ellie worked was certainly one hell of a coincidence. But this latest revelation of someone dating his daughter's best friend had to take this far beyond the realms of any coincidence.

'Dad, what's wrong? You've gone pale.'

'Do you know anything about this guy she's dating?'

'Just that he's an older guy and works at the same lab as she does in Oxford,' Ellie replied.

His blood went cold. 'What sort of lab?'

'They do vaccine research. Part of Zoe's job is to look after the animals they have there.'

Joseph gawped at her. 'Oh shite! This is exactly what Aaron from the Pitt Rivers Museum tipped us off about, that the person responsible might work in a lab where they experimented on animals. And she was seeing this man tonight, correct?'

Ellie's eyes widened. 'You're not saying she's in any sort of danger, are you?'

'Hopefully, it's just one hell of a coincidence and nothing more. But I've got a bad feeling about this, Ellie.'

'Oh, God!' Ellie began pulling the cushions aside as she hunted for her phone.

'Is something wrong?' Dylan said, finally opening his eyes.

'Not sure, but I'm going to check one way or the other,' Joseph replied.

Ellie pulled her phone free and immediately stabbed the screen and put it to her ear. She chewed her lip as she listened. 'Hell, it's gone straight to Zoe's voicemail.'

'Okay, before you panic, she did say he was taking her somewhere, but we should go over to her place and double-check. Maybe I'm just being paranoid.'

Dylan gave them both a worried look as they went to grab their coats.

CHAPTER NINETEEN

As Ellie headed up the steps towards Zoe's house, Joseph paid the taxi that, thanks to a minor miracle, they had somehow grabbed so late on Christmas Day.

The problem now was that one glance at the darkened windows told the detective that there wasn't anybody in. His daughter had already told Joseph that Zoe's housemates were away for the holiday, suggesting there would be no one to ask inside if it turned out she wasn't there.

Ellie pressed the doorbell, and Joseph heard an answering chime deep inside the house as he joined his daughter on the step. When no silhouette of a person appeared on the other side of the leaf-patterned frosted glass, his daughter leant on the doorbell for her second attempt.

'Come on, come on,' she muttered under her breath as she began knocking on the door too.

'I think it's reasonable to assume that no one's home,' Joseph said.

'Damn it, she must have already left for her hot date with her mystery man.'

'Okay, we need to try to work out where she is, because

without dressing this up for you, Ellie, she may be in real danger. Is there any way we can find out where they might have gone?'

Ellie gave a sharp nod. 'Zoe has always been really brilliant at being organised. She makes a point of keeping her calendar updated on her mobile.'

'And that syncs with the calendar on her computer, right?' Joseph asked.

'Right, and she keeps her laptop in her bedroom.'

'Okay, as this is an emergency and I have every reason to believe she's in danger, I'm going to make a forced entry.' Joseph slid the truncheon that he'd deliberately brought with him out of his pocket as he'd had a hunch he was going to need it.

But Ellie reached out her hand and placed her hand on his his. 'No need for that, Dad.'

She headed towards the small front garden overrun with weeds, picked up a psychedelically painted gnome and turned it over. 'Zoe is forever locking herself out.' She poked in her fingers and withdrew a rusty Yale key.

Joseph pocketed his truncheon again as she slipped the key into the lock and opened the front door.

'Yes, a slightly more subtle approach to breaking the door down.'

Ellie nodded as they stepped inside. 'Zoe, are you in?' she called out.

Not so much as a murmur came back.

He reached out and flicked a switch on and an ancient low-energy fluorescent bulb flickered into life, bathing the hallway with a faint bluish glow.

'Where's Zoe's room?' Joseph asked.

'Upstairs, at the back. Follow me.'

Joseph fell in behind Ellie, and as they climbed the stairs, he took in the mouldy wallpaper and the distinct smell of a blocked drain somewhere in the house. He'd seen worse, but it seemed wrong that someone as full of life as Zoe lived here, especially when she had a good job as a lab assistant.

As Ellie headed towards one of the three bedroom doors, Joseph reached out and placed his hand on her shoulder.

'Better let me go in first.'

Ellie spun around to look at him. 'You're not trying to say what I think you are?'

'We can't rule anything out.'

His daughter's hands flew to her mouth. 'Oh, God!'

Joseph squeezed her shoulder. 'Don't panic yet, I'm just being extra cautious.' He tried his best to give her a reassuring smile.

She chewed her lip, but she gave him a small nod.

The detective slipped a pair of latex gloves out of his pocket, which made Ellie's eyes widen.

The truth was, if this was a crime scene and Joseph corrupted any evidence, Amy would drag him over the coals. But based on the panicked expression on his daughter's face, Joseph didn't think confirming his reason would go down very well with her right now. Instead, he kept quiet and took a mental breath as he pushed open the door. Joseph flicked on the light switch and, when he didn't see a body lying on the bed and blood splatter on the walls, he let out a long sigh of relief.

'Thank Christ for that.'

Before Joseph could stop her, Ellie was in the room with him. 'Bloody hell, Dad, you had me worried there.'

'Sorry about that, but also don't take another step into the room. There could still be DNA evidence in here that will need logging. And before you say anything, obviously I hope with every fibre of my being there's nothing to worry about, but I'm also paid to be paranoid.'

'You're telling me, but I promise I'll be careful.'

Joseph scanned the room, taking in the coloured translucent scarves that Zoe had hung on the walls like tasteful bunting. She'd done a pretty decent job of transforming what could have been a dingy room into somewhere that was almost cosy.

Ellie gestured towards the closed drawer in a small desk that was just within reach. Above it was a mirror that had lots of passport-sized photos stuck in the frame. On closer inspection, most of them showed Zoe and Ellie in different outfits posing in the railway photo booth where they'd been taken. Unfortunately, there were no photos of any man among them.

Joseph opened the laptop and, as he'd expected, was immediately confronted by the password prompt.

'Any ideas, Ellie?'

'Knowing Zoe, I can make some educated guesses that it's based on her favourite things. She has a real thing for Ben's Cookies from the market, so start there.'

He typed with glove fingers and pressed return. Apart from the computer beeping and *Two Attempts Remaining* appearing above the password box, nothing else changed.

'Okay, let's try her favourite pet that she's desperate to get, a blue Burmese cat,' Ellie said.

The DI tried that and was once again rewarded with a beep and another message about one attempt remaining.

'You're saying she always bases her password on her favourite things, so I think we're missing something obvious here. Your name.'

Ellie slowly nodded. 'Actually, that's not a bad idea. But if she did that, you better try her pet name for me, *Ellie the brave,* with no spaces'

'I rather like that.'

'Yeah, me too.'

Joseph typed it in and this time when he hit return, the desktop appeared.

His daughter nodded. 'Quite the formidable team when we want to be.'

'You better believe it,' Joseph replied.

He moved the cursor over the calendar application and opened it up. 'Okay, let's see what we have here...'

The first entry read, *Christmas dinner on Ellie's dad's cool boat!* That raised a smile from him, but the second entry pulled his mind back into sharp focus, *Romantic dinner at the stone!!!*

'Is that a pub or something?' Joseph asked Ellie, who'd appeared at his shoulder.

Ellie screwed her eyes up as she tapped her finger on the lips. 'Not that I've ever heard of. Hang on.' She pulled her phone out and began tapping away.

'What are you doing?'

'Just searching for any pubs or clubs in this area with stone as part of the name.' She frowned. 'Nope, not getting anything.'

'Okay, this will make me as popular as a dog's fart under the dinner table on Christmas Day, but I'm going to call this in and put the word out that Zoe needs to be located as quickly as possible.'

'But how will you do that?'

'First thing is to find out the last mobile mast that her phone was connected to. That will narrow down the search area for wherever this stone place is. It could be a cottage for all we know.'

Ellie's face relaxed a fraction. 'Yes, a romantic break in a cottage, especially at Christmas, would be Zoe's idea of heaven.'

'Also, don't forget this could all just be a coincidence, and I could be getting ahead of myself here.'

'Yes, that really could be it...'

But Joseph could clearly hear the uncertainty in his daughter's voice, which was only matched by his own worry that was getting more intense by the minute.

Joseph lowered his gaze from the clock on the office wall, which he'd been watching crawling towards midnight, back to Ellie. She was asleep with her head on Ian's desk, a stone-cold cup of tea just in front of her. At least that was an improvement on her staring out of the windows with a blank expression on her face as she chewed her nails. Joseph hadn't needed to be a mind reader to know what she'd been thinking about because countless nightmare scenarios of what might have happened to Zoe by now kept cycling through his brain.

He'd arrived with Ellie at the St Aldates Police Station via another taxi and had immediately contacted Chris. Despite being initially pissed off that he'd rung him on Christmas Day, the DCI had quickly changed his tune when he'd heard about Zoe. To his credit, he'd escalated things quickly, even though they couldn't be certain she was really in danger, and had rallied the troops. He'd even contacted Derek for high-level authorisation to make the cogs spin at maximum to run a trace on Zoe's mobile.

Megan put her head around the door and glanced across at Ellie and gave him a gentle smile. 'She must be emotionally exhausted,' she whispered.

Joseph nodded. 'I just pray that I'm jumping to conclusions and it all has a happy ending. The best thing I'm hoping for is just wasting everyone's time.'

'No, this was the right call, Joseph. It's what any good police officer would do.'

'I guess you're right.'

'You better believe it. Anyway, I was wondering if there'd been news from the phone company about locating Zoe's mobile yet?'

'Nothing so far, but they're always glacially slow. Even with a grade one request, because of a possible imminent threat to life, it's already been three hours since the SPOC officer contacted them.'

'SPOC?' Ellie asked, blinking and raising her head from the desk.

'Single point of contact officer, a specialist who deals with these kinds of requests,' he replied.

'Oh right, I'm still learning something new every day,' his daughter replied.

'Hopefully, it won't be much longer,' Megan said.

'I certainly hope not, because every minute we wait is a minute too long in my book.'

Megan sighed. 'Yes, I know.'

Joseph gazed at the DC. 'How about you? Any joy on coming up with a list of potential locations for the stone that she mentioned in her calendar?'

'Nothing worth mentioning. By itself, it really isn't much of a lead.'

'Yeah, tell me about it.'

With a chirp, his desk phone rang and Joseph almost tore the receiver from its cradle.

'Hi, DI Joseph Stone?' a woman's voice said.

'Yes.'

'We have that phone trace you ordered, just back from the mobile company. The last registered connection for Zoe Bryce's mobile before it was turned off was with a mast at Chipping Norton at around ten-fifteen PM. I wish I had more precise information for you.'

'At least it's a start, and it will narrow down the search area a bit. Thank you for all your help.'

'No problem and good hunting, Inspector.'

Joseph placed the receiver back on its cradle.

'News?' Ellie asked, now wide awake and sitting up.

'The Chipping Norton mobile mast made the last connection with her phone,' he said. 'Now let's see what we can find out.' Joseph tapped a few keys and pulled up a map as the others gathered round him.

'So what sort of range does a mobile mast have?' Megan asked.

'Up to fifty miles, but it will be less than that, otherwise it would have been picked up by other towers. That will narrow down the search area.'

'We could Google *stones* around Chipping Norton then,' Ellie suggested.

'It's worth a shot,' Joseph replied. He pulled up the search page, entered the information and hit return.

Within a nanosecond, an answer came back from the mighty Google brain and they all stared at the first entry on the screen, *Rollright Stones – English Heritage*.

'A stone circle?' Megan asked.

But Joseph was already grabbing his things. 'Think about it, Megan, it all fits. Especially if we're talking about a connection to the occult. Get the word out to the Chipping Norton Police Station to send a patrol car there straight away.'

Ellie was standing too and pulling her jacket on.

'Where do you think you're going?' he said.

'No way I'm just going to wait here whilst you tear over there. Zoe's my friend and I need to know she's okay.'

'So I'll contact you as soon as I know. Just please stay here and wait for me.'

'But, Dad!'

Joseph held up his hand to stop her. 'No, I'm sorry, Ellie, but this could be dangerous.'

She glowered at him, but he crossed his arms, in their very own version of a Mexican standoff.

When Joseph didn't so much as blink, Ellie finally threw her hands up in the air. 'Okay, okay. Have it your way.' She dropped back down into the chair.

'Good lass.' Joseph turned and rushed out the door with Megan before his daughter could change her mind.

'And the real reason you don't want Ellie to come is?' Megan asked.

'What do you think?' Joseph said with a grim face as they raced down the corridor together.

CHAPTER TWENTY

ZOE OPENED her eyes into nothingness. Then she felt the soft velvet of the eye mask pressed against her face, blacking the world out. Something jagged, hard, and rocky was pressing into her back. Cold air wrapped around her half naked body, the basque and her panties the only thing between her and the elements. What had happened to the rest of her clothes?

She desperately fought the wooziness ebbing through as she tried to form a word in her mind.

'Donald?' she managed to say.

'Shush, it won't be much longer, so just sleep,' he said with the same strange croaky voice, apparently down to a bad case of laryngitis.

But something was wrong, very wrong. She could now feel it with every fibre of her being.

She should have listened to her instinct that something was off with Donald tonight when he had turned up at her house wearing one of the demon masks. That was something that he'd once made her wear when he'd dragged her to a kinky exclusive club he was a member of. She boasted about that to Ellie, trying to impress her about how much she loved that side of her older man. But for all her talk about how she loved risky sex, talk was all it was. The truth was she'd been distinctly uncomfortable at the club, and had refused to join in with any of their *games*. But at least Donald had respected her decision and not forced her to do anything she didn't want to.

She tried to push herself away from the hard rocky surface, but then she felt the tug of the ropes on her wrists that were holding her to it. A sense of utter dread took hold, enough to clear some of the fog filling her mind.

'What are you doing?' she squeezed out through her lead filled jaw.

'Patience, you'll find out soon enough,' Donald replied, his husky voice muffled by the mask.

He'd brought her to the Hawk Stone to see the stars. The last thing she could remember was sipping a glass of champagne with Donald as they had gazed up at the stars... Suddenly, she knew exactly what was pressing into her back.

Zoe swallowed down the awful dryness filling her throat to force the question out. 'You tied me to the Hawk Stone?'

'Indeed, so we could perform the ceremony tonight.'

Ceremony? Panic surged through Zoe. Then she heard footsteps approaching across the field.

'Help me...,' Zoe said, her words trailing away with the effort.

'Don't worry yourself, they're with me,' Donald said.

Zoe pulled harder against the rope, but she was tied fast to the Hawk Stone like some sort of modern day witch.

'Ready to join the party?' Donald said to the newcomer.

But whoever it was remained mute.

Then Zoe felt something that felt like plastic gloves brush against her face. The hand moved down her body, changing pressure as it traced a line down her throat, and over the basque, between her breasts.

'Please stop!' she said as fear fluttered in her stomach.

But the gloved finger didn't and continued its journey down over the basque to her tummy, lingering for a moment before sliding downwards and pausing at the top of her panties.

Her heart was thumping in her chest. Just how far would Donald and his friend take this?

Once again, the finger trailed down and slid inside her panties.

Zoe gritted her teeth. 'No!' she shouted.

Then the hand was withdrawn before the mask was yanked from Zoe's face.

She blinked at the two people standing before her, heads silhouetted by the full moon behind them. The Hawk Stone loomed over them all like a broken tooth, casting a moonlit shadow across the scene.

On the ground was a picnic blanket, a bottle of champagne, and the two glasses, the one that she'd been drinking from empty. Suddenly, she knew what had happened. Her drink must have been spiked.

As Zoe's eyes adjusted to the bright light of the moon, she focused on the two figures. Of all the things she'd been expecting Donald to be wearing, Zoe was shocked to see both people had white coveralls and demon masks. However, it was easy to tell that Donald was naked beneath his outfit because his erection was hard to miss. A shorter figure standing before Zoe reached out and ran a hand slowly over her face.

'So beautiful,' Donald whispered as he watched. Then of all things, he glanced at his watch.

The other person had a syringe in their hand and before Zoe could say anything, they plunged it into her neck. Almost instantly, a warm, numb feeling spread quickly throughout her body.

'Let me go—' Zoe said, a sob cutting off the rest of her words.

'Shush, my darling,' Donald said. 'It will be better for you if you're asleep.'

She stared back at the demon masked man that she had been crazy about, that sense of fear burrowing deeper into her soul.

Her eyelid began to flutter. 'Don't...'

'Shush, don't talk. Just sleep now, Zoe.'

'I'm begging...' But her words faded away and she couldn't summon the energy to continue.

Her masked lover looked at his watch again.

'It's midnight at last,' he said from what seemed like a long way away, his voice no longer husky and strangely different.

The two figures were becoming nothing more than silhouettes as everything faded around her.

'I'm so sorry,' Donald whispered. He leant in and kissed her on the cheek. Then she realised he had turned and was walking away.

She focused on a single thought. *Why?*

The other shorter man who remained was pulling something out of a small cloth bag.

Part of Zoe's mind registered the thin blade. She watched, unable to move now, as he positioned its tip over her forehead, the numbness in her body spreading throughout her mind, as that raw primal fear began to scream inside her.

Then the man extended the dagger upwards towards the moon, the horns of his mask silhouetted as he held the blade aloft. He lowered his gaze to look at Zoe, his eyes visible as he moved the blade towards her forehead.

With the last of her consciousness, Zoe felt the cold steel tip bite into her flesh. Darkness swirled up around her and swept her away forever.

26TH DECEMBER

CHAPTER TWENTY-ONE

Joseph and Megan sped along the narrow lane, hedgerows whipping past and bathed in blue from their flashing lights. Around them, the rolling hills of eastern Oxfordshire spread out, barely a lit house to be seen. No doubt the choice of the Rollright Stones was no coincidence for Zoe's date. Apart from a farm, the National Heritage site was basically in the middle of nowhere, so no eyewitnesses to see what was happening tonight.

Joseph leant in for a closer look at the car's GPS map. 'Okay, we're almost there. Only about a mile to go. Let's just hope we get there in time.'

'You're certain this really is our man, then?' Megan asked.

'He has to be. Too many coincidences in play for it to be anything else, especially working in a lab with all those animals where he's probably been getting his practice in. All we can hope for is that killing Charlie was a one-off event he carried out in the heat of the moment to protect his identity. Maybe he doesn't mean to harm Zoe tonight.'

'The problem is that for a rendezvous, a stone circle in the middle of the night has a definite dodgy whiff to it.'

'I know, and our suspect also obviously has a major obsession with the occult. But let's keep hoping it might not be as bad as we think it is. However, this could also be our chance to arrest the bastard and stop him before it escalates any further.'

'At least we won't have much longer to find out.' Megan gestured towards the brown sign on the side of the road, *Rollright Stones, 100 Hundred Yards - A National Heritage Site.*

Ahead of them was a patrol car already parked up.

'Looks like the local cavalry has beaten us to it,' Megan said as she pulled in behind the other vehicle.

As they got out, Joseph grabbed a torch from his bag. He could see the dark shapes of the stone circle over the top of the hedgerow, almost glowing silver under the moonlight. It wasn't hard to see why it would be the choice of someone seriously into the occult, as it certainly seemed mystical, especially in the middle of the night.

The silhouettes of two police officers appeared over a stile and approached the detectives as they flashed their police warrant cards.

'So, what's the news?' Joseph asked.

'Nothing, sir,' the older officer said. 'We've been all around the site and there isn't a sign of anyone being here.'

A knot of tension tightened in the DI's stomach. 'Oh feck, I was certain that this was going to be the stones Zoe was talking about.'

Megan's eyes widened. 'Not stones, plural, stone as in singular.' She spun to face the officers. 'I don't suppose there are other major standing stones near Chipping Norton, especially ones by themselves?'

The younger officer nodded. 'Actually, there's the Hawk Stone, and it's only a few fields away.'

Joseph didn't know whether it was just his well-honed policeman's instinct kicking in, but somehow he immediately knew that had to be the place.

'You know exactly where it is?' he said.

'Yes, but it will be quicker to drive.'

A few moments later, they were following the PCs' patrol car, tearing along the lanes at breakneck speed.

Less than a couple of miles away, the other car skidded to a stop in the gateway to a field and they pulled up behind it.

With no one needing to be told, they all were out of the vehicle within seconds, had climbed over the gate, and broken into a run. The detectives and the younger officer kept up with each other, but it wasn't long before the older man had fallen behind. It was at moments like this that Joseph was grateful for all his time on his mountain bike.

They raced over a ploughed field, clods of earth picked out like frosty mountain peaks in the moonlight, heading towards a stone at the far side of the field. It was then that Joseph spotted smoke drifting up from a shape tied to a standing stone.

Ice prickling his skin, Joseph realised what they were looking at as they slowed.

'Oh no...' Megan said to the DI as they all stopped.

They all stared at the charred remains of a woman's head-less, naked body, the skin blackened and blistered like overdone crackling.

Without warning, the younger officer turned away and was violently sick. The older officer caught up with them and cast a grim-faced look at the murder scene.

'Okay, radio in for reinforcements,' Joseph said to him. 'Then set up a roadblock at either end of this lane. We don't want anyone coming within a two-mile radius of this crime scene.'

'Yes, sir...' The man's eyes trailed back to the remains of the woman's body with a haunted look in his eyes.

'Oh, and give your colleague one of these. It will help.'

Joseph took out his tube of Silvermints and handed one to the older officer.

He raised his eyebrows at Joseph in a silent question.

'It will take the taste of the sick away.'

'Right...' The man nodded and set off back to the younger officer, who was wiping his mouth with the back of his hand.

Joseph offered another Silvermint to Megan.

'No, I'm good for now.'

He gestured with his head back towards the car. 'You can stay in there if you want?'

Megan shook her head. 'No, I need to do this, sir.'

'Sir, is it? You obviously mean business.'

She gave him a faint smile. 'Let's put it this way, I have to take this step now or I suspect I never will.'

'I understand, so let's do this together then.'

As the detectives headed closer to the victim, despite how awful the situation was, Joseph felt a swell of pride in his chest for Megan. She really was throwing herself in the deep end. Whatever Chris thought of her, it was already clear to Joseph that the DC had real guts and had what it took to make a go of this job.

They were only twenty feet away when Joseph stopped, gesturing for Megan to do the same.

'We can't get too close. Trust me, we don't want to bring Amy's wrath down on our heads if we disturb any forensic evidence at her crime scene,' he said.

Megan thinned her lips. 'To be absolutely honest, that suits me fine.'

Joseph noticed a powerful scent of burnt flesh hanging in the air as wisps of smoke drifted up from the charred remains. Closer to the woman's body now, it was clear that the head had been cleanly removed, whilst her arms were still tied behind her back to the Hawk Stone.

Megan placed her hands over her mouth. 'Oh my God, that poor woman.'

'I know, I know...' Then Joseph's professionalism finally cracked, and tears were suddenly beading his eyes, as he remembered Zoe as she'd been earlier that day at Christmas dinner. 'Bloody bastard!' he hissed.

'Yes...' Without saying another word, Megan handed him a tissue out of her pocket.

The DI dabbed his eyes. 'Sorry, but Zoe shared Christmas dinner with us only a few hours ago. She was so full of life, and now this.'

'It's awful and no one should die like that.'

'And here was me thinking that I was going to have to worry about you attending a gruesome murder scene.'

She smiled at him. 'Maybe time for a Silvermint, Joseph?'

'Aye, perhaps it is,' he replied, returning her smile. He offered one to Megan and took another for himself.

The taste of the menthol worked its usual magic, and his thoughts steadied. 'Right, let's see what else we can find out before the cavalry turns up.'

He turned his torch on and played it over Zoe's corpse. 'It certainly looks like some sort of ritual killing.'

Megan nodded. 'Grim, but...'

Then Joseph noticed in her expression that the raw sense of shock he'd first seen in Megan was slowly being replaced by something else—if anything, an intense look of fascination. Yes, she was already well on her way to developing what it took to do this job. Even if Joseph was currently having a bit of a wobble.

She had her own torch out and was directing it to a secondary smaller pile beyond the body. 'What's that?'

Peering at it, Joseph spotted a fragment of embroidered scarlet fabric, and once again a lump formed in his throat. It had to be the basque that Ellie had given Zoe as a Christmas present.

'That must be the remains of the clothes she was wearing,' he said. 'Our murderer obviously didn't want to take any chances that we might be able to pick up any of their DNA on it.'

'Which was a pointless exercise as we already have it from that hair strand recovered from the goat.'

'That's something for us to know and for them to wonder about for now,' the DI replied. He directed his torch beam back towards the body and an object glimmered.

'What's that?' Megan said, peering at it.

'Keep your torch on it, and I'll take a photo.'

The DC did as instructed and Joseph zoomed in as closely as he could with his phone's camera and took a snap. Then he enlarged the photo until the silver object filled about a third of the screen. Even though it was very blurred, it was clear enough for him to make out the shape.

'Oh shite,' he muttered.

'Joseph?'

He swivelled the screen for her to see. 'It's one half of the friendship cat necklace Zoe gave Ellie. She kept this half for herself. That basically confirms that this really is Zoe.'

'Joseph, I'm so sorry. That's the second victim that you've known personally.'

'Exactly, and it's making me more than a little paranoid. But that aside, how on Earth am I going to tell my daughter what's happened to her best friend?'

'Joseph, if it would help, I'd be more than happy to do it.'

'No, this is my job even if it will cut me up having to break it to her. Those two were as thick as thieves.'

'Then, it should come from you, but the offer is still there if you want it.'

'Thanks, Megan, I appreciate it.'

But Joseph was already running through a mental dress rehearsal of telling his daughter. The only problem was he could see the movie so clearly in his mind of how her soul would shatter into fragments so tiny it would be hard to piece them back together.

To avoid Megan's penetrating gaze, Joseph returned his attention to the remains of the torso and moved the torchlight down from the necklace to the abdomen. It was there that he caught sight of a shape carved into the skin. He kept his torch beam on it.

'Are you seeing what I'm seeing, Megan?'

She peered at it and then snapped a photo with her phone before enlarging it and showing it to him.

Joseph found himself looking at a diagonal line with a second zigzagging line running through it, small circles above and below.

'The symbol for Azrael,' Megan said.

Joseph nodded as a feeling of anger began to burn inside him.

It was then in the distance, he spotted a convoy of blue flashing lights cresting the hill. 'Looks like the cavalry is almost here.'

'Then let's just hope that forensics turn up something useful.'

'If anyone can, it will be Amy and her team.' Joseph turned to her. 'So, if you were the SIO in charge, what would your next step be?'

'Holidays or not, I'd drag in all the warm bodies I could on this case, and chase down the staff details involved in any sort of animal testing at the Oxford research labs where Zoe worked. Then I'd cross reference them to the data from that red light camera near Lord Saxton's home to see if we get a match on a vehicle. If you pardon my language, we have to track this bastard down before they can do this again.'

'Personally, I always think a proper bit of swearing is called for in a situation like this.'

Megan actually managed a grin. 'Me too.'

'That aside, I completely agree with your plan of attack. But if that isn't exactly what our illustrious SIO does, then what?'

Megan scrunched up her eyes at him. 'We do it ourselves?'

'Oh, you're learning so quickly.'

She snorted. 'I'm certainly trying my best.'

The procession of police vehicles appeared at the top of the lane and slowed as they approached the gate.

'Okay, we better go and brief the troops.'

Megan nodded and headed back towards the gate.

However, Joseph hung back for a moment and gazed at the charred remains of Zoe's body. He felt the tension tightening in his chest. The tension that he'd been doing his best to keep suppressed whilst he'd been talking to Megan. It was always the same when he had to deal with the death of a young woman roughly the age of his daughter, because in his mind it was always Ellie's body that he had found.

Joseph wasn't unique in that respect. It was exactly the same for every officer on the force who was also a parent. They always saw their own in these brutal murders of young people. That's why Megan was absolutely right. They would do whatever it took to capture the *bastard* and put him away forever. He made the sign of the cross, almost as a silent vow to himself, and turned away to meet the other officers with Megan.

CHAPTER TWENTY-TWO

THE FIRST GREY light of dawn was creeping into the cabin of Joseph's narrowboat as Ellie cuddled into him on the small bench seat of the boat. The detective had arrived back from the Hawk Stone only an hour before. Dylan had met him outside, where Joseph told him what had happened. It was bad enough breaking the news about Zoe to the professor, but telling Ellie what had happened to her best friend would be seared into his mind forever. As his daughter's hot tears soaked his shirt and stuck it to his chest, Joseph cradled her to him, desperate to take her pain away.

As she shook, Joseph kissed the top of her head. 'I'm so sorry, my love. I wish we could have got there in time to save her. It's hard to get away from the feeling of guilt that this is all my fault.'

His daughter raised her puffy face towards him, eyes glistening. 'Dad, you mustn't. You did everything you could. If Zoe was here, she'd—'

Her voice choked up with wracking sobs, and he pulled her to him again.

'I know, I know, my beautiful lass.'

It was a good few minutes before her crying slowed again, and this time Ellie reached for a tissue from a box he'd put on the table especially for her, and blew her nose.

Then she clasped her fingers over her half of the cat friendship pendant that she was wearing around her neck.

'I just can't believe she's gone, Dad.'

'Tragically, that's often the way of these things. No chance for goodbyes, no time for anything.'

'Just please tell me this heartbreak will get easier?'

She looked at him with such desperation in her eyes, desperate to hear the reassuring words of a parent to tell her all the hurt would melt away. But she was also too old now for him to spin her one of his yarns.

'Only very slowly, I'm afraid, Ellie. She'll leave an empty space inside you, just like the loss of your baby brother did when he passed. But like back then, somehow you will find a way to carry on, taking one step at a time, each and every day.'

Ellie drew in a shuddering breath. 'Yes...' And then she looked at him. 'How could anyone do something like this to another human being, Dad?'

Joseph sighed. 'This is a stark reminder that there are some seriously sick minds out there. It's a big part of the reason that I do what I do, to stop people doing things like this.'

'Then thank God for officers like you,' Ellie said with a sad smile.

'I do what I can to make a difference.' Joseph gazed into her liquid eyes. 'But we need to talk about you now.'

'What do you mean?'

'I mean, that you're going to have to be extra careful.'

She stared at him. 'You think this madman may still come after me?'

'Let's put it this way, if I wasn't your dad but just another police officer, I'd still be advising that you needed protection. As much as I love having you here, we can't afford to take any risks until he's caught. So, I think the time has come to move to your mum's temporarily and take Walker up on his offer to have someone stand guard outside your mum's house until this is all over.'

'It sounds like you're saying I can't even step outside?'

'I'm afraid so. I realise it sounds a bit like house arrest, but this is for your safety, Ellie.' Joseph dropped his gaze to his hands. 'You see, when I saw what that bastard had done to Zoe —' Before he knew what was happening, a big sob of his own rolled up from somewhere deep inside him, stopping him dead from being able to say anything else.

Then it was Ellie holding onto him, rather than the other way around, gently patting his back. 'I know. I know, Dad. You don't need to say anything else.'

'Sorry, I'm meant to be the strong one here, and this isn't exactly helping you.'

'Actually, it is, because it means you really care, and that means a lot.'

She entwined the pendant's chain between her fingers, which brought a fresh lump to his throat as Joseph thought of its twin and where he'd last seen it.

Ellie, oblivious to his thoughts, gazed down at it, her smile a little stronger. 'I'll always wear this as a way to remember her.'

'Yes, I think Zoe would give you a serious earache if you put it away in a drawer.'

A small smile lit up his beautiful daughter's face. 'Yes, she absolutely would if I did that.'

He slowly nodded and drew in a deep breath. 'Right, let's get you over to your mum's.'

Ellie sat up and looked out of the window. 'When exactly did it become morning?'

'No idea, but it's arrived, so I need to get back to the station.'

'But Dad, you need to get some sleep. You've been up all night.'

'Maybe I have, but this case is too urgent for me not to be at the station. And before you nag me, I'll do my best to try to catch forty winks at my desk.'

'That wouldn't be the first time when you're working a case,' Ellie said.

'You're sounding like your mum now. Anyway, get your things together and I'll ring for a taxi and we'll head straight over to hers.'

'I haven't got a choice in this, have I?' Ellie said.

'No, I'm afraid that you haven't,' Joseph replied with a small, sad smile.

───────

Joseph dropped Ellie off to Kate, who had immediately drawn Ellie into her arms. It turned out his ex-wife had already got all the details from Derek, who'd sworn her to secrecy on the promise of a scoop once they went public about the case. But as Kate said, the only thing she was interested in now was protecting their daughter. Thankfully, PC John Thorpe was already on guard outside the house, which had made Joseph feel a lot more comfortable about leaving their daughter there, before he headed off to the St Aldates station.

Now, Megan and Joseph were gathered with at least thirty other officers in the packed-out incident room, which was impressive considering it was Boxing Day. Obviously, the super-intendent, who was also there, was no longer sparing resources on this case. His spreadsheet be damned.

Chris and Derek sat on the edge of the desk at the front, looking at a tablet in the DCI's hand and occasionally shaking their heads. Joseph had caught a sneak peek at what they had been looking at: photos of Zoe's body from the night before. Those made very grim viewing for anybody, even those with the strongest of constitutions.

Joseph spotted the enormous pile of turkey sandwiches that Derek had brought in with him for everybody to tuck into, courtesy of Kate. They were up to her usual legendary quality, topped with bacon and garlic mayo with a layer of iceberg lettuce on granary bread. He was certainly grateful for them as he started his second one. He'd been running on empty, and two cups of coffee hadn't exactly helped, either.

Amy swept in and nodded to Chris, who pushed off from the desk and stood up.

'Okay everyone, let's get this briefing underway. I just got the results back from the autopsy. According to the pathologist, blood work analysis has confirmed the presence of a considerable amount of ketamine in Zoe Bryce's body. The administration agent seems to have been champagne, of which they found trace amounts in her stomach, despite her body being burned, presumably in an effort to destroy the evidence. The presence of ketamine alone would be enough to raise suspicions that this is linked to the Midwinter Butcher. But to remove any doubt, we once again found another strand of grey hair that is an exact DNA match for the hair recovered at the city farm incident. Also, the saw used to sever her head matches that used to decapitate the goat and all the other previous animals.'

Many people were nodding, including him, when Megan leant in towards Joseph. 'No surprise there, but I still don't get it,' she whispered.

'Get what?' Chris asked, overhearing her.

Megan cleared her throat. 'The murderer goes to all the

trouble of wearing a forensic suit, yet twice now they've been careless enough to leave a hair.'

'It wouldn't be the first time, Megan,' Derek replied with his most patient voice. 'Criminals, even the best of them, can get complacent, believing they'll never be caught. But when they do, that's exactly the moment that critical evidence often turns up that will put them away for a very long time.'

She nodded, but with a slight scowl, and Joseph could certainly see her point. Confirmation of DNA evidence was all a little too convenient, but who was he to look a gift horse in the mouth?

Amy looked at Megan with respect in her eyes. She had always liked officers who asked questions, which was probably also why Joseph and Amy had always got on so well.

'I'll hand it over to Amy at this point, regarding the SOC team report,' Chris said.

Amy nodded as her gaze swept over the room. 'The pathologist is still attempting to confirm the identity of Zoe's body, as obviously a lack of a head didn't make that the easy task that it usually is. However, we managed to retrieve partial prints from the victim's hands, despite them being badly burned. Her prints were a match from samples we retrieved from a glass in the room that she rents. We were also able to retrieve hair strands from a brush that were also a DNA match to that of the body found at the Hawk Stone. Then, if we needed any further confirmation, DI Stone identified a partly burned scarlet basque that his daughter, Ellie, had given Zoe earlier on Christmas Day.'

All eyes in the room flicked to him, which Joseph ignored.

'So in summary, we can say with some certainty that the victim is Zoe Bryce.' Amy met their gazes. 'I'll now take any questions that you have.'

Joseph's hand was in the air. 'Have we any idea exactly how

she was killed, because I'm assuming she didn't have her head sawn off whilst she was still alive?'

'According to the pathology report, we can't be sure, but the ketamine dosage was sufficient to knock her out, so she probably knew very little about what was happening,' Chris replied.

A vivid nightmare image immediately flashed through his mind—Zoe trying to scream but not able to as her head was sawn off, her eyes locked onto the murderer's. Joseph wasn't alone either, as a few other officers who'd been eating their turkey sandwiches grimaced and put them down.

No more hands were raised after that, and everyone's attention shifted to DSU Walker as he stepped forward.

'I'm sure I don't need to tell any of you that time is of the essence, and we need to identify, then apprehend our suspect as quickly as possible. If you need any extra motivation, as a precaution we've posted an officer to keep guard outside of the house where Ellie Stone is currently staying with her mother, in case she's the next target.'

Derek dipped his chin towards Joseph and he nodded back. Yes, they were now very much on the same page, even if it had taken them a while to get there.

'So, what's the next step, sir?' Ian said from across the room.

The DSU's gaze alighted on Megan again. 'As I'm sure you heard, Megan came up with an idea during the search of Lord Saxton's mansion. Ten minutes ago, that idea bore fruit. We've just received a list of vehicles back from a red light camera at the junction that borders Lord Saxton's property. The only problem is that it's a list of over five thousand vehicle number plates that were recorded over the span of six months on the nights of the parties held at Lord Saxton's house. However, by cross-referencing, that list has been narrowed down to just over a hundred vehicles that were there for each party night.'

'So, you're saying that we have to trace a hundred different owners and interview them all?' Ian asked.

'No, and that's thanks to Megan's second idea of trawling through the staff list of anyone who worked at any of the labs in Oxford involved in any form of animal research. By further cross-referencing with the vehicle list, if we get lucky, the suspect's vehicle may pop out of the data. So today is all about bums on seats and churning through the information that we now have until we get a match.'

Joseph pulled a face as a thought struck him.

'What is it, Joseph?' Derek asked, spotting his expression.

'It may not be as easy as that. What if the murderer didn't use his own car to go to one of the parties, and instead they got a lift with someone else, or used a taxi even?'

Chris gave him an annoyed look, like Joseph was deliberately trying to rain on his parade. 'If it's a taxi driver, we'll contact all the relevant firms to see if they have a record of who they gave a ride to that particular night, check the credit card records, that sort of thing.'

'And if they paid cash?' Ian said, piping up from across the room.

'Bloody hell, give me strength,' the DCI muttered.

'Maybe we should just interview every person on that list of a hundred vehicles, just to be sure,' Joseph added.

Derek looked suddenly distinctly uncomfortable and waved a dismissive hand at him. 'Let's cross that bridge if we ever get to it.'

There was something in the way he said it that left Joseph with the distinct impression that was his least favourite option. Maybe it was to do with all the time it would take, but the DI couldn't help but notice the knowing look Amy was giving him, which told him that there was something else in play here. He made a mental note to chat with her about it later.

'Okay, if you head back to your desks, we'll be distributing a list of all the staff lab members, which we're hoping to receive in the next hour from Oxford University,' Chris said. 'That's it for now and let's do whatever it takes to catch our suspect before this day is out.'

The moment the meeting broke up, a dozen conversations started as people went into huddles.

Megan turned to Joseph. 'Why the reluctance to trace all the owners straight away? Surely a hundred vehicles aren't too many to trawl through?'

'Aye, it's a good question and I intend to get to the bottom of it. But for now, I've got a different mission for us.'

'Which is?'

'Even though it was our idea, with everyone being thrown into this hunt for the vehicle, I think we're putting all our eggs in one basket. So I was thinking that maybe we should go and do some old-fashioned police work.'

'Which is what exactly?'

'We talk to Zoe's neighbours and see if they ever saw anything of this mystery man of hers. She didn't drive and we've already checked all the local taxi firms, who have no record of any picking her up on Christmas Day. So, I bet our murderer picked her up in person last night.'

'But I thought Uniform had already asked her immediate neighbours, as well as put up an appeal for witnesses with a sign outside her house.'

'Aye, they have, but there hasn't been time to ask more people, as it only happened last night. As it's still early on Boxing Day, there's every chance that people haven't gone out yet and seen the incident notice boards. We can even check the whole road if we have to, rather than sit here on our arses waiting for data to arrive. It certainly can't hurt.'

'Isn't this still a job for Uniform?'

'Not with everyone being pulled into looking at the list of vehicles. So I say we make ourselves useful out there on the front line.'

'In that case, what are we waiting for?' Megan said as she grabbed the car keys from her desk. 'Let's get over there.'

CHAPTER TWENTY-THREE

THE LACK of sleep was seriously getting to Joseph as he and Megan headed along what was starting to feel like an endless residential street. His fatigue wasn't exactly being helped either by the fairly standard response they'd had from those who even bothered to answer their doors. It varied between *'That's just so shocking'* and pitching straight into wanting to gossip about Zoe's murder. Unfortunately, in the twelve or more houses they had already tried, no one had seen or heard anything.

They headed towards the last house on the opposite side from Zoe's, at the junction with Cowley Road.

Megan looked similarly wiped out. 'I don't know about you, Joseph, but I could do with a cup of coffee from that deli round the corner.'

'Not a bad idea. I'm dropping my feet here,' he replied. 'Let's just finish up with this last house first.'

Megan nodded and opened the gate.

Joseph was steeling himself as he pressed the doorbell, ready to go through the same going nowhere conversation, when Megan pointed to the glass-enclosed porch. 'Look!'

The DI looked where she was indicating and saw a small

round white security camera with a glowing red LED on it. He glanced back to where it was pointing, and realised it was roughly pointed towards Zoe's house further along the street.

'Oh you little beauty,' he said. 'Let's just hope it caught something useful last night.'

A few moments later, a guy in his mid-thirties with a neatly trimmed beard, wearing the most striking Christmas jumper with Rudolf on it, opened the door. Just behind him, two young girls dressed in long black capes and with wands in their hands stopped in mid-chase to stare at the detectives.

'Hello, can I help you?' the man asked.

'Hi, I'm Detective Inspector Stone and this is Detective Constable Anderson. I don't know if you've heard about what happened at number thirty-three, but we're making door-to-door inquiries to see if you witnessed anything last night between roughly eight PM and eleven PM?'

'Oh yes, I saw the board outside the house and the appeal for witnesses. Shocking that happening here. Have you had any leads yet?'

Here we go again, Joseph thought. Although, the desire to know more was understandable—who wouldn't when a murder had happened practically on their doorstep—but did they really think they would share all the juicy details with them?

Regardless of that, Joseph fixed his professional mask in place. 'Sorry, sir, we're not at liberty to discuss that.'

'Don't worry, just me being nosey. But to answer your question, we didn't hear or see anything.'

'What about your security camera?' Megan asked.

The man gave her a blank look. 'Our what?'

She gestured towards the Wi-Fi camera in the porch's corner.

'Oh yes, sorry, I forget it's there most of the time. My wife fitted it a couple of years ago after our Amazon parcels kept disappearing.'

'Some people will steal anything that isn't nailed down,' Joseph said.

'Isn't that the truth?' the man replied.

Megan glanced at the camera. 'It looks like it has a good view of the street, is that right?'

His eyes widened. 'You think it may have caught something?'

'Only one way to find out,' she said.

'Sorry, I should have thought to check it before now, But I was a bit preoccupied with our daughters, post-Christmas.'

'You don't need to explain,' Joseph replied. 'Anyway, could we see that footage?'

'Yes, no problem, just give me a moment. My wife, who is a whiz with computers, set up the app for me on my phone.'

He took out his mobile, and then hunted through until he found what he was looking for. Then, a couple of taps later, he handed the detectives the phone.

'I'm afraid you're going to have to hunt through the footage by hand. Even though the recordings are triggered when it detects movement, it practically records non-stop because of all the traffic. That's why we stopped bothering to look at the videos unless we need to, as it records so much rubbish.'

'Hopefully, some of that *rubbish* may be critical evidence,' Megan said.

'Wow, that would be great if it is. But anyway, rather than hang around on the doorstep, why don't you both come in and have a cup of coffee or tea?'

'Coffee please, and the stronger the better,' he replied.

'Same for me,' Megan said.

'Excellent. I just got an espresso machine for Christmas and I'm looking for any excuse to try it out. Also, my wife has just baked some of the best mince pies you'll have ever tasted. I think it's the dash of Jamaican rum she puts in them.'

'Then it would be rude of us to refuse your very kind offer,' Joseph replied with a wink towards Megan. 'Thank you—sorry, I didn't catch your name?'

'It's Craig.' He opened the door behind him and ushered the detectives in under the gaze of the curious eyes of his two daughters, watching them from the stairs, their wands now lowered.

Megan studied the logos on their capes. 'You're both in Gryffindor from Harry Potter, am I right?'

Both girls gave her a disgusted look.

'No, Hufflepuff!' the older one said, only just stopping herself from adding, *stupid!*

'You'll have to excuse them. They've both gone mad this year over everything Harry Potter, and we have all the Lego sets to prove it.'

'I can imagine,' Joseph said, remembering exactly how Ellie had grown up on those stories a lifetime ago.

Joseph and Megan sat in a front room that looked like it had fallen straight out of an IKEA catalogue thanks to the abundance of Scandinavian furniture that it had been tastefully decorated with. However, pride of place went to a Christmas tree in the corner, dripping with decorations. Quite a few of the glitter-covered creations were obviously made by the two girls, who had already informed them that they'd made them at school. That was, until Craig had banished them into the kitchen so the detectives could work in peace.

Now with cups of espresso to fuel them, Megan and Joseph

were taking turns hunting through the large number of video clips that had been recorded the previous night.

Craig put his head around the door. 'Can I get you anything else?'

'No, we're grand, thank you,' Joseph said. 'And thanks for these, they're just as good as you said they would be,' he said, holding up one of the mince pies.

Megan nodded. 'With cooking talent like that, she should be on the Great British Bake Off.'

Craig beamed at them. 'I will let her know.' He disappeared back around the door, accompanied by the cries of his daughters casting spells at each other again.

'Nice family,' Megan said as she helped herself to another mince pie, which Joseph noticed was at least her third.

'They are,' Joseph said as he returned his attention to the video footage.

Although grainy, the clips were surprisingly clear for such a tiny camera.

He watched a taxi drive past, but of course, that had already been ruled out. The DI glanced at the time stamp that said they'd reached eleven PM.

'Damn, we're running out of footage,' he said.

'Still no joy then,' Megan said, obviously concentrating more on what she was eating rather than the task at hand.

'Nothing so far. Anyway, it's about time you took your turn while I have a mince pie before you finish them all off.'

'I can't help it if I've got a bit of a sweet tooth.'

'Have you got a doctor's note for that, saying it gives you the right to stuff your face with mince pies then?'

'No, but I'm sure I can sort something out,' she replied with a grin. She wiped the sugar from her fingers with a napkin and took the mobile from him.

He'd barely had a chance to take a bite of his mince pie,

before Megan said, 'Yes!' She angled the screen so they could both see it and played the video again.

A silver Mercedes urban tank, otherwise known as an SUV, was double-parked directly outside a house further down the road on the opposite side. The driver didn't emerge, and the windscreen was too dark to see into the cabin. But any doubt that this was the right vehicle was swept away when a young woman with red hair emerged from the house.

'That's Zoe, and she looks dressed to kill,' Megan said, taking in the sparkling party dress and high heels she was wearing.

'Or be killed,' he replied with a frown.

They watched her head towards the parked SUV, open the passenger door, and get in.

'Damn, the vehicle is too far away to get its number plate,' Megan said.

'Patience,' Joseph said.

The SUV slowly pulled away, heading towards the camera on what the DI knew would be the last journey Zoe Bryce would ever take in her life.

'Oh great, the hedgerows are in the way now,' Megan said.

'There's a gap coming up where that gate is in front of the neighbour's house, so keep your fingers crossed.'

The SUV was almost parallel to the house when the vehicle reached the gap. They had a brief glimpse of the plate before it disappeared again into another hedgerow.

They both exchanged glances.

'Did you get a clear look at it?' Joseph asked.

'Not sure, I'll back up frame-by-frame—it's that first button,' Megan replied.

The video crawled backwards, the SUV reversing back towards the gap, and she hit pause the moment it had lined up.

The detectives both stared at the letters and numerals, blurred but still just possible to make out.

'Okay, I'm seeing GK20LK, but I'll be damned if I can make out that last digit. How about you?' Joseph said.

Megan chewed her lip. 'Sorry, the same for me.'

'Don't worry, running through the characters we do have, and cross-referencing them with that model of Mercedes SUV, I'd be very surprised if we don't get an exact match.'

Her eyes widened. 'You mean we've got him?'

A small smile filled his face. 'I do believe we might.'

Megan thumped the air. 'Get in.'

'Do you want to tell Chris or shall I?' he said with a wide grin.

'Joseph, it was your idea, you deserve this moment in the sun, so go ahead.'

'In that case, I don't mind if I do.'

He pulled up Chris's name in his contact list and punched dial on his mobile.

The DCI picked up in three rings.

'Joseph, where are you?'

'Rather than hang around the station, I thought Megan and I would make ourselves useful and extend the door-to-door around Zoe's house. And we've struck gold. A home security camera picked up a silver SUV, and we have most of the plate. It's GK20LK, but we're missing the last digit.'

'It's an *A*, Joseph. The list of number plates was finally sent through twenty minutes ago and we almost immediately got a match.'

'You mean you've already traced him?'

'We have. It turns out it belongs to one Professor Donald Thackeray who heads up a vaccine research lab into viral pandemics in Oxford. And we're about to raid his home, if you'd like to meet us there?'

'Damned right I do, Chris. Good work.'

'You too, Joseph. Now let's go and put this bastard away.'

'Too bloody right.'

'I'm sending you the address now and the drinks will be on me tonight,' Chris said before hanging up.

Megan stared at him. 'We're really on the murderer's trail?'

'It certainly looks that way, so let's get our skates on.'

As they stood, Megan helped herself to another mince pie before, with a quick thank you to Craig and instructions on where to send the video file, the detectives headed for the door, just barely dodging a couple of spells cast at them by the girls on their way out.

CHAPTER TWENTY-FOUR

EVEN THOUGH MEGAN drove Joseph to Professor Donald Thackeray's house on Cumnor Hill at a speed that would have even impressed Ian, they were still the last to arrive at the party. Patrol cars and unmarked vehicles filled the driveway as neighbours thronged the pavement, desperate to know what was happening. Megan tooted the horn and a moment later a PC appeared and began herding the crowd aside so they could squeeze the car past them and park.

'Wow, Chris doesn't mess around,' Megan said as she took in all the officers coming and going from the front door. 'This is like Lord Saxton's place all over again.'

'Yes, the DCI's approach isn't the most subtle, but he gets results.'

'Let's hope so on this occasion,' Megan said as they headed to the front door.

Amy was just inside, beyond a boundary tape, already suited and booted in her forensics suit. On seeing the detectives, she gave them a wave.

'How's it going?' Joseph asked as they approached the tape.

'Unfortunately, no sign of Professor Thackeray. However,

plenty of DNA evidence everywhere to make me one very happy forensic officer.' She held up a bag with a comb, silver hairs visible among its teeth. 'I'm going to send this straight off to the lab to see if we can get a match.'

'Any other more immediate clues to link him?'

'Nothing so far, but it's early days.'

'If he's got any sense, there won't be anything here to connect him to the case,' Joseph said. 'But, going for gold, I don't suppose there's any clue where Professor Thackeray might currently be?'

'There was a printout on his desk for an Airbnb in the Lake District, the booking date from today,' Chris said from behind him.

Megan and Joseph turned to find the DCI dressed in a forensic suit.

'We've already contacted the local force up there who have dispatched a patrol car,' he continued. 'It's such a shame we're not going to be the ones to arrest him.'

Joseph could easily imagine how galling that would be for a DCI who wasn't exactly always the best team player. In the past, Chris had never hesitated to make sure he was in the right place at the right time to get the lion's share of the glory. The man had a definite talent for it.

'Ah well, the main thing is that he's taken into custody as quickly as possible,' Megan replied.

'Absolutely.' Chris did his best to smile, but it was a bit like watching a ventriloquist's dummy trying to convey a genuine emotion by rearranging their face to look like they really meant it. He nodded to the two detectives and then slipped under the perimeter tape to join in with the search of the property.

Amy gave them a thinned-lipped smile. 'I'm surprised he hasn't jumped in a car to join them on the arrest.'

Joseph couldn't help but smirk. 'Oh, don't you worry, if he

thought he could get there in time he would have already headed off,' he replied.

'Is he really that narcissistic?' Megan asked.

They both looked at her. 'Yes,' Amy and Joseph said in unison, then grinned at each other.

'Right,' Megan said, shaking her head.

The transformation in Joseph's and Amy's mood was obvious, especially as they were taking the piss out of Chris like usual, albeit behind his back. They were closing in on the killer, and that was what really mattered.

'Okay, it's obvious there's not a lot we can do here,' Joseph said, glancing at his watch. 'I don't know about you, Megan, but I could do with heading home for some serious shut-eye.'

'God, yes. I'm exhausted and no amount of coffee is going to fix that anytime soon.'

'It's alright for some,' Amy said.

'Hey, I know exactly what you're like. You always run on pure adrenaline when investigating a scene for any clues. I'll never forget that thirty-six-hour stint you pulled with no sleep to gather the evidence for those child abductions.'

'Says the man who almost matched me with thirty-four hours without sleep.'

'I'm an amateur compared to you.'

Amy tilted her head to one side. 'I'll take that as a compliment.'

'You should,' he replied. 'Okay, we'll get out of your hair and leave you to do what you were born to do.'

Amy smiled, and with a wave of her hand, turned and headed into an open-plan kitchen, as the detectives made their way back to the car.

'Joseph, I hope you don't mind me asking, but have you and Amy ever been an item?' Megan asked, bold as brass.

He stopped and stared at her. 'Bloody hell, you don't hold back, do you?'

'I'm told it's one of my better qualities.'

'Or just bloody nosey. But to answer your question, no, we've never been together. We're just good mates.'

'What a waste. You two really suit each other.'

Joseph made a *humphing* sound as Megan opened the driver's door. 'If it's all the same to you, I'll pass on the dating advice.'

'Your loss,' Megan said, giving Joseph a knowing look as he got in beside her.

She started to reverse the car towards the crowd of onlookers that had grown considerably in the short time they'd been there.

Joseph gestured at them. 'I just hope no one posts any photos to social media that might tip off Professor Thackeray before he's arrested and taken into custody. If I'd been running this investigation, I would have just sent a couple of unmarked cars in, rather than arrive with the whole travelling circus.'

'Yes, a low-profile approach would have been a better call,' Megan replied.

The PC was just clearing the people away so the detectives could pull out onto the main road when a woman in a cardigan approached the car and tapped on his window.

'Hang on a moment, Megan,' Joseph said as he lowered it.

'Sorry to stop you, but it's hard to ignore that you're searching Donald's house.'

'And you are?' Joseph asked.

'Clare Stepford. I live next door. Never liked the man, always so rude when I try to tackle him about the height of his hedges.'

'Right, well, I really haven't got time to discuss hedges...'

She waved a dismissive hand at him. 'No, not that. But have

you looked in his garden studio? It's hidden right at the back of the garden behind another hedge. I just wanted to make sure you knew it was there, as it's easy to miss.'

'Oh right, and thank you. That's very useful information.'

She gave him a smile. 'Just trying to do my bit to support our local police force.'

'Well, it's very public-spirited,' the DI replied.

'Anytime, anytime,' the woman replied, practically fluttering her eyelashes at him.

Joseph raised the car window again.

'Talk about a busybody,' Megan said with a scowl as she watched the woman, head held high, make her way back through the crowd.

'But a very useful busybody. We better check it out.'

'You mean before Chris gets to it first?'

'I'm not saying a word,' he replied with a smile.

The nosey neighbour wasn't wrong. Even though Joseph and Megan knew it was there, it still took a fair bit of searching to actually locate the garden studio. It had been built into a space behind a very thick hedge and was totally screened from view from the house. Amy was in tow now as well, once they had popped back into the house to let her know.

The building itself was a very modern design and clad in cedar wood. A large bi-fold door filled up most of the front wall, but unfortunately, whatever was inside was hidden behind a blind that had been closed. The only other noticeable detail was a cat flap built into the wall.

Joseph put on the latex gloves that he'd grabbed from the car and offered the other pair to Megan, as Amy tried the door.

'Not surprisingly, it's locked. I'll get one of the team to smash the door down.'

'Hang on, no need for that,' the DI said, taking out a small leather pouch he'd bought with him.

'What have you got there?' Megan asked.

'A lock-picking kit,' he said.

'You're not still using that?' Amy said.

'Yes, as it's proved its use more than once, as you well know.' Joseph turned to Megan. 'You didn't see me do this, right?'

'You really are such a bad influence, aren't you?'

'He most certainly is, and I suppose some might say that's all part of his Irish charm,' Amy said, shaking her head.

Joseph grinned at her as he inserted two of his tools into the lock. As the DI worked his way along the pins, jiggling them into place until they clicked into position, he couldn't help but notice the scratch marks.

He pointed them out to the others. 'See those, those suggest Professor Thackeray has called on the service of a locksmith before, to get this open.'

'He probably just lost his keys or something,' Megan said.

The DI nodded as he felt the last tumbler click into place. Then, with the tip of his tongue showing between his teeth, Joseph used the tools to rotate the lock before withdrawing them again. A brief surge of elation filled him as he turned the handle, and the door swung open.

'You see, so much more finesse than using a battering ram,' Joseph said to his companions.

'You may have a point there,' Amy said.

He reached in far enough to turn on the light and gaped at what was revealed inside.

Behind him, Megan let out a gasp. It looked like something straight out of a horror movie. Animal heads had been mounted on the wall, including a deer's and even a goat's head, which

Joseph was certain was Dumbledore's from the Laithwaite City Farm incident.

But it was what was in a large glass jar, presumably filled with formaldehyde, that made his stomach turn. Zoe's head stared lifelessly out through the glass, her red hair hanging suspended in the liquid as though it had been caught in an ethereal wind.

Joseph heard Megan gagging but, transfixed by this nightmare, he couldn't tear his eyes away from it to check on her.

'Fucking hell,' Amy said, who reserved swearing for only the most shocking moments.

But the DI's attention was now fully on the magnetic notice board to which photos of Zoe had been pinned. There were also photocopies of the symbol for Azrael, as well as a white demon mask hanging from a peg.

Amy just shook her head and turned to him with wide eyes. 'I think we just hit the jackpot, Joseph.'

CHAPTER TWENTY-FIVE

DESPERATE TO TRY and claw back a semblance of energy, Joseph had hunkered down in the car to catch what was supposed to be a quick nap whilst Amy's team searched the garden studio.

A sharp knock drew Joseph out of a dreamless sleep and he opened his eyes to see that it had grown dark outside. Megan peered in at him, alongside a woman probably in her late fifties with grey streaks she hadn't bothered to disguise with hair dye.

The DI glanced at his watch and was taken aback when he realised he'd been asleep for five hours. Opening the door, he clambered out, trying to shake the cobwebs of sleep from his mind.

'Sorry to disturb you, Joseph, but everyone else is caught up in the search, and you really need to hear what this woman has to say,' Megan said.

'And you are?' Joseph asked, looking at the woman as the fog in his brain started to lift.

'Alice Thackeray,' the woman said, reaching out and shaking his hand.

He narrowed his gaze on her. 'Any relation to Professor Donald Thackeray, by any chance?'

'Yes, he's my ex-husband. I came over to feed his... Well, I mean, our cat.'

There was no hardness in Alice's eyes when she mentioned Donald's name and, combining that with the fact she still kept her married surname, that told the DI it had been an amicable divorce. Just like with Kate and him.

'Oh right. And you wanted to talk to someone, because?'

She flapped a hand towards all the police vehicles still crowding the driveway. 'Because of all this. What on Earth are you all doing here?'

'I'm afraid I'm not at liberty to discuss that, as it's an ongoing investigation. Just that your ex-husband is a person of interest in a case.'

'Which is what I tried to tell Ms Thackeray,' Megan said.

She crossed her arms. 'Whatever Donald is, I can tell you for a fact that you've got the wrong man.'

'Yes, I'm sure, but I'm afraid there's a lot of evidence that's already been recovered from his garden studio.'

Her eyes narrowed on him. 'What sort of evidence, exactly?'

'Enough to make it look very bad for your ex-husband,' Joseph replied.

'Really? But I didn't notice anything when I was feeding the cat in there. She prefers to live out in the garden, you see, rather than in the main house. It's probably everything to do with her having a farm cat for a mother.'

Megan exchanged a surprised look with Joseph. 'Hang on. You're saying that you didn't spot all the photos and clippings stuck to the whiteboard, and the animal heads all over the place?'

'Sorry, are we talking about the same garden studio? I was

only there this morning and I can assure you nothing like that was in there then.'

A cog started to turn in Joseph's head. 'Where do you believe your ex-husband is now?'

'Well, that's the strangest thing. He received an email saying he'd won a booking at an Airbnb up in the Lakes. Of course, he thought it was a scam at first. But when he double-checked the booking directly with the owner, it turned out that it was legitimate and that the fee had already been paid in full. Then, not wanting to look a gift horse in the mouth, he headed up there first thing this morning.'

The cog was starting to spin faster. For the first time, something was feeling off here, and the DI's mind was racing ahead towards an obvious conclusion. Donald was being framed for something he had nothing to do with. They also had in front of them someone who could give an insight into Professor Donald Thackeray's real character.

'So, if I asked you if your ex-husband is into the occult, what would you say?'

She gawped at Joseph like he had a hinge loose. 'You're not being serious. Of course he isn't and never has been.'

'What about owning a demon mask?' Megan said, obviously sensing where this was headed. 'Ever seen one of those in his studio?'

Alice snorted. 'Okay, now you're just trying to wind me up. Donald with a mask—I don't think so. Getting him to wear a hat to keep his face out of the sun was always a big enough problem, let alone anything else.'

'What if I was to tell you that these masks belonged to a very exclusive members-only club where anything went?' Joseph asked.

This time, Alice actually laughed in his face. 'We cannot be talking about the same man. Donald, even though I do still love him, has always been one of the most boring people you could hope to meet. His idea of a good time is maybe a couple of glasses of sherry at the staff Christmas party at the lab, and even that would count as racy for him.'

Joseph exchanged a longer look with Megan. It wouldn't be the first time a husband, even an ex-one, had led a double life. But Alice's reaction to what they'd found in the studio was beyond troubling.

'Okay, it sounds like we're going to need to take an official statement from you,' Megan said.

'Of course, anything to help Donald. And I'll tell you again. Whatever it is that you think he's done, you've definitely got the wrong man.'

'Thank you so much,' Joseph said. 'Your information has been invaluable.'

'No problem, anyway I better go and round up this cat, which is probably half frightened to death by now by all this commotion.'

Joseph nodded, and with a wave, Alice headed away.

Once she was out of earshot, Megan turned to Joseph. 'Those scratches on the lock.'

'Yes, I know. It looks like our good professor has been set up to take the fall for Zoe's murder.'

'What do you mean she can vouch for Professor Donald Thackeray on the night of Lord Saxton's parties?' Chris said, on the verge of shouting at Joseph within the confines of his glass-walled office back at the station. It was still loud enough to turn the heads of the people at desks outside in the main office.

'I mean exactly that, Chris,' the DI replied. 'Alice Thackeray has supplied clear alibis for Professor Thackeray during

Lord Saxton's sex parties. She even said that she and the new man in her life had gone over to Thackeray's on one of those nights for dinner. As for the other date, she told us that he was at a viral research conference in Edinburgh, which we independently checked out and confirmed.'

'But even if she isn't just covering for him, that still doesn't mean that he's not a member of Lord Saxton's club, especially as his number plate was caught on that red light camera.'

'Maybe, but something isn't stacking up here,' Joseph replied. 'We have to seriously consider that we've been left a false trail, so we'll pursue the wrong man. We need to change the course of this investigation, and quickly.'

Chris's eyes actually bulged. 'Give me strength. We have more than enough evidence to convict Thackeray, especially as Zoe's head was found on his property. If that isn't enough to convince a jury, Amy just heard from the lab confirming that Donald's DNA matches the grey hair recovered from the city farm.'

'Oh right, I hadn't heard that.' Joseph rubbed the back of his neck with his hand. 'But even with what appears to be overwhelming evidence, I still think we should keep an open mind. For someone who exercised such extreme caution, it seems strange that the murderer got careless enough to leave such damning evidence on his property. Perhaps those grey hairs were deliberately left at the scenes.'

'Or he became so arrogant that he didn't believe the police would ever catch up with him.' Chris gave Joseph such a straight look that it left him with the distinct impression that he thought that was partly his responsibility.

Joseph tried to keep the irritation that was growing inside him out of his voice. 'Until we've interviewed Thackeray, I think we should continue to explore other avenues of inquiry.'

'You're still not listening to me, Joseph. We already have our man, and if you needed even more evidence of that, the final nail in his coffin is that he didn't turn up at that Airbnb in the Lakes. I wouldn't be surprised if his ex-wife tipped him off about the raid on his house and he's gone to ground.'

'With all due respect, Chris, you're making a lot of assumptions there.'

'For fuck's sake. I'm the one running this investigation and if you're not happy with that, feel free to put in for a transfer. Derek warned me what you were like to work with, but I ignored him, thinking that I'd give you the benefit of the doubt. But now I find you in here questioning my judgement. Well, I have a message for you, either get on board or get out. Your choice, Stone.'

The DI felt like grinding his teeth together. This sort of stubborn determination to get a case closed as quickly as possible, even if it meant cutting a few corners, was the same reason he'd fallen out with Derek. Now it seemed like Chris was following in his mentor's footsteps.

Joseph sat up, getting ready to tell the DCI exactly where he could stuff his choice, when a knock sounded on the door.

They both turned to see Megan hovering there. Chris gestured for her to come in.

'We've just been going through any alerts on Donald Thackeray's name and we've got a match that I think we should investigate.'

'Which is?' Chris asked in a considerably calmer tone than he'd just been using with Joseph.

'It's over a month old, but there is a record of a Thackeray hiring a Mercedes SUV that is identical to his own car.'

'But why on earth would he do that?' Chris asked.

'No idea, sir,' Megan replied.

'Maybe he was worried about getting Zoe's DNA in his own car, which could link him to her killing,' Chris said.

'Although why he chose to use the same type of vehicle seems a bit odd.'

The DI knew he needed to play the game if he didn't want to get thrown off the case, especially when they were so close to getting to the bottom of it. Time to suck it up.

'Only one way to find out, sir. I'm quite happy to go and chat with the hire firm to see if they can cast any light on the matter. Maybe we should even impound the hire vehicle to run a thorough forensic sweep on it, just in case.'

'Now that I like the idea of.' The DCI aimed a penetrating stare at Joseph. 'It sounds to me like you still want to be on the team.'

Joseph sighed. 'Aye, it does, so we better get to it.'

The DCI nodded and with a dismissive gesture, pointed at the door.

Megan gave the DI a questioning look as they headed out of his office, tracked by nearly every set of eyes in the room beyond.

———

Joseph and Megan waited as the man behind the vehicle hire desk went through his records.

'Professor Donald Thackeray, wasn't it?' he asked.

'That's the one,' Joseph replied.

The man nodded and tapped a few more buttons. 'Yes, he was in here on 20th December, hiring a Mercedes SUV. According to our records, he still has it booked out until the 6th of Jan.'

'Do you have a credit card payment to confirm that?' Megan asked.

The guy squinted at his screen. 'Actually, according to the information here, he paid in cash.'

'Isn't that a bit unusual?'

'Off the record, not really, although normally it tends to be more your white van driver types, if you catch my drift.'

Joseph made a mental note to tip off their fraud division about that little bit of info and how some surveillance might throw up some interesting results from this particular establishment.

'Presumably, Mr Thackeray gave proof of identity?' Megan asked.

The man pulled a face. 'Of course.' He hit a key on the computer and a printer whirred into life. A moment later he handed them a piece of paper with a copy of Donald's driving licence and an electricity bill for his home.

'I don't suppose you have a photo ID as well, do you?' Megan asked.

'Not in terms of what Mr Thackeray supplied. However...' He pointed up to a small camera that Joseph hadn't noticed before tucked into the bookshelf behind the desk. 'We keep the footage in the back office. Just give me a moment and I can get the video for when he picked up the car.'

'That would be grand, thank you,' Joseph replied.

The man nodded and disappeared through a door.

'Are you still following through on a hunch about the professor being set up?' Megan asked.

'Have you ever heard the phrase, too good to be true?'

'Absolutely, especially when things have lined up just a bit too neatly like with Professor Thackeray.'

'Yes, things are decidedly odd, like the wife's testimony not supporting the idea of Donald being into the occult, let alone anything dodgier like sex clubs.'

'So, are you going to come out and say what we're both thinking?'

'He isn't our man,' Joseph said. 'But someone out there is pulling the strings to make it look like he is.'

Megan blew her cheeks out. 'I agree. But you're sure that we're not stretching things a bit?'

'We should know soon enough when we see the security camera footage.'

At that moment, the door opened again and the guy appeared with a memory stick in his hand. 'Here you go. Good footage of the professor.'

He slid it into the USB slot on his computer and a second later a video window opened on his screen, which he angled towards the detectives.

As the man pressed play, Joseph leant in. He felt a trickle of electricity running down his spine like he always did when he knew he was really onto something.

On the video a figure appeared, wearing a trench coat with the collar turned up. He approached the desk and even though he was wearing glasses and had grey hair, Joseph realised there was every chance that it could be a wig. Despite that, the DI still instantly recognised the man and everything suddenly fell into place.

'There you go, that's Professor Thackeray—I remember him now,' the man said. 'Very polite and even put a twenty-pound note in our charity box.' He gestured towards the red plastic box for a children's charity on the counter.

'That isn't Professor Donald Thackeray,' Megan said, staring at Joseph with wide eyes.

'Who the hell is it then?' the man asked.

'A guy called Aaron Fearnley,' Joseph replied, kicking himself for not seeing it before. 'Has that charity box been emptied since he put that twenty-pound note in it?'

The guy shook his head. 'I don't think so.'

'Good, then I'm going to need to take it for evidence to see if we can lift some prints off the note. And before you ask, don't worry, we'll get it back to you. I'll also need that video footage, too.'

'No problem, but bloody hell, this guy's involved in something dodgy, then?'

'Very dodgy,' Megan said.

'In that case, I'm just glad to be of help,' the man said, handing Joseph the memory stick as Megan picked up the charity box.

The moment they were outside, Megan turned to the DI. 'So you're saying the SUV we saw on the security footage that picked Zoe up was the one that Aaron hired from here, and fitted with false plates?'

'I think it has to be, Megan. For whatever reason, Aaron's been going around pretending to be Donald Thackeray. The question now is, has he been our real suspect all along?' Joseph shook his head, kicking himself for not figuring it out sooner. 'Let's call this in and then organise a search of Aaron's house.'

Megan gave him a wide smile.

'What?'

'Just, sometimes I wonder who's really running this investigation, you or Chris?'

'Let's keep him thinking that he is and everything will be grand.'

Megan laughed. 'Got it.' She took her phone from her pocket and dialled as they headed back to the car.

CHAPTER TWENTY-SIX

THE POLICE CARS and vans had parked up in the industrial estate so as to not tip off Aaron Fearnley that they were about to search his house. Joseph, Megan and the assembled team filed along the footpath that ran parallel to a school like a column of soldiers about to launch an attack, which in so many ways was exactly what they were about to do.

The team now stood around the corner from the shoebox of a maisonette house in West Street near the centre of Oxford. The house itself was immaculately well-kept, with a window box and a freshly painted front door. A bicycle was padlocked to a hoop mounted on the front wall, which hopefully meant their man was home.

Megan gestured at the street lined with more tiny houses. 'With all the money Aaron's made from that book of his, I would have thought we'd find him living somewhere posher than in a tiny house like this.'

'You really don't know Oxford, do you?' Chris replied as he adjusted the straps on his stab vest. 'Don't be deceived by the size because these properties around here easily sell for a price on its way to a million.'

Megan pulled a face. 'But that's ridiculous. I'd expect a small mansion for that sort of money.'

'That's Oxford prices for you.'

'Which is exactly why I have to rent, because I can't afford to do anything else in this city,' Megan said.

'Why do you think I live on a boat?' Joseph replied with a wry smile.

'I might have to look into that as an option.'

Chris's radio beeped, and he pressed its button. 'DCI Faulkner here.'

'All units are in position, sir,' a man's voice replied.

'Okay, let's do this,' Chris said.

A sergeant from the St Aldates station who was leading the raid nodded, as Joseph traded a look with Megan. A sense of anticipation began to build inside the DI as the sergeant walked quickly around the corner with another officer, carrying a stocky red battering ram.

Chris turned towards Megan and Joseph. 'Let's just hope we're not on a wild goose chase here.'

'You wouldn't have signed off on this if you didn't believe the latest evidence was too significant to ignore,' the DI replied.

Chris nodded. 'Thackeray certainly does seem to have disappeared off the face of the planet. According to local officers in the Lake District, he never turned up at that Airbnb. Still, until now, everything pointed towards the professor being our man.'

'It's exactly because the evidence is so neatly stacked against him that we should have been more suspicious,' Megan said.

Joseph felt a swell of pride at her for being so blunt with Chris. As long as the tarnish on him didn't rub off too much on her, the DI was increasingly certain she had a great future ahead of her on the force.

Chris scowled. 'We will soon see, won't we?'

As the DCI returned his attention to the armed officers who had moved into position, from the other side of the door, Joseph winked at Megan and she grinned back at him.

The sergeant gestured towards the officer with the battering ram, who swung it back and then drove it hard into the lock. With a loud crack, the red door splintered and smashed inward as its lock gave way, and the rest of the team swept into the house.

'Police!' one of them shouted out.

Chris, Megan and Joseph were hot on their heels and entered the house as two of the team rushed upstairs, shouting out another challenge. There was a crash of further doors and within twenty seconds, a silence descended over the house.

The sergeant approached the detectives. 'I'm afraid there's no one here.'

'Damn and blast it,' Chris muttered.

'But there's something in a backroom you're going to want to see. Follow me.'

With the sergeant leading the way, they followed him through to the front room, or parlour as Joseph's ma would have called it. As he'd half expected for someone who worked in a museum, the room was full of books. There were also plenty of etchings of naked women, some of which were pretty pornographic. But it was a copy of Aaron's occult book mounted in a gold leaf-covered box frame that took centre stage. However, the sergeant didn't stop there, but carried on through a doorway into a rear room.

The moment they entered it, they all came to a halt.

A large notice board took up an entire wall, and on it were numerous newspaper clippings about the murder of the goat at Laithwaite City Farm.

On a desk in front of it, apart from a computer, was what

looked like a 3D printer with a transparent orange Perspex box above it.

But Joseph's attention snapped back to the pinboard and specifically a photograph of Zoe, all smiles and blowing kisses at the camera. It was one that Ellie had once shown him on her Instagram feed. If only she'd realised the danger her friend had been in. Below that photo was one of the real Professor Thackeray

'Joseph, did you see this?' Megan said, pointing to the opposite end of the pinboard.

His gaze immediately zeroed in on a Post-it to the left of the board upon which had been written, *'And so it begins.'* Beneath that was another newspaper clipping that Joseph recognised, with a photo of a SUV. It was from an article about the accident sixteen years ago that had claimed the life of his son. The car had been his family's.

The DI felt a pulse of anger and clenched his fists.

'I'm so sorry, Joseph,' Chris said. 'It looks like your instinct was right, and this time we really have discovered the identity of the real Midwinter Butcher.'

'Aye, it looks that way,' the DI said, not feeling any joy for having been right. 'We better not disturb anything and call Amy and her team in. I think they're going to have a field day in here.'

Chris nodded, but Megan was looking at the machine on the desk. 'That's a 3D printer, and there's a memory stick still in the slot. Do you mind if I have a look at what Aaron's been printing in case it's relevant?'

'We should really wait for Amy,' Chris replied.

'Don't worry, I've got my latex gloves on so won't contaminate any prints.'

Chris frowned, but still nodded. 'Go ahead.'

Megan pressed some buttons on the control panel at the base of the machine.

'You actually look like you know what you're doing with that,' Joseph said.

'I have an older brother to thank for that. He's a designer and mucks around with these 3D printers all the time. It's incredible some of the things he's created with his.'

'So why does Aaron have one?' Chris asked.

Megan's eyes widened, and she pointed at the display on the machine that had just lit up. 'Because of that.'

Joseph squatted in front of the machine and found himself looking at a 3D model of a very familiar demon mask on the machine's display.

'Are you trying to tell me Aaron printed that damned masked himself?' Chris said.

'It certainly looks that way,' Joseph said. 'This is increasingly looking like an attempt by Aaron, to set Donald up by wearing the demon mask when he murdered his victims. But that also suggests that the professor really was a member of Lord Saxton's exclusive little club.'

Megan sighed. 'So Alice Thackeray really doesn't know her ex-husband as well as she thinks she does.'

'Okay, but why did Fearnley want to set up the professor at all?' Chris asked.

'Maybe he has a history with Thackeray and this was all some form of revenge,' Megan suggested.

Chris sucked the air between his teeth. 'Could be, but one thing's for sure, we'll need to run a deep check into Aaron Fearnley's background and quickly.'

'We have a much more urgent priority,' Joseph said. 'We now know Thackeray is missing, and if Aaron is trying to frame him as the Midwinter Butcher, he may be tidying up loose ends right now.'

Chris stared at him. 'You mean he's going to kill the professor, too?'

'Why not? He's obviously planned all of this meticulously, down to planting evidence at the professor's home and deliberately placing his DNA evidence at the crime scenes. My money is on Aaron having abducted Thackeray. I suggest that we run a trace on the number plate for the professor's car since we now know that Aaron has cloned the plates for it. If we find that, we find him.'

'I'll order a trace right away and issue a warrant for Fearnley's arrest,' Chris replied.

'Do it, because if we're not too late already, we're almost certainly Donald's last chance.'

Joseph was leaning against the Peugeot sipping a coffee that a friendly neighbour had furnished him with, watching the front door. Inside, Amy's team, with Megan in attendance, were conducting a thorough examination of the property. Chris had long since melted away, intending to coordinate the search for the vehicle that Aaron had hired, both with its original plates and the cloned ones from Thackeray's car.

Megan emerged from the house in a forensic suit and pulled off her face mask as she approached him.

'Has Amy's team turned up anything else?'

'Not as such, although she's hopeful about retrieving some data from his laptop.'

His phone pinged and Joseph looked at the screen to see it was a message from Chris. When he opened it, he saw a grey image of the Mercedes SUV driving through a set of lights. Then the DI's mobile rang, and he picked up.

'Hi, Joseph. The image I just sent through is the only hit we have on the professor's number plate,' Chris said.

'When was this captured?' Joseph asked, peering at it.

'Well, good news there. It was taken just a couple of hours ago at the bottom of George Street. After that, none of the cameras have picked the vehicle up again.'

'So, either Aaron has once again swapped the plates, or he's still somewhere in Oxford.'

'Exactly. I've organised roadblocks on all roads out of the city and also car-to-car searches, as well as concentrating foot patrols on the streets. If he's still here, it won't be long till we catch him.'

'I hope so, Chris.'

'Me too...' The DCI paused before speaking again. 'I just wanted to say I think I may have misjudged you, Joseph. In the future, I'm going to make a point of listening to you more than maybe I have in the past.'

'Good to know, and it turns out you're not too bad yourself.'

Chris chuckled at the other end of the line. 'Look, you've had a long day of it and I could do with you fighting fit for tomorrow, so why don't you take yourself off home and catch up on some sleep? I'll ring you if we get any strong leads.'

'That sounds like a great idea just now.'

'Good, then I'll see you in the morning.'

As the call clicked off, Megan arched an eyebrow at him.

'You heard most of that conversation then?' Joseph asked.

'Yes, I did, especially the bit about what amounts to high praise coming from Chris.'

Joseph smiled. 'I didn't dream that part then?'

'If you did, then I did too. Anyway, let's get you back home for some very well-earned rest.'

Joseph and Megan drove through the streets of Oxford, where barely anyone was out in the small hours, apart from a few lone taxi drivers ferrying drunks home from the clubs.

'I keep wondering why Aaron targeted Donald at all?' Megan said as she drove.

Joseph shrugged. 'Maybe because he thought he would be the perfect fall guy as he experiments on animals, so we might think that he would get his kicks killing them.' A thought occurred to him. 'You don't suppose it's worth checking his lab, in case we can find any leads there?'

'Surely it's closed during the Christmas holidays?' Megan replied

'But there's bound to be a security guard on site, no matter what time of year.'

Megan raised her shoulders. 'It's less than half a mile away and we could do worse than to swing past and check out the lab. But shouldn't we call it in first to Chris?'

'Not unless we find something. I don't want to break this winning streak that I seem to be on at the moment with the DCI.'

Megan nodded. 'Okay, you're the boss.'

A short time later, they pulled up outside the Kingston Research Lab, a reasonably nondescript modern building for Oxford, made out of polished granite blocks. It also had dark-tinted windows, none of which were at ground level, that accentuated its brooding presence in the street. Its solid grey metallic gates looked like the only way in.

'This place looks like a fortress,' Megan said as the detectives got out of the car.

'It needs to be because of animal rights protesters. Hence the lack of any signage about it being a lab. It's anonymous because they really don't want anyone to know what they get up to in there.'

Joseph scanned the street, and apart from a lone black BMW SUV parked up on the opposite side of the road, there was no one around.

'So how the hell do we get in?' Megan asked.

'We ring the doorbell, of course.'

He headed up to a steel doorway with a number pad next to it and an intercom mounted below that. The DI leant on the buzzer until a man's voice answered.

'Hi, how can I help you?'

'I'm Detective Inspector Joseph Stone and I'm with Detective Constable Megan Anderson. Do you know if Professor Thackeray happens to be working in the lab tonight?'

'First of all, I'm going to need to see some ID. Just hold them towards the camera above the panel.'

Both detectives held up their warrant cards.

'Thank you, and to answer your question, yes. I had to buzz him in earlier as he managed to forget his PIN for the car park gate.'

Megan's eyes widened.

'Was there anyone with him?' Joseph asked.

'Not that I could see.'

'Can you confirm if he's still in the lab now?'

'Let me just check the camera for the car park...'

Joseph held his breath.

'Yes, his SUV is there right next to the lab entrance. Would you like me to go and get him?'

'No, don't do that, we'll—'

The DI's response was cut off by a sharp scream, although muffled, coming from an upper-story window, the only lit one in the entire building.

'Oh shite!' Joseph said. 'Right, buzz us in now. Does the professor's lab happen to be on the third floor?'

'Yes, it is. Why, is there some sort of problem?'

'I'm afraid so, and get ready for half the Oxford police force to turn up here any moment. Now open this bloody gate.'

With a buzz, the door hinged backwards. Megan and Joseph ran through it as she radioed for backup, Joseph's heart thundering in his chest as they raced towards the door.

CHAPTER TWENTY-SEVEN

MEGAN AND JOSEPH tore up the stairs with the security guard who had joined them, a burly guy in his mid-thirties. The DI had so much adrenaline surging through his system that he had a metallic tang in his mouth.

They reached the landing where they found a door propped open with a fire extinguisher. A muffled whimpering was coming from the room beyond.

'Do we wait for backup?' Megan asked as they took up positions on either side of the door.

Joseph gave a sharp headshake. 'It could be too late by then, and for the moment at least, we can hear someone alive in there.' The DI took a deep breath, his grip growing clammy on his baton. He kicked the door hard, and it flew open.

The DI led the way with his baton ready to swing into whatever skull he had to. The two detectives rushed into a large open-plan office, computer screens glowing in the dark. But as soon Joseph entered he spotted a grey-haired man slumped in a chair that he'd been tied to. Bright red slits had been sliced into his wrists and blood was running down his fingers and dripping onto the floor to form glistening pools of red.

The guard stumbled to a stop behind them, as Joseph and Megan rushed to help the man.

The DI knelt before the man, immediately applying pressure to the two open slits, but the blood still bubbled up between his fingers. Megan had dashed to a first aid cabinet, yanked it open and grabbed several lengths of bandages, before rushing back.

'Let me take over,' she said.

But the moment Joseph withdrew his hand, the man's blood started pumping faster again. Megan was already wrapping the bandages around his wrists.

'Ring for a bloody ambulance,' Joseph shouted at the guard who was just standing there, gawping at them.

The guard blinked and then pulled a phone from his pocket and began to dial.

For the first time, Joseph looked up into the man's face to find himself staring at Professor Donald Thackeray, who had his eyes shut. Joseph immediately pressed his finger to his neck, and relief swept through him when he felt a pulse, faint but still there.

Joseph took hold of the man's shoulders and gently shook him as Megan finished tying off the bandages. 'Donald, can you hear me?'

The professor slowly cracked his eyes open as his gaze focused on his face.

'They...attacked...me,' he said, his voice trembling.

'They?' Joseph exchanged a startled look with Megan.

'Was Aaron Fearnley one of them?' she asked.

'Don't know...names, but were wearing forensic suits. Attacked me at home...drugged me, brought me here.'

'Okay, we understand. Help is on the way, but you need to hang in there,' Megan said.

'Doing...my...best.'

Joseph glanced around the bright white room, but there wasn't a shadow to hide in. There was a door at the far end though.

'The man who did this to you, where is he now, Donald?'

But the professor's eyes had closed again.

'No, stay with me. Fight this, man, fight it with everything you've got.'

His eyes fluttered open as Megan shot the DI a grim look.

Donald stared at him. 'One is still here... He was putting a letter on a desk over there. He rushed off into the lab when he heard you coming.'

Scanning the desks, Joseph soon saw the letter with *I'm sorry* written on it.

Joseph turned to the security guard, who was ashen-faced as he stared at the blood on the floor. 'Where is the lab?'

The man raised his gaze. 'Just through that door, at the back of the room.'

'Okay, you stay with the professor and do everything you can to keep him alive till the ambulance gets here. Raising his arms above his head would help.'

The guard nodded and, although he paled even more as he approached the blood-soaked professor, to his credit, he squatted by him and placed a hand on Donald's shoulder and started talking to him to keep him awake.

'Right, Megan, you're with me,' Joseph said,

She wiped the back of her hand across her brow, leaving a trace of blood. 'Let's do this.'

They were about to head off when his mobile rang and the screen displayed Kate's name.

Joseph hit the call accept button.

'Oh, thank God, you picked up,' Kate immediately said. 'Ellie's been taken.'

'What? How? I thought John was guarding the house?'

'He was, but when I got back just now, I found him knocked out, and the front door was wide open.' A note of hysteria crept into Kate's voice. 'There's no sign of Ellie, and there was a struggle, as the hallway table has been knocked over.'

Joseph's blood turned to ice as his darkest nightmare came true. 'Have you called Derek?'

'Already done, but he said that you might be closer to the suspect?'

'It's complicated, but yes.'

'Then go and stop him, whatever it takes, Joseph, before he has a chance to harm our daughter.'

'Leave it to me,' the DI said, ending the call. 'Come on Megan. Aaron, and whoever his accomplice is, have abducted my daughter and if it wasn't already before, it's bloody personal now.'

They ran together towards the lab door. The DI's heart was thumping hard in his chest. What if they were too late and Aaron or his accomplice had already murdered Ellie before heading over to the lab with Donald?

Nausea swirled through Joseph's gut at the very thought. He tried to push the thought away as, batons drawn, the two detectives headed through the door into a blindingly white lab. Animal cages lined the wall and immediately a cacophony of monkeys started crying out and rattling their cages.

Joseph could immediately see the parts of the puzzle slotting together in his mind. This was where Zoe had once worked, and was probably one of Donald's assistants. What better way to set up a perfect false trail of breadcrumbs in order to frame the professor for her murder, than to stage his own suicide here when he hadn't been able to handle the guilt?

The DI's eyes darted around the room, but there was no sign of anyone here either, although there was a pile of metal boxes visible through a partly ajar door at the far end. The perfect hiding place.

Joseph leant in towards Megan. 'Just follow my lead,' he whispered.

The DC nodded, gripping her baton tighter.

He cleared his throat. 'Armed police, come out with your hands up.'

Megan gave him a surprised look, and Joseph just shrugged as he took up a position to the side of the door, ready to slam his baton down onto the man's head the moment he appeared. Megan stood to the other side, baton also raised, ready to strike.

Even though they were both ready, the demon masked man still managed to catch them both by surprise. The door was shoved open hard, and it swung into Joseph, knocking him to the ground. In that split second, the man in the forensic suit erupted from the gap with a metal cylinder in his hand. He slammed hard into Megan's midriff like a rugby player, toppling her backwards and slamming her head against the edge of the desk. As he jumped back to his feet, Megan collapsed to the floor, her eyes closing. However, she also had the man's demon mask in her hand. She'd managed to tear it off to reveal Aaron's face, his eyes wild.

The man swerved away, heading towards the door to the accompaniment of the monkeys howling at him.

Joseph scrambled to his own feet and raced to Megan. Her eyelids fluttered open as he grabbed her shoulders.

'Fuck, that hurts like hell, but I'm okay.' She tried to stand, but slouched down again.

'Don't try to move,' the DI said.

She nodded and grimaced as she clutched the back of her head. 'Just get the bastard for me.'

'Oh, don't you worry, I intend to.'

The DI jumped back to his feet and raced after the man

who'd already disappeared out of the door. Joseph reached the stairwell just in time to hear a door below slamming shut.

Joseph ran down the stairs two steps at a time, skidded onto the landing and hurtled towards the door. He thumped the release button, his body slamming into the door as he charged through. As the detective emerged from the research lab, he spotted Aaron. He had jumped onto a tree planter and was leaning across, trying to grab hold of the top of the gate as the sound of sirens in the distance grew louder.

The detective rushed after Aaron as he clambered over the gate and disappeared over the other side. Adrenaline was well and truly powering Joseph's system now and the detective followed the man's route, up and over. Whatever Joseph did, he couldn't lose Aaron, as he and his accomplice had Ellie, and there still might be a faint chance she was alive.

Joseph dropped down the other side just as the man raced towards the parked BMW on the other side of the road.

Shite, his accomplice is already back in a getaway car, Joseph thought to himself.

Fists pumping the air, the DI raced after Aaron, but the guy had too much of a head start. There was no way that Joseph could catch up with him before he reached his car.

Then everything changed in a heartbeat.

The headlights of the parked BMW blazed into life. Wheels scrabbling for grip, the car shot forward straight towards Aaron as he waved his arms at it. As the BMW closed the distance at a shocking speed, Joseph suddenly realised that the driver wasn't slowing.

Aaron let out a guttural yell as, too late, he tried to jump out of the vehicle's way. With a sickening *thunk* and the crunching of breaking bone, the BMW crashed into him, sending him flying up over the bonnet and into the passenger side of the windscreen, cracking it.

As Aaron tumbled away onto the ground, the car swerved towards Joseph.

The DI just had time to leap aside as the vehicle skimmed past. Pure experience kicked in and somehow despite almost being killed, he managed to keep it together. The detective immediately pulled out his phone just in time to snap the BMW number plate as it sped around the corner.

Then Joseph raced over to Aaron, who was lying on the ground, his legs bending the wrong way from his body. His forensic suit was ripped open at the chest to reveal the Eye of Horus amulet lying on his chest. The good the charm's supposed protection had done to save the man.

Aaron looked up at Joseph as blood dribbled from his gaping mouth. He took a gurgling breath and tried to say something.

Joseph leaned down. 'Who did this to you?'

'She killed all the others and she'll kill Ellie now,' Aaron whispered, his voice fading fast.

The DI grabbed his shoulders. 'Where?'

'Pitt Rivers. Basement in a storage room. Please know the deer was—' A gasp cut off the rest of Aaron's words and, with a rattling breath, his eyes rolled up into his head. Joseph immediately checked for a pulse, but found none.

The detective sat back on his haunches, his mind already racing. He had to find Aaron's female accomplice and get to Ellie before it was too late. But he also wouldn't make it on time on foot to the museum, as Aaron's accomplice already had a serious head start.

It was as Joseph stood that he spotted Megan's Peugeot still parked outside the lab.

Without even thinking, he raced back to it, opened the door, and jumped into the driver's seat.

Keys!

With a tsunami of relief, Joseph saw that in their haste to get into the lab, Megan had forgotten to remove the keys from the ignition.

Oh, you little beauty. Normally, of course, he would have had to have a serious word with the DC about being so careless, but not today.

With a slight tremble in his hand, Joseph turned the key and the car's engine rumbled to life. His palms were already clammy again, a sick feeling swirling through his stomach, as he put the Peugeot into first gear.

You can do this, Joseph. You have to, for the sake of your daughter.

A grim determination took hold, and he floored the accelerator. The engine roared almost as loud as his heart as he sped away down the road in the vehicle, heading towards the museum. In his rear-view mirror, he spotted two police cars and an ambulance racing towards the lab and coming to a sharp stop outside it.

Maybe they could still save the professor, but there was another soul Joseph was focused on saving.

I'm coming for you, Ellie...

CHAPTER TWENTY-EIGHT

As HIS FEAR for Ellie spun round Joseph's mind, he skidded the Peugeot to a stop in front of the entrance to the Natural History Museum. There was no sign of the BMW anywhere.

Shite!

The detective's eyes tore to the satnav map. There was a small service road that the Pitt Rivers Collection backed up to at the rear. Aaron's female accomplice would want the car as close as possible, so if she really was about to execute Ellie, she could make a speedy getaway. The one thing playing in his favour was that she wouldn't know that Aaron had told Joseph where to find her, and he needed to play that to his advantage.

Joseph shoved the car back into gear and moments later he was speeding down a narrow lane between the buildings, doing his best to avoid the bins scattered along either side of it.

Then he saw it, the black BMW dead ahead and parked next to an open door.

As the detective parked up behind the other vehicle, his mobile rang.

'Where the hell are you, Joseph?' Chris said the moment the call connected.

'I've pursued a second accomplice to the Pitt Rivers Museum. Aaron told me that whoever the woman is, she is the real murderer. Now she's come to the museum to kill Ellie in the basement where she's being held captive.'

'Bloody hell, I can see your location from your phone's signal. I'll be there with backup as soon as possible.'

'I can't wait for you, Chris. I have to get in there now before it's too late. Just hurry.'

'Joseph—'

The DI hit the end-call button before the DCI could talk him down off the ledge. He pocketed the phone and raced through the door into a darkened corridor. There was a door opened at the end where a faint light was coming from.

Joseph headed towards it, gathering himself for what he was about to get himself into. He hadn't been able to save Eoin sixteen years ago, but he'd be damned, whatever the cost, if he wouldn't save his daughter this time around. Ellie was the only remaining light in his life. If she was extinguished, then his life would be over, too.

A short time later Joseph was walking out into the Pitt Rivers main exhibition hall. Only dim lighting illuminated the space, reducing the display cases to a collection of glass cabinets with nothing but shadows inside. His footsteps seemed impossibly loud in the darkness as he headed through it.

Joseph took a deep centring breath. Going in alone was always going to be dangerous, but he had no choice.

It was only then that the detective realised the distinct lack of an alarm screeching that should have been triggered by the rear door to the museum being opened. The woman must have had time to deactivate it. But how? It was almost like she had an intimate knowledge of the museum to even gain access to the building at all. Maybe a colleague of Aaron's? If so, what had happened to the guard who should have been patrolling? Had she already murdered them, too? The only positive out of that grim line of thinking is that it would have slowed her down, so there was a chance that he could still save his daughter.

The detective needed to think fast, because there was no obvious direction that the woman had gone in. Aaron had told Joseph before he'd died that Ellie was being held in a storage room, in the basement of Pitt Rivers. Also, when he and Megan had first met Aaron, the museum curator had taken them to a subterranean meeting room somewhere roughly beneath where the detective was standing now. The DI vaguely recollected dozens of other doors down there, too. The most likely thing was that behind one of them was where Ellie was now being held. But also, of course, it being Boxing Day meant the museum wasn't open, so there was even less danger of Aaron's accomplice being disturbed.

Joseph set off at a run to the door in the corner that Aaron had taken them through before, leading to the stairwell. He rushed through the glass doors and down the steps two at a time. The blood pounded in his ears, as his imagination filled in what he might be about to discover with gruesome details that made his stomach muscles clench.

The detective reached the bottom of the stairwell and raced along the corridor, flinging open doors as he went, including that to the meeting room where they had first spoken with Aaron, but all were empty.

Where are you, my beautiful lass?

Then at the end, Joseph at last spotted a door that hadn't quite latched properly. A few moments later, he headed through it to find himself on a set of metal steps leading down into the bowels of the museum.

The DI slowly descended the stairs, baton ready, his mouth going dry. If that woman had harmed a single hair on Ellie's head, God help him, he wouldn't be responsible for his actions.

Pipes ran along the ceiling towards a large industrial-sized boiler at the far end of the corridor. The DI began to walk along it, and spotted a door to one side that was slightly ajar. His heart leapt as he heard Ellie's muffled voice coming from the room beyond.

She's still alive!

His daughter's words were inaudible, but her tone was growing increasingly agitated by the second.

Joseph crept as silently as he could towards the door, his baton greasy in his hand. He had to maximise the element of surprise so the woman didn't have a chance to use his daughter as a hostage.

He reached the door and peered through the crack in the doorway to see Ellie tied to a chair, a gag in her mouth. Behind her was a large symbol for Azrael, daubed on the wall with what looked suspiciously like blood. The final sacrifice, dreamt up by the twisted mind of a psychopath, to gain her god's approval? Or was this simply the woman tying up loose ends?

Although Joseph still couldn't see Ellie's captor, he could see his daughter watching someone with wide eyes as they moved around the room, screened from his view by the door. He finally caught sight of a gloved hand and a white sleeve of a forensic suit, as the woman reached forward and lit two candles that had been placed at either end of a table. But it was the other objects that chilled his blood to the core of his being. There was a fine-toothed steel bone saw, and an ornately designed stiletto dagger. That had to be the murder weapon that Aaron's accomplice had used to kill Charlie and Zoe.

Bile filled the back of Joseph's throat. Everything about this had the feel of a makeshift temple, with the table as the altar that Ellie was about to be sacrificed upon.

'It will make it so much easier on you, if you drink this first,' a woman's voice said.

Joseph had heard that voice somewhere before, recently too, but for now he couldn't place it. Then a goblet was placed on the table before his daughter.

'I'm going to take your gag off so you can drink, but there's no point in screaming for help because there's no one to hear you,' the woman continued, as she moved behind Ellie, her face hidden behind a demon mask. Then she ran her fingers through Ellie's dark hair.

'Such a waste of a pretty thing. Not that I was ever going to let you live as I have a god whose approval I need and they need your blood.'

Ellie jerked her head away from the woman's touch. Her eyes snagged on Joseph's, peering through the crack in the door at her, and she stiffened.

It was all the warning the woman needed, as her own gaze tore towards the door.

Joseph leapt immediately into action. It might be his only chance.

But even as the DI crashed through the door, in a lightning move, the woman had already snatched the stiletto dagger from the table and was now standing behind Ellie, holding the blade to his daughter's throat.

'Take one more step, and so help me, I'll slit her throat from ear to ear in front of you,' the woman shouted.

Joseph froze as Ellie desperately tried to break free of her bonds. The woman pressed the blade tighter against her throat.

'It would be better for your health if you didn't struggle,' the woman said.

Joseph held out a hand and gestured for his daughter to calm down. 'Do what she says, Ellie.'

Ellie's gaze clung to his as she stilled again.

'See, that's much better,' the woman said, with something that bordered on amusement.

The sick fecker is enjoying herself! Joseph thought to himself.

He tightened his grip on his baton, desperate to drive it into the woman's skull. 'So what happens now?'

'Well, if you want your daughter to live, I'm going to head out of here with her, and you're going to let me.'

'We both know I can't let you do that.'

'Can't you? Are you really sure about that, Inspector? Surely, losing a son was bad enough, but losing a daughter too would be downright careless.'

He glared at her. 'You killed my boy?'

'No, that was all Aaron's doing, albeit an accident when he sacrificed the deer to satisfy an itch. He told me all about it on the dark web chat forum where I found him. For what it's worth, he was mortified by that.'

The detective thought about Aaron's last words, *Please know the deer was—*

He glowered at the masked woman. 'So you were responsible for all the murders?'

'I suppose it doesn't matter if you know now, as I'm simply going to disappear after this and you'll never be able to find me when I adopt another assumed identity. But yes, Aaron just didn't have the stomach for any of that. Animals, yes, but people, no. He couldn't bring himself to step up his game to human sacrifice, the big baby. So I had to step in and handle it myself.'

'Which included sacrificing Charlie and Zoe?' Joseph asked.

'Well, Zoe's murder was a planned one during the full moon over the Hawk Stone.'

'But why her?'

'Because there was a beautiful symmetry to all of this, Inspector. When Aaron ran into Ellie at Laithwaite Farm, somewhere I told him to target because she worked there, that was what actually put the idea into my head that your daughter could be one of our sacrifices. In many ways it felt like destiny coming full circle after Aaron killed your son by accident all those years ago. So what better way to complete that circle than by him also killing your daughter. Then when I started to do some research, I quickly discovered that Ellie's best friend, Zoe, worked at a lab where there was animal testing. An idea began to hatch when I began following her and quickly discovered she was dating the professor, who also took her to Lord Saxton's sex parties. Once I knew that, I realised the little slut had it coming and deserved to be killed. Anyway, that gave Aaron and me the perfect way to frame Donald as an animal killer and sex pervert, who had taken Zoe's life. Then he would take his own life in an extreme fit of guilt, his suicide letter ready to be found at the lab. I even got Aaron to plant the idea in your minds that someone who worked in an animal research lab might be responsible. Wheels within wheels. The only tricky thing was that Aaron needed to pretend to be Donald by picking Zoe up that night from her house whilst wearing a demon mask so she wouldn't recognise him. But Aaron played his part well and he successfully lured Zoe to the Hawk Stone, where I took considerable delight in killing her and then sawing her head off. But tonight, right at the last hurdle, all Aaron had to do was get out of the lab without being spotted, but he couldn't get that simple thing right.'

Joseph glared at her, realising just how calculating the bitch standing before him was.

'So why kill Aaron, too?' the DI asked, as Ellie stared at him with shocked eyes.

'That was always my fallback plan if the police ever realised that Professor Thackeray was actually innocent. Then everything would point towards Aaron being found guilty of being the one and only Midwinter Butcher, especially when traces of your daughter's blood would be found here in the museum once I tipped the police off. Of course, I had forged a confession in his handwriting, saying Aaron was responsible for everything. However, when you clocked him and chased him from the lab, I needed to take Aaron out before he could tell you all my dirty little secrets and spoil the grand finale of my plan. So to cover my tracks as your daughter spotted me without a mask when she managed to rip it from my face, I still needed to murder her. Do that and then I could melt away into the shadows and start my fun all over again in another city. Anyway, that's all the information I'm going to give you, as it's time for me to make a move.'

Joseph was acutely aware of the time ticking past. He resisted the temptation to glance back at the door. How long would it take Chris and the reinforcements to get here? Maybe if he could keep this woman talking just a few moments longer...

The detective peered at the woman. 'So what about Charlie?'

'Oh, you mean the homeless guy. Wrong place, wrong time. Thankfully, I was with Aaron finishing the scapegoat ritual, when he stumbled across us. Aaron would have just let the old man go, of course, but the guy had seen us. That would've blown the whole cover story apart as had he lived then the police would have been looking for two people, not just one. After that, I really didn't have any choice. Besides homeless people like that old man are the scum of the earth, parasites who just need to be exterminated. I did the world a favour. Anyway, you should have seen the way his dog tried to protect its master until I kicked him aside. It was tragically heroic.'

Joseph felt a cold fury burning inside him. He'd dealt with his fair share of killers in his time, but this woman, apart from being a twisted psychopath, almost seemed like she was actually boasting about what she had done.

'Anyway, that's as much as I'm going to say,' she continued.

'Can't make life too easy for you with your investigation. So...' Then, still holding the dagger to Ellie's throat, she unbound his daughter from the chair, and made her stand. The woman went to move towards the door with Ellie, but Joseph immediately stood in her path.

The woman glowered at the detective through the eyeholes of her demon mask. 'Just let me go and I will release your daughter the moment I'm out of the museum. How does that sound, Joseph?'

So, she knew his name. For a psychopath who planned everything so meticulously, of course she did.

'That isn't going to happen,' Joseph replied in a cold tone.

'You really believe that?' The woman pressed the blade hard enough into Ellie's throat to open up a small cut, which immediately bled.

His daughter panted hard against her gag, her eyes wild.

Joseph held up his hands. 'Okay, I get the bloody message. But why do any of this?'

The woman shrugged. 'Why not? I love killing things, always have, and Aaron's whole thing with the occult really turned me on and was a new angle for my own interest in the subject. Anyway, that's the end of our cosy little chat. Now, you're going to let me walk out of here, Detective.'

Joseph raised his hands. 'Then let's take this nice and slow.'

'That's the attitude,' the woman said. 'Out of my way, and don't even think about trying anything, or I won't hesitate to kill your daughter, and oh, how tragic that would be.'

Joseph slowly did as he was told and stepped aside. 'It will be alright, Ellie,' he said as his daughter's gaze clung to his.

'Maybe it will, or maybe it won't, it's all down to you now,' the woman said. 'Okay, Joseph, back up to the wall and don't get any ideas about being a hero or things could get messy for everyone. And none of us want that, do we, sweet man?'

The DI stared at the woman as she edged towards the door with his daughter, the blade pressed into her neck. Damned if he tried, and damned if he didn't. Joseph weighed everything up in a fraction of a second, but it was the instinct of a father who had to protect his daughter that overrode everything else. He was getting ready to leap at the woman and knock the knife from her hand when Ellie acted first.

With a driving backward blow, his daughter stamped her heel hard into the woman's shin. At the same moment, her hands now free, Ellie spun around and drove her arms upwards and then outwards in a move designed to break an opponent's hold from around one's neck—a move that Joseph had taught her when she'd been only twelve.

Everything after that happened in the blink of an eye. Joseph grabbed Ellie and pushed her behind him as his daughter tore the gag from her mouth. Snarling, teeth bared, the woman regained her balance and lunged at the detective, dagger raised. As she tried to drive the thin, spike-like blade towards the DI's chest, he just managed to grab hold of her wrist.

As they desperately grappled, Joseph kicked out hard into the woman's knee, making her leg fold. As the woman collapsed, he tried to hang onto her dagger hand, but she yanked her hand free, before she tumbled away and landed face down on the floor, with a sickening crunch of bone.

The DI got ready to pin her down, but the woman jerked violently before she stilled.

'Dad?' Ellie said with a strained voice as she peered down at her.

Joseph crouched and rolled the woman over. Ellie gasped as they both saw what had happened. The woman had fallen onto her own dagger, the pommel striking the floor first, and driving it backwards into her chest.

As they stared at the dead woman, her breathing having

stilled with a final gasp, they heard running footsteps rapidly approaching.

'Where are you?' Chris shouted from the corridor outside.

'Here!' Joseph called back.

A few seconds later, Chris and two armed officers charged into the room.

'Are you both okay?' the DCI asked, his face pale as Ellie turned and threw her arms around Joseph.

'We are thanks to my rather bloody amazing daughter,' the DI said as he hung onto his daughter, kissing the side of her head.

Ellie swallowed hard and her eyes met his. 'You're not too shabby yourself, Dad.'

One officer was already kneeling by the woman, checking for a pulse in her neck. Then he rested back onto his haunches as he looked up at them and shook his head.

'So who the hell is this?' Chris asked.

Suddenly Joseph knew, finally able to place the voice. He broke away from Ellie, and knelt by the dead woman, pulling the mask from her face.

'Her name's Helen and she works here in the museum,' he said as he closed her eyelids.

'So, she knew Aaron, then?' Chris asked.

'She was his work colleague and also his accomplice, but she took credit for the actual murders themselves. She just told us that Aaron didn't have the stomach for it.' Joseph looked at the occult symbols on the wall. 'It seems Azrael ended up getting his sacrifice from her tonight, after all. Although, perhaps not Helen's first choice.'

Ellie looked down at the dead woman and shuddered.

'Yes, I know, lass,' Joseph said as he wrapped his arm around her shoulders. 'Time to get out of here.'

Chris nodded to the DI as he passed him, leading his daughter away from the place where she'd so nearly lost her life.

Joseph sat in the back of an ambulance as Ellie's shallow throat wound was dabbed with antiseptic by the female paramedic.

'Ow, that really stings,' his daughter said, pulling away.

'If you stop squirming, this might go a little faster,' the woman replied, her tone brisk.

'Sorry, doing my best here,' Ellie said, a bit more contritely.

He shook his head at her. 'They say that doctors make the worst patient, but maybe daughters of policemen are going to have to be added to that list, too.'

Ellie managed a smile, but grimaced as the woman used a stitch bandage to pull the sides of the cut together. Then her gaze locked onto something beyond his shoulder and Joseph turned to see a body bag being loaded into another ambulance.

Ellie grimaced.

The DI reached out and squeezed her shoulder. 'I know. I wish you didn't have to witness any of that. But I'm very proud of the way you dealt with Helen.'

'It seems not taking any *shite* runs in our family.'

Joseph managed a soft chuckle. 'Isn't that the truth.'

Ellie nodded, but then she narrowed her gaze at him. 'What's this I hear about you driving over here in a police vehicle? Since when have you started doing cars again, Dad?'

'Since your life was on the line. The only thing that mattered was getting here in time to rescue you; my phobia of driving be damned.'

His daughter nodded as another unmarked police vehicle joined the dozen that had already arrived. Megan got out of the passenger seat and headed over.

'Bloody hell, you're a sight for sore eyes,' she said as she reached them.

Joseph examined the bandage wrapped around her head. 'You too. How's your injury?'

'Thankfully superficial, although I may have a decent scar beneath my hairline.'

'Shouldn't you get it stitched?'

'Later, I just wanted to check you were both okay,' she said, turning towards his daughter.

'Sorry, Dad's rubbish at making introductions, and you are?' Ellie held out a hand.

'DC Anderson, but to you, Megan,' she said, shaking the offered hand.

They all heard a car approaching at high speed and turned to see an old battered Porsche coming to a screeching stop outside the museum. Kate jumped out, and spotting the group, rushed straight over as Joseph headed out to intercept her.

'Please tell me that Ellie is alright,' Kate said the moment she reached him.

'Relax, she's fine,' Joseph replied, gesturing towards the ambulance behind him.

Kate's eyes widened as she saw Ellie climb out of the vehicle, her throat now bandaged. In three strides, Kate had rushed up to their daughter and enveloped her in her arms, sobbing.

'Maybe you better get involved with that reunion, too, Joseph?' Megan said as she joined him.

'Aye, maybe I should.'

He gazed at the young DC for a moment. Yes, she had acquitted herself very well on this case. Whilst his stock was still riding high with Chris, he would make sure she stayed working with him from now on. He had to admit he rather enjoyed working with a partner again, especially when they were so capable and had such a sharp mind.

'What?' Megan asked, looking back at Joseph.

'I was just thinking about how well you've done.'

She beamed at him. 'Thank you, and you're not too shabby yourself.'

Chuckling, Joseph patted her on the shoulder as he turned away to join his family.

NEW YEAR'S DAY

CHAPTER TWENTY-NINE

'A MEMORIAL BARBECUE is a new one on me,' Joseph said, sipping the very large G&T Dylan had poured for him, as he sat next to Ellie on the roof of his boat.

Dylan flapped away the cloud of smoke currently enshrouding him like some sort of ethereal apparition, as White Fang watched and licked his lips. 'Personally, I think it's a great idea,' the professor said.

She beamed at him as she dangled her feet over the side, drumming her heels gently on the side of Tús Nua. 'I know for a fact that Zoe would have loved it.' Then she shivered in the wind that had an edge to it, sharp enough to cut glass.

Joseph slipped off his coat and gave it to her.

With a grateful smile, Ellie wrapped it tight around her shoulders. 'I just wish it was a little warmer for this.'

'You mean, break the tradition of alfresco dining in perishing weather in this country?' Dylan said. 'I don't think so.'

Ellie laughed, but then looked down at her pendant with its reunited black and silver cats. 'I meant to say, Dad, thank you so much for persuading Derek that the police no longer needed this for evidence.'

'It wasn't a problem. Amy and her team already had a mountain of material from the crime scenes along with evidence from Aaron's house. Besides, it's not like there's going to be a court case when both suspects are dead.'

'I've been meaning to ask you about that. Have you been able to find out anything more about why Helen was as crazy as she was?'

'Strictly off the record, Amy's team contacted the internet providers who logged all the IP addresses for any websites that Aaron's laptop had accessed over the last twelve months. One site on the dark web immediately threw up a red flag.'

'Which one exactly?' Dylan said.

'Once again, in complete and utter confidence, Aaron hung out on some pretty dodgy forums. It was on one of those that he was contacted three months ago by a user called *Melpomene*.'

'The Greek muse of tragedy,' Dylan said.

'Exactly, and we now believe that Melpomene was Helen. The problem is, because we're talking the dark web here, there's no way to confirm any of it. Anyway, Amy had someone on her team infiltrate the message boards that Aaron used, with login details and a password that Aaron wrote down in a notebook— God bless him—it turns out there are several groups dedicated to the occult and even satanism on there. Aaron had probably been swapping animal murder ritual notes on there when he was first approached by Helen, who had taken her love of the occult way further than he ever had.'

'Are there any other leads?' Ellie asked.

'Well, there's plenty of evidence at Aaron's flat directly linking him to all the animal killings. It turns out that he borrowed the murder weapon from one of the display cases at the Pitt Rivers Museum. At the time, it didn't raise any red flags as it was a ritualistic dagger, well within his area of witchcraft and occult expertise. It was only when we approached them that they realised the likely significance and drew our attention to it.'

'What a great place to hide a murder weapon in a museum on open display in a case in plain sight of everyone,' Megan said as she appeared behind them on the towpath with a bottle of champagne. She gave Joseph a pointed look. 'Discussing the case with civilians, are we?'

He waved a dismissive hand at her. 'You must have been hearing things. Anyway, it's about time you turned up. We started half an hour ago.'

'Oh, I'm an old hand when it comes to barbecues,' Megan said, boarding the boat. 'People always light them thirty minutes too late.'

Dylan smiled at her as he took the bottle and stuck it in a bucket of ice. 'You have a wise partner in crime-busting.'

Joseph snorted. 'Aye, it would seem that I have.'

'Just as well, as somebody needs to keep you in check,' Megan replied. 'Anyway, I thought you'd like to know that I bring news about Professor Thackeray. He's just been discharged from the hospital.'

'That's great to hear and, in no small part, down to your swift actions, Megan.'

'I'm just pleased I could put my basic medical training to some use.'

'You do realise that you're in danger of being named employee of the month by Chris?'

Megan shrugged. 'That may be true, but we both know it should be you.'

'Nah, I haven't anywhere to put a trophy on my boat.'

'There's a trophy?'

Joseph gave her a wide grin.

'That will be the famous Stone humour I've heard so much about,' Megan said.

'What can I say? I like to hide my comedy gold away, so I don't dazzle you all too much.'

Megan laughed as she turned to Ellie. 'But seriously, your dad is one in a million.'

'Don't I know it,' Ellie said as she hugged him.

Joseph kissed the side of her head. 'You're not so bad your-self, kiddo.'

Dylan was smiling at the two of them as he turned over the ribs that he'd been cooking. 'Okay, these look done to perfection. I hope you're all hungry as we have an awful lot of food to get through.'

'Like a horse,' Megan said.

It was then that they heard a bark and turned to see Amy heading towards them with a dog on a lead.

She waved to them as she approached. 'I'm not too late, am I?'

'No, we're just about to serve up, so perfect timing,' Joseph said. 'Hang on, isn't that Max, Charlie's dog?'

'It is indeed,' Dylan said, stepping off the boat he knelt before the dog. White Fang joined him in greeting the new arrivals.

Amy handed the lead over to the professor. 'The vet says Max has made a complete recovery and is ready for his new foster home.'

Joseph looked between them. 'You're taking Max on, Dylan?'

'Of course I am. It's what Charlie would have wanted, and White Fang will enjoy the company.'

His dog didn't respond with a bark to agree, but only because he was too busy smelling Max's arse, and vice versa, in the dog equivalent of a handshake.

Amy discreetly gestured for Joseph to follow her. A few moments later, they had headed a short distance from the boat.

'What is it?' Joseph asked the moment they were out of earshot of the others.

'Just an interesting little titbit of information that needs to stay between us.'

'Okay, I'm all ears.'

'I've found out exactly why our DSU was keen on not digging too far into the membership list for the Asmodeus club.'

Joseph stared at her. 'You're not going to tell me that Derek Walker is a bloody member, are you?'

'No. But he did confide, if only to stop me from digging any further, that some highly influential people are on that list, including some very senior officers on the force.'

Joseph gawped at her. 'You're telling me it's the sex equivalent of a masonic lodge?'

She laughed. 'Now there's a description that I'm not going to forget in a hurry. But to answer your question, maybe. Certainly, that membership includes people with plenty of money and power, probably using their influence to help each other.'

He shook his head. 'The same old, in other words. But there is one thing I still can't get straight in my head. Is Professor Thackeray really a member?'

'Let's just say that Donald isn't quite as boring as his ex-wife thinks he is. Anyway, that meat smells absolutely delicious and I'm famished.'

'Then no more talking shop; let's go and feed our faces.'

When they headed back to the boat, Ellie was holding a glass of champagne out to each of them. 'I just wanted to say something to everyone,' she said.

'Knock yourself out, kiddo,' Joseph replied with a smile.

Ellie nodded, twiddling the cat necklace between her fingers as she looked at all of them. 'Okay, before we all tuck into the feast that Dylan prepared for us, I'd just like to propose a toast to Zoe. She was one of the most alive people that I've ever met.' She looked up at the ribbons of blue sky just visible between the rolling grey clouds. 'And if you're up there, Zoe, I hope you're still seriously partying.' She raised her glass. 'To Zoe.'

'To Zoe,' they all repeated, clinking their glasses.

Joseph gazed at his daughter with enough love fit to burst. She had gone through a lot, they all had, but here she was, having lived through it, still smiling. The one thing he knew was that he would rest a lot easier than he had for over sixteen years. He took a sip of the champagne and beamed at Ellie who had so much to look forward to, her life once again bright with possibilities, just as it should be.

JOIN THE J.R. SINCLAIR VIP CLUB

Get instant access to exclusive photos of locations used from the series, and the latest news from J.R. Sinclair.

Just click here to start receiving your free content: https://www. subscribepage.com/n4zom8

PRE-ORDER A FLOOD OF SORROW

DI Joseph Stone will return in
A FLOOD OF SORROW

Pre-order now: https://geni.us/AFloodOfSorrow

Or read on for Chapter One....

CHAPTER 1 OF A FLOOD OF SORROW

The rain hammered down onto the roof of Alex's narrowboat, *The Kraken*, becoming more deafening by the second.

Tracey tore her attention away from the laptop screen she'd just been watching with Alex. They'd been attempting to finish the last episode of the Netflix crime show they'd been binge-watching for the past two nights, but with the current heavy rock downpour that really wasn't an option anymore.

She cast a withering look towards the ceiling. 'Oh, I give up! I can barely hear myself think over all that racket.'

Alex paused the episode. 'I could sort out a Bluetooth speaker...' He frowned, spotting something move past the cabin window. No, not something but *everything* sliding past the porthole and at an increasing speed. That was a problem because right now *The Kraken* was meant to be safely moored to their regular spot on the embankment.

He jumped to his feet and rushed to the window. The bushes and trees that lined the towpath were now under at least a foot of water.

Alex grabbed his waterproof cagoule and shrugged it on over his shoulders.

'What is it?' Tracey asked as she surfaced from beneath the blanket that only a moment ago they'd been snuggling up together beneath.

'That bloody flood that they've been warning us about has just ripped us from our mooring,' Alex called back as he headed to the door.

As he walked outside the air caught in his throat. He took in the transformation of the Isis, the name the locals gave this section of the Thames that snaked its way through Oxford.

Rain hammered down into the rolling surface of the river like a hail of gunshots. The towpath had already disappeared under the rapidly rising floodwater. The river was swollen and running fast, carrying a flotilla of broken branches and rubbish— and his home—right along with it.

Alex sucked in the air through his teeth, trying to assess the situation without panicking as dark storm clouds scudded over-head, sucking all the colour out of the world.

A few seconds later, Tracey appeared on deck wrapped in her yellow waterproof jacket. 'Bloody hell, this has turned ugly, real quick.'

'I know, I know, and I only have my own pig-headed-ness to blame. I heard the warnings. But unlike our neigh-bours who sensibly moved their boats over to the Oxford Canal, I honestly thought we'd be fine on the river. I even took the piss out of them last week, pointing out the fact that a boat was probably the safest place to be if it did flood.'

Tracey shrugged. 'No biggie, just power up the engine, and we can find a new mooring to ride this thing out.'

He smiled at her. 'Yes, you're right, there's no need to panic. What would I do without you?'

She grinned at him. 'Get your knickers in way too much of a twist.'

He laughed, leant over and kissed the top of her head. 'Isn't that the truth.'

Alex reached down to the control panel and turned the key to the start position. Immediately the engine began to turn over, but three seconds became ten as the engine refused to catch. As their narrowboat began to gather speed in the fast-flowing river, so did Alex's heartbeat.

'Come on,' he muttered to his boat.

'You did get the engine serviced like you said you were going to?' Tracey asked.

He grimaced. 'It's been on my to-do list, but I never had a chance to get round to it. You know how busy I've been at work.'

She shook her head at him as the whir of the starter began to slow as the battery drained.

He returned the key to the off position, threw out a silent prayer to the river gods, and tried again.

Three spins of the starter and then, with a glorious gurgling cough, the engine burbled into life with a puff of blue smoke.

'Ta-da!' Alex said, patting the top of the cabin.

'I had every confidence in you,' Tracey replied with a shrug.

He winked at her. 'Yeah, I so believe that.'

As the engine settled into a steady chugging, he threw the engine into reverse and gunned the throttle.

With a roar from the diesel engine beneath the deck, *The Kraken* started to slow, but she was still being carried forward by the strengthening current.

'Is it too late to try and turn her round?' Tracey asked as the wind start to howl around the narrowboat, driving the rain into a slanting angle.

'No dice, in this torrent. The moment I try that the boat will probably be pitched over. The best we can do is ride this thing out until the river slows.'

'Okay, but we're so looking at buying a flat after this. So

much for the romantic life on the water you pitched to me when we first met in that bar over a year ago. Not one mention of chemical toilets and having to empty them practically every week, more often if you've had curry.'

He grinned at her. 'It must have slipped my mind.'

Tracey gave him a mock punch in the arm and shook her head at him.

The banter was a good distraction because Alex didn't want to let his girlfriend realise just how worried he really was. Even in full reverse, *The Kraken* was moving as fast as a speedboat by the time Iffley Lock appeared in the distance. It was then that Alex realised why the current was getting even faster. Both lock gates ahead of them had been left wide open by the keeper, no doubt to let the storm water pass through to avoid flooding across Oxford. He sailed through Iffley Lock many times, but this wasn't going to be the usual slow-speed crawl through it. It would be more like riding an out of control runaway express train.

'Jesus, can't you slow this thing down any more than this?' Tracey asked, her eyes widening as they were sucked towards their imminent possible destruction.

'I've already got the throttle wide open in reverse as it is,' Alex finally admitted. 'This is as slow as it gets, so you better hang onto something and keep everything crossed that we make it through in one piece.'

His girlfriend shot him a lip chewing look as she grabbed hold of the railing.

With his heart thumping in his chest like a drum solo, Alex began to make rapid adjustments to the tiller. All he could do was aim for the rushing torrent of water being channelled through the middle of the lock and pray they made it through in one piece.

The open gates rushed towards them at a shocking speed

and suddenly they were inside the roaring waters rushing through the lock. There was absolutely nothing Alex could do to keep *The Kraken* on a straight path, and suddenly it began to slip sideways.

With a huge bang, the prow hit the wall, almost pitching them both overboard. Adrenaline made his blood hum as a brief sound of splintering wood scraping over brick echoed off the walls of this manmade canyon. But then with a rush of spray, the narrowboat shot out of the other side of the lock into the vast expanse of calmer flood water beyond.

Alex sucked in a breath as he took in the lake where there was no sign of the shores of the river anywhere. The Isis had well and truly burst its banks, spreading far and wide into the flood plain of fields that surrounded Oxford. Trees pointed up out of the water like the gnarled fingers of old men.

After the deafening noise of the roaring water, the sudden silence that descended over them was almost as shocking. No longer contained, the river's flow had dropped to a crawl, and the narrowboat finally began to slow. It was then that Alex realised that there wasn't even the sound of the diesel engine running.

'No, no, no,' he said as he tried the key again.

But apart from a clicking noise coming from the engine compartment beneath his feet, nothing else happened. Without power, *The Kraken* quickly began to drift out into the newly formed lake.

Tracey pointed ahead towards a large oak tree directly in their path.

Alex shook his head. 'Don't worry. Even without the engine, I can still use the tiller to steer us round it.'

Tracey nodded. 'Okay, but all I'm asking is that you get us and our home through this in one piece.'

'No pressure then,' he replied, forcing a smile. But as he

deftly manoeuvred *The Kraken* around the obstruction, his heart finally began to decelerate, as he began to consider their predicament.

Their boat was effectively adrift without power. The hull almost certainly had significant damage from the impact with the lock. In the longer term, Alex had no idea how the hell was he going to pay for the repairs. In the shorter term, how was he going to get them out of this situation?

'So what happens now?' Tracey asked as she loosened her white-knuckled grip on the railing.

'I would say we should ring emergency services. But which one? Police, the fire brigade, or the bloody coast guard?

Tracey snorted, but then her eyes widened when she caught sight of something ahead. 'Actually, that might not be necessary.'

Alex looked to where she was pointing to see that their narrowboat was being carried towards a grassy island rising above the floodwater, but he was pretty sure was actually a raised section of the river embankment.

'You"re saying we could ground the boat on that?' Alex said, gesturing towards it.

'Exactly, then all we have to do is wait for the water to go down and get someone to give us a tow back up the river.'

'You mean, we're not going to end up in the middle of a dry field like some sort of modern-day Noah's Ark?'

Tracey laughed. 'Now there's a thought, although someone must have forgotten to load all the animals.'

Alex laughed as he steered the narrowboat towards the island.

After everything they'd just been through, it wouldn't have been too much to ask for things to go smoothly. But no, the river wasn't finished having its fun with them, just yet.

At the very last moment, as they closed in on the embankment, an invisible current caught hold of the *The Kraken* and started to turn the boat at an angle to the island. Despite leaning hard on the rudder, there was nothing Alex could do to slow the narrowboat as hit it hard, gouging out a great chunk of the embankment. As a landslide of mud and turf, slid into the water with a whoosh, they finally came to a shuddering rest.

Alex immediately jumped off the boat and drove metal stakes into the embankment, securing ropes to the narrowboat as Tracey threw them across to him.

As the adrenaline ebbed away from his system, he looked at their new mooring. Then he laughed as a massive sense of relief surged through him.

'What?' Tracey asked.

'The lads at work aren't going to believe me when I tell them about our white water ride on a canal boat.'

But the smile that started to form on Tracey's lips fell away as she looked down at the gap between the boat and the embankment. 'What's that, Alex?'

He peered down at the object bobbing on the surface of the water. It was heavily covered in mud but had patches of blue showing in between. He was used to seeing no end of flotsam sailing past on the Thames, everything from milk cartons to used condoms. But there was something about this that was different from the usual rubbish.

'Pass me the pole from the roof and I'll fish it out,' he said.

A few moments later Tracey had handed him the pole they usually used for keeping the narrowboat away from the walls of the lock. Alex used the end of it to guide the object within reach. He lifted the mud covered thing clear of the water, and dropped it by his feet. A moment later he had cleared enough of the mud off to reveal an expensive-looking blue running shoe, a woman's going by the size of it.

Alex shook his head. 'The things people sling into the river.'

Tracey frowned. 'Actually, I think it might have been buried in that mud we just knocked into the river. But how could it have got there in the first place?'

Before Alex could reply, a series of bubbles came from the same spot in the water where he'd just recovered the running shoe from. Almost in slow motion, something much bigger broke the surface.

It took several heartbeats for Alex's brain to catch up with what they were both now staring at. A human hand floated on the surface, its mottled grey bloated fingers pointing to the sky like an echo of the flooded tree branches all around them. Then, like a mermaid rising from the depths, the rest of body surfaced as well.

Alex found himself gawping at a woman's lifeless face, her mouth frozen open as though she'd been gasping for breath, her eyes shrivelled to grey marbles. Strips of flesh hung from her ribcage like ribbons of grey seaweed rippling in the water.

As his brain rebooted from the shock, it took him a moment to realise that Tracey was screaming. He scrambled back up the embankment, nausea spinning through stomach. The moment he stood, breathing hard, Tracey threw her arms round him, sobbing. As she buried her head into his chest, Alex yanked his mobile from his pocket and rang the police, looking anywhere but at the dead woman floating in her watery grave and staring up at them with those cold dead eyes.

GO BEHIND THE SCENES

If you are intrigued to learn more about real life locations in Oxford and the surrounding area, from The Dead Of Midwinter, author J.R. Sinclair has created an online gallery of images with brief notes for each image.

See everything from the Radcliffe Camera, to the Hawk Stone itself, in an ever expanding gallery of photos.

Get your access to the **Location Photos** here: https://www. jrsinclair.net/vip-club

ACKNOWLEGDEMENTS

There are some key people that I need to thank in no particular order: Barry Hutchison, Tom Gillespie, Jonathan Mayhew, Hanna Elizabeth, Merry-Ellen Unan, and Joy F Saker. I wouldn't be able to do any of this without of support of my wife, Karen and our two cats, Jesse and Joey, especially for their creative help with the typing by walking across my keyboard. Such is the life of the author. Also a special thanks to Mark Buckland for suggesting moving the sacrifice scene from the Rollright Stones to the Hawk Stone. As a location it was absolutely perfect. A huge thank you to all my beta readers, who are too numerous to mention, but you know who you are. Your contribution was absolutely invaluable. Also, whilst I'm at it, I can't begin to express just how grateful I am to Patrick FitzSymons who did such an astonishing job bringing Joseph and all the others to life for the audiobook adaption. It really is very special.

Last but not least, a huge thanks to you, dear reader, for taking the plunge and reading the first book in my DI Joseph Stone series. I hope you really enjoyed the book as much as I did writing it and are eager for more, because I certainly am. Onwards.

Made in the USA
Monee, IL
11 September 2024